T0046771

SING A SONG OF SUMMER

SING A SONG OF SUMMER

A Roxanne Calloway Mystery

RAYE ANDERSON

Doug Whiteway, Editor

Signature
EDITIONS

© 2023, Raye Anderson

All rights reserved. No part of this book may be reproduced, for any
reason, by any means, without the permission of the publisher.

Cover design by Doowah Design.
Photo of author by Michael Long.

This book was printed on Ancient Forest Friendly paper.
Printed and bound in Canada by Hignell Book Printing Inc.

We acknowledge the support of the Canada Council for the Arts
and the Manitoba Arts Council for our publishing program.

Library and Archives Canada Cataloguing in Publication

Title: Sing a song of summer / Raye Anderson ; Doug Whiteway, editor.
Names: Anderson, Raye, 1943- author.
Description: Series statement: A Roxanne Calloway mystery
Identifiers: Canadiana (print) 20230210430 |
Canadiana (ebook) 20230210457 |
ISBN 9781773241210 (softcover) |
ISBN 9781773241227 (EPUB)
Classification: LCC PS8601.N44725 S56 2023 | DDC C813/.6—dc23

Signature Editions
P.O. Box 206, RPO Corydon, Winnipeg, Manitoba, R3M 3S7
www.signature-editions.com

1

IT WAS GOING to be another hot summer day, a cloudless sky and not a drop of rain. Sasha Rosenberg woke early in her tiny cottage at Cullen Village as a yellow sliver began to peek over the horizon of the big lake near where she lived. The birds joined in chorus to welcome the morning. She reached for the phone on her bedside table: 5:14 am, she read. Her window was wide open, to allow cool night air into the house. It also let in all that loud, cheerful chirruping. She wasn't going to get back to sleep.

Sasha kicked off the light sheet that covered her. She might as well get up. She was wide awake now, and this was going to be the best time of day to walk her dog. Her basset hound, Lenny, was twelve years old, arthritic and overweight. It would be too hot for him to go anywhere by mid-morning and although he was slow, he did love to go for a daily wander. She hauled herself out of bed, found loose cotton pants, a T-shirt and sandals, reached for a leash and her sunglasses. Lenny rewarded her with a slow wag of his long tail.

"C'mon then," she said and pulled the door closed behind them. She would take him to the lakeshore while it was fairly cool and walk along the berm at the water's edge, then come home for breakfast. She could have a nap later to make up for the early start. Lenny would snooze the rest of the day away in a shady spot in the backyard.

They strolled past sleeping cottages and boats berthed at the marina, Lenny stopping to sniff at the bottom of every post and tree. This early, there was not a single cottager or boater to be seen.

Soon the village would be busier. The influx of summer cottagers to the Manitoba Interlake had come early this year, along with a heatwave. Cullen Village was an easy hour's drive north of the city of Winnipeg. People had been cooped up the last couple of years because of a pandemic. Now it seemed that every person who owned a summer cottage by the lake had escaped town and headed here, where the air smelled fresh and the virus was less invasive. Cottagers had arrived in droves and installed themselves by the May long weekend.

Usually, they only came Friday to Sunday, for the weekend, but this year many of them were working from home and home schooling their kids. A lot of them had stayed. Their computers and other devices overloaded the local broadband service. They walked and biked the paths and lanes of Cullen Village, many of them ignoring advice to wear a medical mask, and got together and partied, even though they weren't supposed to visit beyond their selected "bubble" of trusted friends or relatives. Twelve people, max. The quiet life that Sasha and her friends enjoyed had been disrupted.

She herself carried a mask folded in the pocket of her pants, ready to cover her nose and mouth, just in case she met a solitary jogger who wore one, out as early as she was. Or another dog walker. But she saw no one.

By the time she reached the lakeshore, the sun had become a bright semicircle, sending a golden shaft of light that fanned out across the surface of the water. The sky was a spotless blue and the lake a placid, shining mirror. The path that ran along the top of the raised, grassy berm was a popular place to walk. You could go all the way around Cullen Bay, from the point furthest north to the south end of the village, following the shoreline. And there were trees, to provide some shade.

Sasha still had the whole place to herself. Even the pelicans hadn't roused themselves yet. They roosted on a rocky outcrop at Maxwell Point, named for a cottage built there in the early

1900s, when Cullen Village was just a good idea dreamed up by a railwayman who realized that this could become a great resort area for the nearby city. Accordingly, he had put in a railroad line. It had succeeded beyond his dreams. Winnipeggers had flocked here in their thousands. There had been a dancehall and a fairground, all gone now, but summer cottages remained popular. John Maxwell wouldn't recognize his modest cottage now. It was painted bright green and had grown to three times its original size with large, glossy windows, stone patios and a huge double garage. It was no longer owned by the Maxwell family. Some rich folks from the city had bought it and done a major renovation.

Sasha unhooked her dog from his leash. No one was around to see her break the rule that said she could not. Some villagers were sticklers for those but none of them were awake this morning to see Lenny amble, loose, past their houses. The sun was now two-thirds up, the flat surface of the water shone silver and gold, and Sasha was glad of her sunglasses. This day was going to be a scorcher but for now it was just pleasantly warm.

She reached a long wooden pier that jutted out, almost thirty feet, over the water. Several of those dotted the shore of Cullen Bay. They were built of spindly poplar beams, barely three feet wide, room for two people to walk side by side or for one cautious person to go down the middle reaching out to the railings on either side for support, the water lapping below them. Crossing them made some people giddy. A village crew put them up in the spring and took them down again in the fall before the lake iced over. They were swimming piers. Cottagers made their way along their rickety length to a fenced platform. It was seven feet down from the end. Jumping off of it into the lake was a summer ritual for the kids who came here. The platforms were edged with benches, a pleasant place to sit on a summer evening. A ladder reached all the way down into the water so you could swim out from the far end, avoiding the stones that washed up along the beaches that lined the shore. But not this year. There had been a month without rain already.

The level of the lake had dropped, exposing sandbars. Sasha had never seen the water so low, not in all the twenty-something years she had lived here. Instead of reaching down into the invitingly cool lake, the ladder on this pier stopped a foot or so above the lake bottom, which stretched out in front of her, interspersed with puddles, right along the curve of Cullen Bay. Sasha surveyed it, north to south. It might be possible for her to walk all the way from where she was to the southernmost point. She'd have to wade occasionally from one sandbar to the next but the water would barely be more than ankle deep by the look of it. She could walk quite far out from the shore. She'd never done that before. It would be fun.

Going down the ladder at end of the pier was beyond Lenny, but there was a path just two houses along, beside a small boat launch, near the house where her friend, Margo Wishart, lay in bed sound asleep. Sasha made her way to the launch and clambered down to the beach, past large yellow rocks placed there to reinforce the side of the berm against days when the lake stormed. Lenny followed her, then puttered along the grassy edge of the beach, staying where the sand was bone dry, sniffing out where other animals had been. Feral cats, skunks, rabbits, coyotes all lived around here. Sasha let him wander as he pleased, took off her sandals, rolled up her pant legs and paddled through an inch or so of lukewarm water to the nearest sandbar. She turned her face to the sun, feeling its warmth, welcome in the coolness of the morning, her eyes almost closed against the light. Moments like this were why she chose to live here, in beautiful Cullen Village.

The sand was pleasantly damp. Her toes and heels left imprints as she walked, the only ones on the pristine surface. Her long shadow stretched behind her. She would have to cross back onto the beach a couple of times to avoid some long stretches of water but that was okay. She needed to check up on Lenny, anyway.

Sasha seldom saw the village from the lake side. Neat wooden houses nestled among the trees, painted in different colours, all of their inhabitants still asleep. Windows caught the sunlight and shone back at her, so the cottages looked like they were smiling. She turned her back to the sun so she could see Lenny, his nose to the ground, big ears trailing in the sand. She'd need to cross back to the shore soon and wait for him to catch up but right now he was within eyeshot.

The sun was entirely exposed now, a glowing orb. A flock of birds rose into the sky to greet it, silhouetted black against the clear blue of the sky. She strode along the damp sand, her sandals swinging from her hand at her side, paddled through another stretch of water, deeper this time, to the next stretch of sand.

Another of the long piers stretched out into the bay. She walked toward it then along the posts at its base, where there was a stony patch of shore. The debris that the lake washed up sometimes contained treasures that Sasha could use in her artwork, pieces of coloured beach glass, worn dull and smooth by the water, interesting pieces of driftwood, lucky stones, ones with a hole at the centre. She beachcombed while Lenny caught up to her and reached into her pocket for her phone to check the time. It wasn't there. She must have left it at home, on her bedside table, but that was okay. She had no need to call anyone this early, and she had a couple of pieces of glass to take home, plus some pretty shells.

She paddled once more through lukewarm water to one of the longest sandbars. It led all the way to a third pier, right at the middle of the bay. The sun shone even more brightly on the water. Sasha wished she'd thought to bring a water bottle. Maybe this was as far as she should go. She would go back to the shore soon, walk back home through the village and have breakfast. Sasha didn't care much for cooking but this perfect day demanded that she make an effort. Scramble up an egg. Make a pot of tea.

Hazeldean Pier was like all the others, long and narrow, built out from a cluster of rocks. It was named for yet another of those old cottages built by a founding father of the village more than a hundred years ago. In this light, the pier was silhouetted above her against the immaculate sky. If she had remembered to bring her phone she could have got a good shot of it and sent it out over the airwaves when she got home. That was too bad. It looked quite spectacular this morning, perched up above the edge of the sandbar in all its spindly glory, water puddled at its base. She looked more intently, raised her hand to better shade her eyes from the sun's glare. What was that she was looking at, hanging off the end of the pier?

Her heart sank. She knew perfectly well what she was seeing, and here she was, all alone out on a sandbar in the middle of the bay, without her phone and only her ancient hound for company. She turned and ran over the wet sand, splashing through ankle-deep water.

Margo Wishart's house was more than half the way back along the berm. She could wake Margo up and use her phone to call 911. Lenny stood at the edge of the water, watching as she ran toward him. She leashed him once more, frustrated that he'd slow her down. Then she realized that she didn't need to rush. She was still the only person around and the body hanging from the end of Hazeldean Pier wasn't going to go anywhere.

2

MARGO WISHART PULLED on a sundress and found a hat while Sasha talked on the phone to the RCMP. A police car was on its way, she heard. Sasha would meet it outside Hazeldean, the cottage by the pier, so she could show the RCMP what she had seen.

"I'll come with you," Margo said, suspecting that Sasha was more disturbed by what she had seen than she was letting on. "I can wait until you are done talking to them."

They left the dogs in the cool, air-conditioned house and retraced Sasha's steps along the berm. It ran along the shoreline, a raised grassy dike built to protect the cottages from stormy water. The path along the top led straight to Hazeldean. It wasn't long before they caught sight of the body, hanging off the end of the pier. A woman, slightly built, dressed in yellow, with a mop of curly blond hair, shone in the early morning sun like a well-lit puppet. Her head was tilted to one side, her arms dangled, the toes of her bare feet turned slightly in.

Margo thought she recognized her, that she had seen her occasionally at Hazeldean, pre-pandemic, but she couldn't be sure. Margo had only lived in the Interlake for a few years. Hazeldean was a summer cottage. People came and went from May long weekend until Canadian Thanksgiving, in October, then the house was shuttered up for the long winter months. It was usually knee-deep in snow by December and remained like that, not a human footprint to be seen, until the spring thaw.

She had seen a man there a couple of times recently, out doing yard work. She'd said hello in passing as she walked by with her dog. But she hadn't seen this woman, not this year.

The promised police car drew up. Margo waited on the berm as Sasha went to talk to a young woman in uniform who looked far too small and too young to be a policewoman. She watched them walk along a path between the cottage and a garage, then over the parched lawn toward the pier. Another constable, wearing a turban and carrying a camera, followed them. Margo was glad she'd thought to bring the sunhat. It was going to get hot as the morning wore on.

The back door of the cottage next to Hazeldean opened onto a veranda facing the lake. Her neighbour, Herb Appleby, came out, in a beige robe and slippers. He must have wakened early, too, or the unusual activity outside his cottage had disturbed his sleep. He frowned when he saw the police, then his face brightened as he noticed Margo. He padded across his lawn and strode up the grassy side of the berm. Herb had to be close to eighty but he was in decent shape for his age. He'd taught phys-ed earlier in his life, played golf regularly, and liked to brag that he walked the course. No riding around on a golf cart for him. He curled in the winter, too.

"What's going on?" he asked, then he spotted the body and the two women climbing down the steps that led down from the end of the pier, one of them a uniformed member of the RCMP. The ladder didn't reach all the way to the bottom. They jumped down the last few feet or so to the ground. "Oh, my!" He squinted into the sunshine. "Isn't that Donna Borthwick? It can't be." He took a step back, reluctant to believe what he was seeing then he peered again. "But it is!"

"Who is Donna Borthwick?" asked Margo.

Herb raised a hand to shade his eyes so he could get a better look. "She's a daughter of the house." He was a tall man with a thick head of hair, still distinguished even in his pyjamas, a good head taller than Margo. "The Borthwick family co-own that cottage, Donna and her brothers and a sister."

"Do you think she's hanged herself?" Margo had also raised a hand to look. The little policewoman was standing right below the body. Sasha was watching from a patch of sand beside the rocks.

"Donna? She wouldn't have." But it certainly looked like she had. Wasn't that Sasha Rosenberg, the potter, down there with the Mountie? Herb asked. What did she have to do with this? Margo explained and told him how she'd promised to wait until Sasha had finished talking to the police.

"It's getting hot out here. You can't wait out in this sunshine," said Herb. "Let's go onto my deck so we can sit in the shade. The Rosenberg woman might be ages yet, they'll need to take a statement." Margo looked again. She could see Sasha pointing out over the water, in the direction that she had taken as she had approached the pier. The male Mountie was up on the platform, photographing a cord that was knotted there, holding the body.

They walked over to the Applebys' deck where there were comfortable padded chairs. Herb put up a shady umbrella, telling her all the time about the woman who had died, who once had been called Donna Borthwick. Now she was Donna Palmer. Married to Gordon Palmer, the politician.

Margo knew who that was, a federal MP representing a riding south of Winnipeg, a Conservative Party stronghold. Herb wandered in and out of his house, fetching coffee. June, his wife, he said, was still asleep, she could sleep through anything, but not him. He'd been awake for hours already. He'd noticed Margo and Sasha walk by and wondered what was going on, so he'd come out to find out what was happening. He'd never expected to see what they had just seen.

Herb's eyes were still good. He could see without glasses. The top of the pier was visible but not the body below. The turbaned Mountie had gone down the ladder now. "Constable Anand," Margo told him. She had been involved with the Fiskar Bay RCMP in the past. Sergeant Roxanne Calloway, who ran the detachment, was a friend.

Herb Appleby had known the Borthwick family most of his life, he told her as they waited. His family had bought his own cottage when he was a boy. He had spent the summer here every year since. He'd known Donna Palmer since she was little, her and her sister and her brothers.

"There's four of them. Jay, the youngest, is the one that's been around lately. You've seen him?" Margo had. "He used to be a chef. Had a restaurant in Winnipeg. Called The Sleeping Dog or something like that."

"The Sleepy Fox?" Margo suggested. She remembered it. She had eaten there, once, about three years ago. It had been a popular spot before the virus had shut it down, got great reviews and you couldn't get a table without making a reservation well in advance. One of her friends had been asked to curate some art done by local artists to decorate the walls and had invited her to go see. It had been a pricey little place, with an adventurous menu featuring locally sourced ingredients and fantastic desserts. The meal had been memorable. If Jay Borthwick had cooked it, he was a talented chef. The Sleepy Fox had tried to survive the pandemic lockdown by offering a takeout menu, she believed, but it hadn't lasted. It must be over a year since it had closed.

"I don't know what Jay's living on these days," said her neighbour. "Maybe one of those government handouts for people who lost their jobs."

"He's been staying at Hazeldean since the spring?" asked Margo.

"Coming and going. Good man, Jay. He's tidied the place up a bit. It sure needed it."

That was true. Hazeldean looked in need of a lick of fresh paint, but it had a shabby kind of charm. It was more than a hundred years old and still in its original state. "He opened up the cottage, took down the shutters, got the water turned on. He was here yesterday. Wonder where he's got to? There's no sign of his car."

Herb hoisted himself up and went to the end of his deck to check. Jay Borthwick drove a red Jeep SUV, he reported back. The only car in the driveway was a silver Honda.

"Jay has one of the shares in the cottage." Herb's mane of hair and thick eyebrows were white, above a curved nose. He reminded Margo of one of the bald eagles that migrated here each year. "So does Donna and her sister, Leslie. Leslie lives in Saskatoon. Maybe it was Donna's turn to be here. They do that. Take turns to have the place in the summer. Donna's done well, you know. Sells houses. Business must really be picking up for her. Places are suddenly selling fast here these days." He was right. Any houses that had sold lately in the Interlake had gone quickly, for well over the asking price. "I still can't see why a woman like her would want to kill herself. She was always such a live wire. Her and Leslie. Loved a good party."

"Maybe the pandemic's been hard on her," Margo suggested. She herself had quite enjoyed being cooped up. She'd taught a couple of university courses online, which was not the best situation but she hadn't had to commute to the city. She'd read lots and got work done on a book she was writing about women who made fibre art. But friends who liked to be out and about, who needed active interaction, had had a hard time, not being able to socialize.

"Maybe, but why kill herself now?" Herb said. "The lockdown's beginning to ease up. Look at us, sitting here, face to face, with no masks on. We couldn't have done this a few months ago. Things are finally improving."

Margo could see his point. She looked over at the pier once more. Sasha and the policewoman had hoisted themselves back up onto the steps. The Mounties both wore white masks and Sasha must have had one in her pocket. Now it covered her nose and mouth. She watched Constable Anand walk to the police car, his phone to his ear. Sasha and the woman remained on the platform, sitting on one of the benches that lined its sides. The policewoman was writing down what Sasha was saying.

"Why is the cottage called 'Hazeldean'?" she asked. She was Scottish, she knew the old song, "Jock O'Hazeldean," a romantic Border ballad penned by Sir Walter Scott and sung to a popular tune. Herb knew how that had happened.

"When June came here she thought it must have been named for a couple of kids called Hazel and Dean, but it wasn't that at all.

"William Borthwick, a Scottish railroad man, friend of John Maxwell, built the place, way back when Cullen Village was first founded. It's got heritage status, you know, because it has a special fireplace."

Margo had noticed a sign out front of the old cottage, made of wrought iron with the name and a date, 1904. CULLEN VILLAGE HISTORICAL SOCIETY: HERITAGE SITE was written below it.

"Back in the days when they first came here, people would get together on a Saturday night to entertain one another. They played music and sang. Told stories, recited poems, ones they knew from the old country. William Borthwick must have liked that old song, 'Jock O'Hazeldean,' and called the cottage that to remind him of home."

Borthwick was an old Scottish Borders name. That made sense.

The first name, William, was always handed down to the eldest son. Donna Palmer's father liked to be called Will. He and Herb had played together when they were kids. Jumped off that pier into the lake many times. Will had gone into insurance. He'd done well but he had died, years ago. Lois, his wife, was still alive the last they had heard but she had Alzheimer's. They had all been friends, Lois and Will, himself and June.

"Usually, the house gets passed on to the oldest son, but Will and Lois's oldest, Fraser, has been a bit of a disappointment. Got himself into a bit of trouble in his teens. Drugs. Stuff like that. He hasn't been seen around here in years, but he'll have a share in the place, too."

"He's called Fraser, not William?"

"William Fraser. Goes by his second name."

"It doesn't look like they've spent much on the cottage," said Margo. "It's in poor shape."

"Too true," Herb Appleby agreed. "Old Will would have a fit if he saw the state it's in now." He'd had a word with Donna about it, two, three years ago, before the pandemic locked them all up. "She said they had plans for it but she wouldn't say what they were. I said to her, you're not planning to sell it, are you, Donna, and she just laughed. Look, there's your friend coming back. And it looks like the police are going to seal off the place."

Sasha was walking back from the pier toward them across the crisp, dry grass. The two RCMP constables were unspooling yellow police tape.

Sasha liked to pretend she was tough. She sculpted with metal, after all, and welded it into giant angular figures. She looked angular herself. But she drooped as she walked, her shoulders down, her hands stuck deep in the pockets of her sweatpants.

"I'll go get another cup of coffee," Herb offered, getting to his feet. But Sasha didn't want any.

"I'd as soon go pick up Lenny and get myself back home," she said. So Margo thanked her neighbour for the conversation and walked back to her own house with her friend.

"I've never seen anything like that before." Sasha shuddered at the memory. "Her face is all distorted and purple."

The dogs were happy to see them, oblivious of the drama being played out close by. That cheered Sasha up momentarily. The police had wanted to know why she was out on the lake, so early, and exactly what she had seen, she told Margo. They had asked if anyone else had been around. Constable Anand had taken lots of photographs. She'd been warned not to touch anything, not even the railings of the pier. They had said a forensic team would be coming out from the city to check everything out and nothing should be contaminated.

"It must have happened last night. She was wearing pyjamas."

"Herb Appleby was able to tell me who she was." Sasha listened to what Margo had learned and soon she changed her mind about that coffee. Maybe she could eat an egg after all, she decided. It was hours since she'd got up. Then she'd take her dog home, go to her studio and do some work. She needed to try to rid her mind of the image of Donna Borthwick in her yellow silk pyjamas hanging off Hazeldean Pier.

3

ROXANNE CALLOWAY COULD have let the constables who worked under her do the basic legwork at site of the alleged suicide, in Cullen Village. Ident, the Forensic Identification Unit, had arrived already. Everything was proceeding as it should. It wasn't as if Roxanne didn't have enough work of her own to do, running the local RCMP detachment this hot Sunday morning. Last night had been busy. Two men lay in the cells in Fiskar Bay, the town just north of Cullen Village where Roxanne worked, hungover and bruised from a bar fight. Her team had broken up a late-night beach party and pulled in a suspected drug dealer. A young driver had driven into a ditch in the early hours of the morning, not wearing a seat belt. He and his passengers had been injured and had needed to be taken by ambulance to hospital. It was going to be like this every weekend, all summer long. And now there was this.

But Roxanne liked to get out of the office and she wanted to see for herself. She parked under a small wrought iron sign with the name of the cottage, HAZELDEAN, in curly letters, and a date, 1904, and some more information about its origin. Aimee Vermette, the youngest constable who worked under her, was directing traffic outside. Both she and Aimee wore short-sleeved shirts and lightweight pants, the RCMP's only concession to summer as far as uniform was concerned. It was still before ten in the morning, but a steady stream of cars had begun to crawl by. Walking past here had suddenly become popular too, and there were several bikes. All eyes turned toward the cottage.

The Ident van was parked in the driveway behind a silver Honda SUV. Corporal Dave Kovak ran this forensic unit. Roxanne had last worked with Dave four years ago, pre-pandemic, when there had been a series of murders in Fiskar Bay. Before then, she had been a member of the Major Crimes Unit and they had met regularly.

"The body's down at the beach," he told her while she stood on the veranda of the cottage, pulling on regulation protective clothing. It was going to be steamy inside a white plastic suit in this heat. It was hard to breathe inside the mask that she was already wearing. "The medics are on their way from Winnipeg to collect it."

The Provincial Medical Examiner's Office had had a busy weekend too. There had been a shooting in the north end of the city last night and a four-car pile-up on the perimeter road that circled Winnipeg. This was only one more body to add to their list.

Old Dr. Gaul, a fixture in the Fiskar Bay Health Centre, had been by already to pronounce death. They knew that the woman had not been hanging from the end of the pier at nightfall the previous evening. A couple had phoned in to say they had walked the beach, right past Hazeldean, near eleven when it was almost dark, and they had seen nothing suspicious. So, death must have occurred sometime during the night.

"She used the cord from a bathrobe. One end was tied to the top rail, over at the far end of the pier"—Dave nodded in the direction of the lake—"then she must have looped it around her neck, stepped up onto the bench inside the railing and jumped off the top. I'm surprised that cord held her. It's not all that strong. She's small and can't weigh more than 120 pounds, but she'd have fallen fast. She mustn't have had a clue what she was doing. Didn't know a thing about the right kind of knot. It looks like she strangled." A hangman's knot would have snapped the woman's neck so that death would have been instant. That had not happened. Donna Palmer would have hung from the pier for some time before she died.

The Major Crimes Unit had been informed but they were overstretched too this busy June weekend and this case seemed a pretty straightforward suicide. The woman had placed her sandals side by side on the wooden platform at the place where she had jumped, the toes facing out toward the water. There was no note lying in any of the obvious places but there was a laptop in the cottage and a phone. Maybe they'd find something on one of them to explain why she had chosen to kill herself.

Roxanne walked across crisp dry grass toward the pier in her plastic bootees. The body had been cut down and was below the pier. She climbed down to a stepladder, set up to cover the gap between the bottom of the pier steps and the lakebed. Roxanne preferred to jump down. A tent protected the remains from the hot sun and the flies. Ravi Anand lifted the flap to let her in. The woman lay on her back on a mat, her arms by her side. She seemed to be in her forties, about five feet, three inches tall, no fat on her at all. She had thick, curly fair hair, bleached at the ends, and wore yellow silk pyjamas. She'd had a recent pedicure. Her fingernails were painted gold, with a bit of sparkle. There were rings on her fingers and golden studs in her ears. The end of the cord that had strangled her was still tied around her throat, the knot at the back, the cord cutting deep into her neck. Her face was a livid purple, in sharp contrast to her yellow clothing. Her mouth hung open, her tongue protruding out one side. Someone had closed her eyes. There were traces of eyeshadow and mascara on her lids. Above them, her brows were drawn in brown arches so she looked faintly astonished.

Roxanne felt a wave of nausea. That surprised her. She'd seen much worse than this in her time with the MCU. Ravi Anand gave her a puzzled look. "You okay, Sarge?" he asked. "You've gone white."

"Must be the heat." It was stifling inside the tent and the body had begun to smell. She stepped outside into the blazing sunshine and pulled down her mask so she could gulp in some air. There wasn't a breath of wind. A boat from the marina at the north side of the bay cut its engine and drifted to a halt out on the water. The couple on the deck passed binoculars back and forth. One of them held up a phone to take a photo.

"There's been a few of those." Ravi stood beside her. "Can't do much to stop them from here. They don't look like press." But it was hard to tell. He'd had to chase away several curious walkers. The police tape stretched down the beach, hanging limply in the sunshine. It didn't provide much of a deterrent. Someone had let a couple of dogs loose and taken time calling them back in, getting a good look while they did so. A group of teenagers had thrown a ball across the sand, then pretended to try to get it back. Ravi had tossed it back to them.

They heard a clatter up on the pier. Two medics were bringing down a stretcher. Soon the body would cease to be an object of curiosity.

"Good," said Roxanne. "Once they are gone, you are done for the day."

Ravi had worked the night shift. It was long past time that he was off duty. She needed him back on highway patrol that night. The cottagers who needed to get back to city jobs began the drive to Winnipeg by late afternoon on Sundays throughout the summer season. So did the day trippers. Not all city drivers were good on the highway. They were impatient to get home and sometimes passed a slower car when they shouldn't. The RCMP knew from experience to prepare for accidents.

She waited until the medics had carried the empty stretcher down the narrow wooden steps then climbed back up to the wooden platform above. It was about seven feet square with a bench all round where cottagers loved to sit on a summer evening above the cool water. Right now, there was no water below, the sun was high in the sky and the temperature had to be in the thirties. Birds were roosting on the rocks along the shore, silent watchers. It was too hot for them to sing. She looked out over the sandbar to the silvery water thirty feet away. Right now, there were people working at this site, like herself, and plenty of onlookers, but last night this would have been a quiet and lonely place to die.

Donna Palmer had left a tote in one of two bedrooms on the main floor, and an open bag with clothes spilling out. The ones that she had worn during the day were thrown on a chair. Her driver's licence confirmed her identity. It showed her as bright eyed and very much alive, trying not to smile at the camera. The Honda parked in the driveway was licensed to her.

A man had been living in the other bedroom. There was underwear in a dresser drawer, shirts and shorts, a casual jacket and pants in the closet, sneakers on the floor. Containers from the local Chinese restaurant were stashed in a garbage bag under the kitchen sink. The receipt told them that Donna Palmer had paid for the food on her debit card. There had been enough for two, most of it eaten, and an empty wine bottle stood on the kitchen counter. Two unwashed glasses sat beside the sink. There were unpacked bags of food in the fridge, a jug almost full of milk. A crate of wine bottles lay in a corner of the floor, more shopping bags beside it.

"So, she ate dinner with someone who was maybe staying here as well?" Roxanne asked.

"Her brother, James, but it looks like he left here yesterday," an Ident technician replied. "There are four siblings who co-own this place. We've talked to a neighbour opposite, says she's a village councillor, name of Halliday."

Roxanne knew Freya Halliday of old. Freya made it her business to know everything that went on in her village. It seemed that she had been her usual informative self. James went by the name of Jay, the Ident technician reported. He drove an SUV, a dark red colour, some kind of Jeep. Doug, her husband, would know what kind it was. Jay had stayed out here quite often since the spring. He was a nice man, friendly. Not all cottagers were, she said, but Jay had helped Doug start their car one morning. And he'd done a little to try to clean Hazeldean up. Raked the lawn. That had needed to be done—you didn't want snow mould. He sometimes had company on the weekend. Had one of his visitors died? she had asked.

So, word that the body was that of Jay Borthwick's sister, wife of the prominent Member of Parliament Gordon Palmer, had not reached Mrs. Halliday yet. That was one bit of good news.

The Hallidays had been in Winnipeg yesterday evening. They'd parked their car behind their house when they got home and gone to bed shortly after. Freya had noticed the Honda out in front of Hazeldean when they locked up. Jay's Jeep had still been in the driveway then. He must have left after 10:00 pm, and the Honda moved to its present place.

Freya and her husband slept at the back of their house. There were often a lot of comings and goings in the village on a summery Saturday night. Parties on decks. Bonfires in backyards, but they were going to be banned soon if this drought continued. Loud music. They hadn't noticed anything like that at Hazeldean. It had been quiet.

"It's a pity they've let this old place go." The technician ran his fingers along a window frame. The blue paint was flaking. The door frames were in just as bad shape. Most of the appliances in the kitchen looked like they dated back to the fifties, though there was an almost new espresso machine and a stand mixer on the counter. The cupboards looked like they hadn't been painted since the fifties either and the glasses and the dishes inside them seemed to be from the same era. The linoleum on the floor was scuffed and curling up at the edges.

Roxanne walked across a dingy hallway and into the living room. A big grey stone fireplace dominated the room, its massive mantel reaching up to the ceiling, a basket half full of logs beside it. The grate was empty of ashes. A blue sofa that had seen better days, big armchairs, and a table with chairs were arranged throughout the room. Bookcases lined one wall, full of old paperbacks, board games, jigsaw puzzles. It was in need of a good clean but the room looked well-used and comfortable. Donna Palmer's laptop had lain on the tabletop, she was told. It was stashed in the Ident van.

She climbed a flight of narrow stairs. Two small bedrooms were at the top, under a sloping roof. The mattresses on the beds were bare. There was nothing much else to see. She creaked her way downstairs. The bathroom was on the main floor. The bathtub was fitted with a makeshift shower, a hose that ran from the taps. Well water had left rust stains in the tub and in the sink and the toilet. Hazeldean must not have a water softener. A toilet bag rested on top of the cistern, containing the usual—toothpaste, deodorant, lotions and creams. The cord was missing from a white terry bathrobe that hung behind the door.

Roxanne walked down the dim hallway and through the screen door that led onto the veranda at the back of the house. Outside, a wicker sofa and matching chairs were missing their cushions and an ancient bike was propped against the railing. She checked the tires. They had air in them. The wooden walls of the cottage were painted a faded blue and the white trim, like the window frames inside, was flaking. This cottage definitely needed some attention before it started to rot.

The body bag was being carried on a stretcher to the back of a white van parked on the street. A cluster of cottagers watched in respectful silence, Freya Halliday among them. Roxanne did not want Freya to recognize her and start quizzing her. She went back behind the house to the veranda and peeled off the plastic suit, bundled it up and left it inside the back door, glad to get it off, but kept her mask on. Corporal Kovak was walking across the dry lawn. His guys would dispose of it, he told her.

"Why would she choose to use a bathrobe cord?" she asked him. "Isn't there anything stronger around here?" There was. A technician had spotted hanks of rope hanging inside a shed at the side of the house behind a garage. "If she co-owned this cottage, wouldn't she have known where to find them?"

"Maybe she acted on impulse." They stood in the back doorway, where there was shade.

"She walked all the way out to the end of that." Roxanne pointed across the back lawn to the long length of pier shimmering in the strong sunlight. "She would have had enough time to think about what she was doing, don't you think? And you haven't found any note, have you?"

Dave Kovak laughed. "What are you saying, Roxanne? Are you trying to make out this is more than a suicide? Are you getting fed up with life out here in the boonies?"

He knew that Roxanne had given up a career as a successful investigator years before. That she'd developed a reputation for being good at tracking down murderers, then quit the Major Crimes Unit after an incident where she had almost died. She still bore the scar from that attack on her throat. She'd spent the last four years keeping the peace in Fiskar Bay instead.

"Forget it," he told her. "All we need to do is find the reason why she did it, and I'll bet it's on one of her devices. This case will be all wrapped up by tomorrow."

Roxanne squinted into the sunshine. Was he right? Was she in need of some excitement? She knew how her job at Fiskar Bay worked, and she'd been told that she was good at it. Life was fine. She and her son, Finn, had moved in with Matt Stavros a couple of years ago, into a big house Matt had built not far from here. Matt had once worked for the RCMP but he'd been in law school when they had started seeing one another, and he had just started work as a lawyer in an office in Fiskar Bay. She had been extraordinarily lucky. She had loved her first husband, Jake, the father of her son, and she'd found another guy, just as good. He got along great with Finn and she was happy. She and Matt would live and work here for the rest of her time with the RCMP, probably for the rest of their lives. She'd stay a sergeant and that was fine with her. She'd never wanted to move up to inspector anyway. That job was all administration, not her style at all.

She looked at her phone. There were no urgent messages from her office at the detachment. She said goodbye for now and walked away, not back to her car but along the berm. She was thirsty. She'd see if Margo Wishart was home and maybe get something to drink in her cool, air-conditioned house. She trusted Margo's opinion. It might be worth finding out what she had to say about Donna Palmer, just in case Dave Kovak had got it wrong.

4

GORDON PALMER, MP, had been in Ottawa when he was informed of his wife's death. He'd caught the redeye back to Winnipeg that night. Sergeant Izzy McBain of the RCMP's Major Crimes Unit was tasked with visiting him first thing on Monday morning. She found the Palmer residence in a well-established neighbourhood in Winnipeg. It was a large, white, three-storey house with pillars at the front door, built to impress a hundred years ago. Giant pots full of spiky red flowers were at the front steps. Izzy had no idea what the plants were called but she guessed they were expensive. A florist's van was parked in the driveway and a young woman was signing for a bouquet when she arrived.

"Sergeant McBain, Major Crimes Unit, to see Mr. Palmer," Izzy announced.

The woman at the door eyed her up and down. Izzy did not look like a cop. She liked to dress casually. Jeans and sneakers were her thing. She used to have a ponytail. She'd got her hair cropped when a guy she worked with had warned her that it was easy for a criminal to grab. Now it was short, really short.

This woman was not dressed like Izzy at all. Dark skirt, crisply laundered shirt, high-heeled shoes, hair cut perfectly along the jawline, and black-framed glasses on her nose. Izzy produced her warrant card and the woman switched on a smile.

"Maria Smith, Mr. Palmer's assistant," she said, and led Izzy inside to a large sitting room. Flowers must have been arriving all morning. There was an arrangement of lilies on a table at the window, another of white tulips on a bureau. Mr. Palmer would be with the sergeant shortly, she was told. Would she like coffee or tea? Maria Smith backed out of the room and closed the door behind her.

The room was minimally furnished in white leather, steel and glass. It was not at all what you would expect in a house of this vintage. The light fixtures were sculptural and a large painting of red poppies almost filled one wall. Izzy tried out a couple of chairs as she waited. They looked great but were not comfortable, she decided. Maria Smith came back with a tray and apologized for the delay.

"Important call," she said and disappeared again. Izzy helped herself to a piece of biscotti and dunked it in her coffee. She sat and looked out the window at the big elm trees that lined the boulevard. The lawn was a vibrant green, the shrubs leafy. It must take a sprinkler system to keep them this healthy in this dry, hot season, but those were banned because of the drought. Maybe being the home of an important person made this house exempt.

The man himself finally appeared, looking exactly as he did on TV, smooth and well-groomed even although he couldn't have caught much sleep last night. He was dressed for business—tailored suit with a black silk tie. He must once have been a handsome man. Now he looked to be about fifty years old, greying at the temples and beginning to bloat, perhaps from too many corporate dinners. But his manners were impeccable.

"So sorry. Ottawa. Some things must go on." He needed to talk to his party leader later today by phone and meet with people at his constituency office. Set up a contingency plan in case he needed to take extra time off.

He'd already told their boy, Graeme, who was asleep upstairs. The sergeant didn't need to disturb him, did she? His daughter shared an apartment with a friend. They'd moved recently. He didn't have their new address but he did have a phone number and had been in touch. Amelia was lunching with him later. It sounded like he was describing a business meeting instead of two family members gathering to commiserate after the sudden death of their wife and mother.

Did he have any idea why his wife would have wanted to kill herself? He did not, but there needed to be a reason. He didn't know everything about her day-to-day life or her work. He did his thing, she did hers. She had been busy, so had he. She had been good at her job, he knew that. Donna had restarted Bricks and Sugar, her business, these past few months. She knew how to make a house look its best. That, Izzy thought, explained the décor in the room.

He had last seen her ten days ago and had been in Ottawa since. She was fine then, nothing unusual. He wasn't surprised she had left no note. Donna tended to act on impulse. It was one of the things people liked about her. She was full of surprises, but this certainly was unexpected. Had she been drinking? he asked.

"Did she?" asked Izzy. "Drink?"

"She liked a glass of wine."

"Too much?"

"My wife liked to party. She loved people, Sergeant. She was sociable." He lowered his voice as though what he was about to say was confidential. "Being shut in the house all day during the pandemic was hard on her. This lockdown has played havoc with people's mental health. I have access to the current data on that," he said. "Isolation wasn't good for people like Donna, who can't stand being alone. That policy has come at a cost." Even under circumstances like these, he managed to make a political point.

"You believe it was suicide?" asked Izzy McBain

"What else would it be?" He raised an eyebrow. Izzy noticed fine pink lines in the whites of his eyes. They were bloodshot. From grief or from lack of sleep?

Gordon Palmer had known that Donna was going to the Interlake for two weeks. That was nothing unusual. She liked being at the cottage and she was hoping to get work done on a couple of houses while she was in the area.

"So, her business had picked up again?" asked Izzy.

"I believe so. In the first year of the pandemic, showing houses in-person was impossible and Donna specialized in providing personal, customized services to her clients. That was hard. But she adjusted. She sold some houses online. Now things are picking up and she was getting Bricks and Sugar back on track again, but my wife was not a person who liked having to repeat herself."

Had she said anything about being worried lately? He didn't think so, but he was gone for weeks at a time these days. The way the present government had spent money was going to cause a financial crisis. There was work that needed to be done to hold some people accountable. He was on his party's finance committee. This was not a good time for him to be away.

Meantime, he assumed, there would be an inquest. The number of people allowed to attend a funeral service was still limited but something would have to be arranged. And, of course, his wife's affairs would need to be attended to.

"You need to hold off on all of that, sir," said Izzy. "There will have to be an autopsy first. It may be some time before the body's released. And we may want to look at Mrs. Palmer's accounts ourselves."

"That's inconvenient, officer." His tired eyes looked at her across the top of his coffee cup.

"Like I said, we haven't found a reason for your wife to have killed herself so far." Izzy drank what was left of her coffee. She'd learned as much as she needed to know, here. It was time for her to go.

Her boss, Inspector Schultz, had called her late last night.

"There's a problem, Isabel," he had growled. He was one of the few people who got away with calling Izzy by that name. She was careful to keep on Schultz's good side, so she put up with it. "We don't know why she did it. There's no note, no nothing. They haven't found a thing on her phone or in her computer so far. Go find the reason she offed herself and let me close the book on this case, soon as? Keep a low profile and get right back to me with anything you discover. That Palmer guy's got connections. Big buds with the premier. Dines with her, regularly. If that woman had some messy secret, they're not going to want any of the dirt attaching itself to him, or the party. Got it?"

She had. She didn't think Schultz needed to worry. Palmer had a watertight alibi. She might not like him but he was so sleek that any dirt would roll right off him.

Izzy had done well in the past three years. She was young to be a sergeant and she had worked hard to earn her stripes. Schultz liked her. He trusted her with cases like this. She just hoped she wouldn't have to go to the Interlake and spend very much time there. Izzy had grown up near Fiskar Bay. It was where she had worked as a constable before she'd joined the MCU. And she'd lived for a few years with Matt Stavros, now the partner of Roxanne Calloway, who ran the Fiskar Bay detachment.

She'd thought it was kind of cute when Matt and Roxanne had started dating not long after she had left. She hadn't thought that it would last. But there they were, quite the happy couple from what she had been told. Her mother kept her up to date.

"Roxanne's got to be at least five years older than him, maybe seven," Mary McBain never failed to point out. She'd been disappointed when Izzy had chosen to leave Matt. Mrs. McBain had had high hopes for that relationship. "She saw what a good catch he was. He's finished law school, you know. Starting work in Derek McVicar's office this summer. They're saying he'll be a partner in no time at all."

Matt's life seemed to be going exactly as he had planned. He would become Fiskar Bay's family lawyer, doing wills, estate sales. Have a safe, reliable career. A quiet life. Little wonder Izzy had left.

But Roxanne? It looked like she had settled for the same. She and her boy had moved into Matt's big house outside Cullen

Village, the one Izzy had helped build. That surprised Izzy. She'd thought Roxanne was more ambitious. She'd certainly been a good investigator. Izzy had learned a lot from her. Roxanne had been a kind of mentor. Women in an organization like the RCMP needed those, to show the way, and Roxanne had done that, but then she had stopped. Stepped sideways, right off the ladder.

Four years ago, Inspector Schultz would have sent Roxanne north to nose out the truth in a sensitive case like this. She'd tracked down a few killers in her time. If Izzy had to go back to Fiskar Bay to investigate, she'd have to work beside Roxanne. Roxanne's career had stalled at the level of sergeant and now Izzy had caught up to her. Working alongside her now would be weird. She hoped that didn't have to happen.

She called Dave Kovak at Ident and filled him in, briefly, about her meeting with Gordon Palmer.

"He thinks it really is suicide?"

"Seems pretty sure she did it. Says she didn't do well being stuck at home by herself during the pandemic and might have had a mental health problem as a result, all the government's fault for causing the shutdown. He hinted that she drank."

"Well, she sure took a lot of alcohol with her to the lake for one person. A boxful, but maybe she was stocking up. Or she planned to socialize. She shared a bottle of wine with someone before she died."

"There's still nothing on the phone?" There was nothing yet. Just work calls and texts. Her kids. Chat with friends. Stuff like that. "Can you dig deeper? Check her finances? Find out how the business was doing?"

She heard him sigh. Things were busy. There were other cases that had priority, he reminded her. There had been several suspicious deaths on the weekend, two of them actual murders.

"Schultzy wants this one cleaned up real fast," Izzy reminded him. So did she, but she wasn't going to tell Dave that.

"We do what we can, Izzy," he said.

Jay Borthwick, brother of Donna Palmer, was her next call. Izzy drove across the river. The suburb here had been built around the same time as the one where Gord Palmer lived, but the lots were half the size, the houses closer together. Still, they reached three stories high, had inviting porches out front and the streets were lined with elms that were just as tall. Some of them reached so high that they met above the street. She squeezed into a parking spot. Jay Borthwick was home.

"Do you mind being in the kitchen?" he asked her. Something aromatic simmered in a pot on the stove, a Moroccan bean soup he was trying out, he told her. A bundle of rhubarb lay on a counter. He brewed an espresso for her. She didn't have the heart to tell him she'd just drunk coffee, he was so keen to make it for her. Did she want a latte? A cappuccino? No, she said. Straight up was fine. He wiped down the table and made a place for them to sit. He lifted a spice loaf out of a tin and cut her a slice. His partner Jennifer, the baker in the family, had made it. She was working at a local bakeshop. Too bad Izzy couldn't meet her, too. He slid the cake across to Izzy like he was offering her gold.

"I can't believe Donna killed herself," he said, finally sitting down. He was a wiry guy, his ginger hair cropped to a fuzz. He had pale, freckled skin and light eyelashes. "She was fine when I left the lake."

"When was that?"

"Not sure. Saturday night. The sun had just gone down. After ten."

"She wasn't unhappy?"

"Not at all. She was looking forward to having the cottage to herself for a couple of weeks. She always liked being out there."

"You spent the evening together. What else did you talk about?"

"Just stuff. Nothing important. How the kids were doing. We hadn't seen each other in ages. Needed to get caught up. She was glad to be working again, doing the stuff she really liked doing. Said she was going to get some work done on a house she was going to sell while she was out there. It sounded like her business was right back on its feet. I tell you, Sergeant, she was doing okay. She was happy. We picked up some Chinese. Had some dinner and then I left. She said she was going to have an early night."

"How much did she have to drink?"

"Not much. We opened a bottle of wine. Maybe a couple of glasses."

"So, you can't think of any reason at all for her to kill herself?"

He shook his head. "No. Nothing. Not a single thing."

"You've been out there quite a lot lately."

"Sure." He was between jobs right now so he had the time. It was better than being stuck in the city and the cottage needed cleaning up. But Donna had wanted to have her turn. They shared the place, every summer, he and Donna mainly, their sister Leslie, sometimes, but not often. Leslie lived in Saskatoon. And Fraser never showed up. Fraser was the oldest of them.

"Leslie's pretty upset about this, Sergeant. We all are. And I managed to get hold of Fraser. He's in Toronto. Leslie can drive. She'll get here soon but Fraser's maybe stuck. He never has much cash. I thought I could lend him some but Les says he'll just blow it all on drugs. Fraser has a bit of a habit. How long will it be before we can get back into Hazeldean?" he asked. "I've got more work I'd like to get done there."

"You want to go back, even although this has just happened?"

His face puckered up. Jay got up and fetched a paper towel. Blew his nose. Tears gleamed on his straw-coloured eyelashes.

"It's awful," he said. "Jennifer and I talked about that. We'll maybe do a ceremony for Donna out there. Burn some candles. Sing a song. I hope that jerk, Gordon, lets us put her ashes into the lake when the time comes. She would like that."

"Don't you like your brother-in-law?"

"I don't like his politics. Look, Sergeant." He scrunched the paper towel. "Donna was full of life. She was fun. There's no way she would kill herself. Something's wrong here. You've got to promise me you'll find out what's happened so my sister can rest easy." Tears welled up once more.

"We'll do our best," Izzy said, hoping that what he was saying was not true. "But if we end up investigating it as a suspicious death, you may not be able to get back into the cottage for a while longer."

"I guess." He mopped his eyes and blew his nose.

"If we find out something soon," she promised. "I'll let you know."

She went back out to the car. What if Jay Borthwick was right? He sounded sincere. She was inclined to believe him, more than she believed Gordon Palmer, for sure. He certainly seemed more upset about his sister's death than his brother-in-law. What if he was right and Donna Palmer hadn't killed herself at all? Maybe she did need to go out to Cullen Village and look for herself, to eyeball the place, just in case this developed into a more complicated investigation. Izzy didn't want that at all. She liked being Sergeant McBain of the Major Crimes Unit. Going back to the place where she'd grown up, where everyone knew her as "Izzy the Cop" didn't sit right with her at all.

5

ROXANNE DID NOT feel like eating breakfast that Monday morning. She left Matt frying bacon and eggs for himself and Finn and left early for work. Finn was registered for summer day camp. Matt would drop him off on his own way to the office an hour later.

She had just reached the highway to Fiskar Bay when Ravi Anand called in.

"There's a truck pulled up outside that cottage. Hazeldean." His voice rang out over her car phone. "Will I stop in and see?" Ravi was on overnight highway duty. Detouring through the village to check that everything there was fine was part of the routine. It had just gone eight, time for him to clock off.

"Don't worry about it," she told him. "I'll swing by and have a look." She stopped at an empty driveway, turned her car around and drove to Cullen Village. Ravi's car passed, going in the opposite direction, when she was almost there. He flashed his lights in recognition. She flashed back.

He was right. A dirty beige Ford truck was parked in the driveway, nosed right up against a strip of police tape. Roxanne stopped her car and walked past the garage to the back of the cottage. A man stood up on the berm at the end of the lawn, looking out over the water. Police tape blocked his way to the pier.

"This property is off limits, sir!" Roxanne called to him. He jumped at the sound of her voice. Consternation registered on his face when he saw a woman in an RCMP sergeant's uniform walking towards him. He raised both hands to show he meant no harm. Roxanne couldn't see much of his face—it was shaded by a brown ball cap and he was wearing sunglasses—but she could tell that he was fairly tall and had the weathered, muscled look of a man accustomed to hard, outdoor work. He wore knee-length brown shorts and a beige tee, a leather belt. They matched his truck. His leather work boots were worn and sock cuffs were folded at his ankles.

"Where's Donna?" he asked. "What's happened here?"

"We have a case under investigation." Roxanne wasn't going to explain, not until she knew more about who this was. "Who are you?"

"Charlie Cain." The man lowered his hands. "I work for Donna Palmer. She told me to meet her here this morning."

"That right?" Roxanne stopped and looked up at him. "We should talk." She glanced around. There were no prying eyes out here right now but that might not last long. "You'd better meet me at the RCMP detachment. In Fiskar Bay."

He looked alarmed at the suggestion. Was he supposed to have done something wrong? "We can't talk here?" he asked.

She had no keys to the cottage.

"No problem. Donna told me where to find one." He pointed. The veranda stretched along the back of the cottage, the steps dead centre leading up to the back door. On either side was a flower bed full of dirt; nothing planted there so far this year. Each was edged with pieces of rock. "Third stone on the left," he said. They ducked under the tape and went to look. There it was, a metal tag in the shape of a letter 'B' attached to it, nestled in the dry soil under a smooth lump of grey granite. Ident had never thought to search there.

Roxanne held it in her hand and looked up at him.

"How long have you known about this?" she asked.

"Just since Friday. Donna said she liked to go out in the morning while she was here. Go for a walk or a swim. Said to let myself in if she wasn't here and make myself some coffee. She wouldn't be long. Just what's happened to her?"

"Let's go inside." Roxanne went up the steps and unlocked the back door. He followed her into the kitchen. They sat down. She described what they had found. He rubbed his hands on his knees and shook his head when he heard.

"You've got to be kidding," he said. "Kill herself? Donna? No way."

"You drove up here, early, from Winnipeg?" He nodded. "Why were you supposed to meet her out here?"

"I'm her fixit guy," he explained. "I help her get houses ready for selling. We were going to go look at a place on the lake, somewhere between here and Fiskar Bay. We were supposed to meet the couple that own it this morning to decide what work needs to be done to their house."

"What kind of work?"

"Well…" He'd removed his hat, revealing short, thick brown hair. Deep lines on his tanned face creased as he spoke. "Donna isn't your average real estate person, y'know. She helps people get the house fixed up real good before she lists it. That's where I come in. We haul stuff to the dump. Put things in storage. Do repairs. A bit of painting. Bumps the price of the house right up."

"Must do, if she's paying for you to come all the way from Winnipeg to do the work," Roxanne commented.

"There's two more houses out here need fixing," Cain said. "Maybe three. I was supposed to stay over and get everything done so she could sell them by the end of next month. Donna would persuade the owners of a house to put some money into making the place look its best. Then she'd call me in and we'd figure out what it would cost before we got started. That's what I'm here to do. It's not just me she has on the payroll. She's got other real estate folks working for her. A couple of women do the cleaning. She contracts the movers and takes care of everything so the sellers don't have to lift a finger. She's brilliant, Donna." He rubbed the knuckles of his well-worn fingers, anxious and puzzled.

"Tell me." Roxanne looked around the shabby kitchen. "If that was what she did for a living, why is this cottage in the state it's in?"

"She had it on her list." Charlie Cain looked around too, like he was assessing what needed to be done. "She was crazy busy. But you know how it is. Your own house is the last one to get done.

"And we're just coming out of the pandemic. She had to lay most of us off, back then. She managed to sell some houses online. Got someone to make videos and did virtual tours, but we couldn't get in to do all the fixing-up. It wasn't the same. The money just wasn't coming in the way it used to. And she hated having to work from home. Donna liked to be out meeting people, helping them figure out how to get the best buck for their house and how to find a new place that was just right for them. She was real glad when things began to open up again. She hired us back, soon as she could. Got back in the game, and she was doing just great. We've been run off our feet since February."

"Well," said Roxanne. "It looks like you're not going to be fixing up any houses out here now."

"I suppose." He fished his phone out of his pocket and checked the time. It had just turned nine. "I'd better go tell the couple we're supposed to be meeting today that it won't be happening. They'll be at the house right now. Can I get going?" He didn't have a name for the sellers of the house, but it was on the highway and he had a number. He'd find the place.

"Where would you have stayed if you had to work out here?" she asked him.

"Got a trailer," he replied. He fished a business card out of his wallet. CH CAIN CONSTRUCTION, it said. She gave him hers.

"She really died out there?" he asked, when he got to the door and could see all the way to the far end of the long, narrow pier.

"Afraid so."

"I can't believe it." Charlie looked sad and perplexed. He hadn't just lost his boss, he was fresh out of a job. "Hope you find out what happened to her real soon," he said as he shook her hand.

His was calloused and rough. He ducked under the yellow tape again, climbed into his truck and backed it out of the driveway in one smooth move.

Roxanne went to her own car. There were latex gloves in the trunk. Then she went back inside the house and started a search of her own, in case anything else had been missed. The box of wine was now stored in the bottom of a kitchen closet. It contained eleven bottles, five red, six white, from a speciality wine shop in Winnipeg. A bag from the same store sat beside it, containing gin, vermouth and a bottle of single malt whisky. In the fridge she found pâté and six kinds of cheese. There was tenderloin steak, cut thick, ready for the barbecue. Fruit. Packaged salads. The freezer section was stacked with gourmet meals, all oven ready, from Winnipeg's best known and most expensive deli. Donna Palmer had intended to eat well for the next couple of weeks. There was enough food here to feed many people. Perhaps she'd been going to entertain guests.

She walked into the room where the woman had planned to sleep and opened the bag that lay on the bed. It contained the usual things: clothes she would have packed for the lake, a swimsuit, shorts, tank tops, flip-flops. Lacy underwear. A couple of thongs and a silky shift of a nightgown. Roxanne let the material run through her fingers and remembered the yellow pyjamas, also silk. She dug further into the bag and found a smaller one containing makeup. There was lipstick, eye makeup, foundation. Another bag held skin cream, suntan oil, a bottle of massage oil. She held that bottle in her hand. Who had been going to do the massaging?

She walked down the shady hallway and out onto the veranda once more. The sunlight blazed on the shimmering lake, the pier etched against it a linear, angular shadow.

Had Donna Palmer planned to spend her week at the lake with company, a special friend? Was that the reason for the sexy lingerie and massage oil? Her husband, Gordon Palmer, had been in Ottawa, so who would have been her guest? And why was Charlie Cain trusted with knowing how to unlock the house?

Her phone beeped. Aimee Vermette had texted from Fiskar Bay. *Sgt McBain here from MCU*, it said. Roxanne closed the door, replaced the key under the stone where it had been found, got into her car and drove north.

Izzy McBain hadn't changed a bit, apart from the hair.

"I like it," said Roxanne, as Izzy pulled up a chair opposite Roxanne's desk. She caught sight of Aimee Vermette watching from the outer office, taking in every move. Someone must have told her that Roxanne and Izzy McBain were old acquaintances. Maybe she knew that Roxanne's partner, Matt Stavros, had once lived with Izzy. Roxanne closed the door.

"Easier to keep when it's shorter." Izzy had noticed that they were being observed as well. This was what always happened around her hometown. Someone would call her mom and tell her that her daughter was in town, for sure. Mary McBain would know Izzy was here by the time her she had finished talking with Roxanne.

"And you're a sergeant now?" Roxanne sat back behind her desk.

"I am. I've caught up to you," said Izzy. "Just got my stripes a couple of months ago." She couldn't resist grinning, pleased with herself.

"So has Schultz sent you to investigate? Officially?" Usually if one of the Major Crimes Unit was going to be working out of her detachment, Roxanne would have been informed. She hadn't been told a thing.

"He wants this one dealt with quietly. And quickly. I'm supposed to find out why Donna Palmer killed herself, ASAP." Izzy reached out a hand and helped herself to a wrapped candy from a dish that Roxanne kept on her desk for visitors. "Then he can close the case and we will be done." She unwrapped a lemon drop and popped it in her mouth. "How's Matt doing these days?" she asked.

"Fine," Roxanne replied, matching Izzy's easy tone. "He's down the street right now, in McVicar's law office if you want to stop in and say hi."

"That's okay. You're still living in that big house he built?"

"We are. Me and Finn." Roxanne knew that Izzy had had some say in the design. If she had stayed with Matt, she would still be living there. "We like it there. Lots of space." That wasn't entirely true. Matt had inherited money and the land he had built it on from a favourite aunt. Her ashes were buried under a tree near the house. Roxanne would have preferred to live in Fiskar Bay, close to work and Finn's school, but she knew that her partner was never going to budge. "You know Matt's got himself another dog?"

Matt had adopted a scruffy terrier mix called Joshua when he was still living with Izzy. He now also had a yellow Labrador that he'd named Maisie.

"Figures. And you haven't got married yet?" Izzy knew the answer to that, perfectly well. Her mother would have told her if there had been a wedding.

"We like things the way they are," Roxanne responded and decided it was time to change the subject. "So where are you at with this case?"

Izzy sucked on the candy and told her. "Ident hasn't found a single thing to prove that Donna Palmer killed herself. Her husband, the politician, is trying to tell us that she could have committed suicide. He's talking about mental health issues and hinting that she liked to drink, but nobody else is. I'm not sure I believe him, he's too smooth to be true. Not that he could have killed her, if it happens to be murder. He was in Ottawa when she died. Her brother Jay says she was happy when he left her at Hazeldean on Saturday night. She was looking forward to a couple of weeks all by herself out at the cottage."

Roxanne was about to open her mouth to suggest otherwise—to tell her about the lingerie and all the goodies that Donna had brought out to Hazeldean and also about her encounter with

Charlie Cain—when Aimee Vermette tapped on the door and stuck her head around.

"Phone call, Sarge," she said. "From Freya Halliday, at Cullen Village. Thought you should know there's a car just arrived at Hazeldean and a woman's just wheeled a suitcase inside."

"Oops," said Izzy. "Best be on my way." Within minutes she was out the front door and into the sunshine.

Roxanne's observations would have to wait until later. A few years ago, she would have been the one whose job was to check out the new intruder at Hazeldean, but now that job had fallen to Izzy. Hopefully, Izzy would keep her informed.

Right now, she felt mildly queasy. She recognized the symptoms. She had to be pregnant. It had happened like this before, when she'd had Finn. She didn't throw up; she just felt sick at first in the morning, then later in the day she wanted the kind of food she never usually ate. Greasy fries. Bread with butter. Carbs and fat. It was early, she must be five weeks gone at most. This would be a January baby if she was right.

She knew what this meant for her job. RCMP policy regarding pregnant members was clear. Desk work only until she left on maternity leave. The force wasn't going to risk the life of an unborn child in the line of duty, so going out and about, investigating, would be forbidden, as soon as her superintendent knew. She'd be stuck in the office, while anything interesting, like this present case, was developing in her area. These were early days, she reassured herself. With a bit of luck, the baby wouldn't show for another three months. She could just keep quiet about it and not let on until she had to.

How did she feel about having another baby? She wasn't at all sure. She'd become used to the idea that Finn would always be an only child. A newborn baby was going to disrupt her life. But she knew that Matt would be excited. He'd want the whole world to know, Finn too; and while Matt might be persuaded to keep their secret for a few weeks, her son would blab, for sure.

So she wouldn't say anything to anyone, just yet. Wait until she was certain. She couldn't get a pregnancy test done right now. Buying one locally was out of the question. The pharmacist might be trusted not to spread the word but you couldn't say the same for his cashier. She'd have to wait until she could get into Winnipeg before she could pick one up. In the meantime, she would carry on and hope that Matt wouldn't notice her change of appetite.

She left her office and walked out onto the baking hot tarmac. She might as well go down to the law office and let him know that Izzy was back in town before someone else did. She could have called him but she'd rather tell him face to face.

6

LESLIE BORTHWICK LOOKED a lot like the photos Izzy had seen of her sister, Donna, but in those Donna had smiled. Leslie did not. "I drove all the way here from Saskatoon. Left as soon as I heard the news. It took me twelve hours. I am tired. I need to sleep," she complained to Sergeant McBain.

"You can't do that here, ma'am."

"Why ever not?" She stood in the hallway of Hazeldean, frowning at Izzy through her glasses. They had thin, gold rims. Leslie was dressed smartly in summer business wear, white pants and a matching jacket, a blue top underneath. Her suitcase stood in the hallway. "I know you've got yellow tape up but you're done here, aren't you?"

"This is still a crime scene. We don't know for sure that your sister took her own life. We're still investigating."

Leslie's lips pursed as she thought about what that implied.

"Hello!" A voice rang out behind Izzy. Freya Halliday stood in the open doorway, silhouetted against the bright light outside. "Why, isn't it Izzy McBain?" she asked.

"Sergeant McBain these days, Councillor Halliday," Izzy corrected her. "Major Crimes Unit."

"Glad to hear you're doing so well, Izzy. Your mother must be so proud of you." Freya flashed Izzy a patronizing smile and took the opportunity to peer further into the cottage. "And aren't you Leslie Borthwick?" She took another step inside.

"You can't come in here, Councillor." Izzy blocked her way.

"Just wanted to offer my condolences." But Freya did as she was told. Izzy was RCMP, after all, and cooperating with the police was always a good idea. She waved a hand as she left. "I'm here to help, anytime."

Izzy bit her lip. She was not sure if the offer to help was for her or Leslie, but she was fairly sure Freya had heard her say that suicide might not have been the cause of Donna Palmer's death. That news would be all around Cullen Village by nightfall.

"I need some water." Leslie strode past her into the kitchen and helped herself to a bottle from the fridge. She did look tired, but not as weary as she should if she had driven overnight from Saskatoon. Maybe that wasn't true and she had stopped off on the way. The eyeliner and mascara behind her gold frames were well applied and her lipstick was freshly pink. There were rings on her fingers and heeled sandals on her feet. Leslie appeared prosperous. She drank from the bottle and took an iPhone, gold coloured to match her sandals, from the pocket of her pants.

"I suppose I'm going to have to find somewhere else to stay," she sighed. "Not that there's going to be anything decent available out here at such short notice."

"Your brother-in-law, Gord, has a huge house in the city. He could maybe spare you a room?" Izzy suggested. Leslie scrunched up her nose at the suggestion. "Have you talked to him?"

"Briefly." Leslie put away the phone and drank some more water. "He didn't have much to say. Never does, not to me, anyway. It was my brother, Jay, who called me and told me what had happened. He said that Donna was found hanging off the end of the pier out there." Her voice began to waver and she suddenly teared up, just as her brother had done the previous day. "How can my sister have committed suicide?" she cried and sank down onto a kitchen chair.

"We'll know more about that, soon," said Izzy. She hoped that was true, that the body wouldn't sit in the morgue for days until it was autopsied. She passed over a roll of paper towel and watched

Leslie rip off a sheet and wipe her eyes. Now her mascara was smeared. Izzy suddenly felt sorry for her.

"You and your sister were close?"

Leslie nodded, unable to speak. Her hair was as fair as Donna's would have been without the bleaching. Straighter. A no-nonsense short cut.

"Let's find you a hotel," Izzy said. She would try to be helpful and having Leslie Borthwick feel that the RCMP was on her side might be useful. She phoned the Fiskar Bay constabulary and asked the young woman constable she'd seen working the front desk if she knew of anywhere that was available. By the time she had finished, Leslie had wiped off most of her eye makeup. It had left dark smudges. She'd also got her breath back.

"Sorry about that," she said.

"That's okay. When did you last talk to your sister?"

Leslie wasn't sure. It had been a while. She and Donna didn't phone much. Christmas. Birthdays. Mostly they emailed or texted. They had messaged last week. Donna had said she'd been looking forward to spending some time out here, at Hazeldean.

"We all love this cottage," she said. "Why would Donna go and do this to herself here? It'll never be the same again. We'll always know that she died out on the pier." Tears oozed onto her cheeks again. She wiped them off, dried her glasses and put them back on.

Donna had been doing okay, she said. Her business had suffered during the pandemic but she had plugged into a government assistance program when she'd needed it, and she'd sold some houses from home. It wasn't like they didn't have money coming in. Gord had a regular paycheque. Donna had coped, like she always did. Now Bricks and Sugar was up and running again.

As far as she knew, both Donna's kids were fine. "Graeme's a world class athlete," she said. "He's doing great. Donna was so proud of him. And Amelia had joined her in the business. Everything was going Donna's way again. There was no need for her to die. Do you think someone might have done this to her?" she asked between sniffs.

Aimee Vermette called in time for Izzy to avoid answering that question. There was a vacancy at the hotel at Fiskar Bay. Some family had tested positive for the virus and had cancelled at the last minute. There was a waiting list for rooms, but since it was the RCMP calling, the hotel would hold the room for them for two hours.

"I'd best go check myself in. Got to make myself look presentable first, though." Leslie went to her suitcase, snapped it open and produced a makeup bag. While she was at it, she gave Izzy her business card. BORTHWICK FINANCIAL SERVICES, Izzy read. Leslie Borthwick was an accountant. She looked the part. She went to the bathroom, wiped off what was left of her makeup, reapplied it, then ran a comb through her hair. She went back to the kitchen and helped herself to one of the wine bottles from the cupboard before she closed her suitcase once more.

"I can take one of these?" she asked. Izzy didn't see why not. Leslie reached into her pocket and pulled out a set of keys.

"You have your own?" asked Izzy.

"Of course," Leslie said as she pulled her wheelie bag to the door. "We all do. You're not going to stay here, are you? I can lock up?"

Izzy helped her hoist the suitcase into the back of her car. She was leaving, too. Leslie had said nothing to help her prove that Donna Palmer had killed herself. She might have to stay out here, in the Interlake, herself. She could always go sleep in her old room in her parents' farmhouse outside Fiskar Bay tonight, but she'd as soon avoid that if she could.

Matt Stavros was not in his office. He was out visiting a client, Derek McVicar told Roxanne, a farmer's wife, newly widowed and not confident about driving because her husband had always insisted on taking the wheel. She was unable to get off the farm by herself and was having to figure out whether she should sell it or not. Matt had said he'd go out there to advise her.

"Kind man, your husband," Derek said.

"We're not married," Roxanne reminded him.

"But as good as." Derek McVicar had a long face and thinning hair. He'd worn a suit to work, in this summer heat, looking every inch the trusted family lawyer that Fiskar Bay believed him to be. "I was just going over to the Yacht Club for a bite to eat. Care to join me?"

Roxanne still wasn't hungry, but she knew better than to refuse an invitation from Matt's new boss, and he might be able to tell her something useful about the Borthwick family. The clubhouse was a short walk away.

As past president, Derek McVicar was ushered to a table at a window overlooking the yachts in the harbour, his sailboat, the *Shirley*, among them. The fish here was always excellent, he assured her, fresh out of the water this morning.

"No, thank you," said Roxanne. "I'll just have a salad." She swallowed some cold water and declined the offer of a glass of wine. "I'm working," she reminded her host.

"Never bothered your predecessor," said McVicar, shaking out his napkin. Then he looked across the table, rueful. Sergeant Bill Gilchrist, who had held the post of RCMP team commander at Fiskar Bay before Roxanne, had come to an unfortunate end four years ago. Roxanne had uncovered his killer. That was the last time anyone had died under suspicious circumstances in this quiet part of the world, as far as either of them knew.

A yachting buddy stopped at the table and was introduced. The clubhouse was a place where the residents of Fiskar Bay who sailed and summer visitors mingled. No one seemed surprised that the town's longest established lawyer and the local head of police were lunching together. Many business meals occurred at these tables. The boat owner didn't stay long, Roxanne's salad arrived, and a steak for her host.

"You're the Borthwick family's lawyer?" she asked.

He was. Always had been. Derek McVicar's father had set up his firm. It went back almost as long as there had been Borthwicks in the Interlake and McVicar's had always taken care of things for them. Sad business about Donna. She'd always been a lot of fun. Just like Lois, her mother. Looked just like her. So did Leslie, her sister, but Donna was the one that took after Lois personality-wise.

And Leslie didn't? Roxanne asked.

"She can be good company when she wants to be," McVicar replied.

"All the siblings own the cottage?" Roxanne picked at the salad. Derek was slicing into a piece of meat with gusto. It was rare. Blood oozed from it.

"They do," he said. "It's an interesting situation." He took on his lawyerly voice. "That cottage has been passed down, father to eldest son, every generation since the first William Borthwick built the place, over a hundred years ago. Will, the father of Donna and her siblings, broke with that tradition. It's shared equally by the four children."

A man in casual sailing clothes, deck shoes on his feet, walked by and said hello. There was some talk of an upcoming regatta. Roxanne picked up a slice of crusty bread and tore off a chunk. She fancied eating that more than the salad. She spread some butter on it.

"Why didn't Fraser inherit it himself? As the oldest son?" she asked, when the yachtsman had moved on.

"Fraser has not done well." David McVicar chewed his steak. Roxanne looked out the window. She could see a boat heading out of the harbour towards open water. McVicar swallowed the meat. "Old Will didn't want to cut him out completely so he did that four-way split. It's not unusual, these days. Both parents are usually working so families don't spend the whole summer at the lake like they used to. This way, each of them get a few weeks instead and they split the costs. Most times it works. If they all get along."

"Do you think they didn't?"

"I'm not saying that." Derek McVicar looked at her archly. Like many lawyers he liked having an audience, even it was only one person. "The Borthwicks are different from one other. The girls are the smart ones. They've both done well for themselves. Lois knew that they were the most capable. She gave them joint power of attorney, when she knew she was going to need that. You're not eating your salad?" he asked. Roxanne picked up some lettuce and nibbled on it to oblige.

"You know, I thought Donna was doing well." He placed the fork on his plate and washed down what he had eaten with a mouthful of red wine. "She ran a successful business and was married to an important man. I've been told that they have a beautiful home in Winnipeg. Her children are both coming along nicely. Graeme's a rower, you know. We got him started, right here, and now he might make Canada's Olympic team." He looked around his club, proud of that accomplishment. "If she was in difficulties, I think she would have found a way around them. She was always resourceful."

"So, you doubt that she would have killed herself?" Roxanne asked.

"That's for your people to decide." McVicar was smart enough not to try to answer that question. "I've been in touch with Donna and Leslie occasionally these past few years but it hasn't been often. Usually Donna, since she was the one still living in Manitoba. Sometimes decisions had to be made about their mother's care. Now Leslie will have sole control of what happens to Lois unless a second person is appointed. Lois still lives here, you know. In Harbourfront House." He pointed toward the window. "Just across the street from here." Harbourfront House was Fiskar Bay's home for the elderly.

"She does?" Roxanne couldn't conceal her surprise. "Why is she not in the city? Close to Donna and Jay?"

"Because"—Derek McVicar leaned in, confidentially—"she's Lois Sigurdson. Married Will Borthwick when she was a teenager.

Her family is local. She grew up here. Her sister Sylvia lives in town. Lois chose to go into Harbourfront, when she knew she was losing her mind. She said she wanted to be where she belongs. Told me that herself. Last time I saw her she had failed a lot but she made the right decision. It's her sister's family that looks out for her. They visit regularly. I drop in, not often but I keep her up to date on what is going on with her affairs. Not that she knows what I'm talking about but I do it anyway. Her daughters haven't seen her since the pandemic started. Not their fault, but I've been told they hardly ever visited her before that. Too busy, I suppose. They just paid the bills when they were asked and left her alone. Stopped in when they had their stint at the cottage and that was it. That happens such a lot these days. You're really not going to finish that?" He watched the server take away the remains of the salad. "All you've eaten is some bread."

"I'm fine," Roxanne assured him. "Just not hungry." And no, she didn't want dessert. "They haven't taken very good care of Hazeldean," she said. "It could use having some money spent on it."

"So I've been told." McVicar nodded sagely. "I'm not sure what that's about, especially since Donna was in the real estate business. I heard from one of her clients today. She said they'll be putting their own house on the market in a few weeks."

"They've found a new realtor, already?" A pot of tea arrived for Roxanne, coffee for MacVicar.

"Not at all." He reached for the cream. "Bricks and Sugar is still going to handle it for them. It seems Donna's daughter, Amelia, will inherit the business and she's going to try to keep it going. The house is a big bungalow, you'll have seen it, halfway between here and Cullen Village, on the lake side. Stone wall. It will fetch a good price."

Roxanne knew exactly which house he meant. Stone walls were rare along the lakefront. She felt her phone vibrate in her pocket and looked. "It's Matt," she said. "Do you mind?"

McVicar did not. He sipped his coffee and looked out at the boats while she took the call.

"Have you heard the news?" Matt asked her. "Donna Palmer's death's just been announced. Suicide. Wife of prominent politician. The premier's made a statement. Heartfelt condolences, respect privacy, the usual."

The Provincial Medical Examiner's office must have fast-tracked the autopsy after all. This result would close the case. There would be no investigation. Everything would return to normal. Roxanne felt a moment's disappointment. She suppressed it as she told Derek McVicar the news.

"Really?" he said. "It's hard to believe but it's better than it being murder, isn't it? We don't want any more of those around here."

Roxanne thanked him for lunch and called Izzy McBain as soon as she got outside.

"That's right." Izzy's voice came through loud and clear. She was in her car, on her way back to Winnipeg, glad that she didn't have to stay in the Interlake after all. The coroner had found in favour of suicide.

"For what reason?" asked Roxanne. She stood outside on the pavement as tourists walked by, conspicuous in her uniform, her cap shading her eyes from the relentless sunshine.

"Mental health issues. Stress. Result of the pandemic. Anything to be able to close the case if you ask me. But that's it. Nice seeing you again, Roxanne. Say hi to Matt for me." And Izzy ended the call.

That was that. Case closed. Roxanne walked back to her office. She stopped when she got to her car. The police tape needed to come down at Hazeldean. She might as well go do it herself, then she could forget about this interesting episode and get on with her real job. And start to think about how life was going to work with a new baby in it.

7

LESLIE BORTHWICK FELT much better the following day, after a good sleep. Her hotel room was pleasant, with a view out over the lake, and she'd been able to book a massage at the spa downstairs. But now, since her sister's death had been declared self-inflicted, Hazeldean was no longer a crime scene. The police could not object if she moved right back in and reclaimed what belonged to her. She checked out before noon and drove the fifteen kilometres south to Cullen Village.

She'd planned to get back home to Saskatoon on the weekend but an email from Gord Palmer's personal assistant, Maria, had informed her that they were hoping to cremate Donna's remains by next Friday. She would have to stay in the Interlake until that happened. That was okay. She could work from the cottage, and she had things to do while she was here. She'd need to check in with the lawyer and find out what happened now that she was the only person in charge of her mother's affairs. She'd have to go to the care home too and visit, although Mom had no idea who Leslie was any more.

When she got to Hazeldean, the yellow tape was all gone and the cottage was deserted. She dragged her suitcase once more to the back of the house and up the veranda steps. Seeing the pier, outlined against the shining water, made her catch her breath again. Donna had chosen to die, here? It still didn't make any sense to her. She shook off that thought and took out her key.

A heap of Donna's belongings still lay on a chair in the bedroom. Those would have to be dealt with sooner or later, but she wasn't ready to do it just yet. First, she'd go make herself a cup of coffee. She went in search of coffee beans. Donna would have brought some with her, she was sure of that.

There was so much good food in the fridge! It was too bad the tenderloin would have to go. It must have been bought almost four days ago. The pâté too. The lettuce was wilting, but the cheeses were fine, and the bread could be toasted. There were eggs. It was too bad she'd paid for breakfast earlier.

She rooted around in a cupboard and found the coffee. An espresso machine sat on the counter. Jay must have brought that out from the city. It looked complicated. She wasn't sure how to work it. Two old percolators lay on a shelf. She didn't intend to use either of those. She continued to search, finding things that had been here since they were kids, and discovered a dusty Bodum coffee press. She filled the kettle from a big, blue water bottle, set up on a water dispenser. It was almost full and must be heavy. Jay would have lifted it up. Another full bottle lay on the floor beside it, enough to last Leslie a couple of weeks if she needed to stay that long.

She heard a motorbike roar up outside and went to look. An older man hoisted himself off the back seat and removed his helmet. He had long, grey hair, looped back into a ponytail, and an untrimmed beard. He passed the helmet to the driver. "Thanks, Wes," she heard him say, then he unbuckled a backpack from behind the pillion and untied a walking cane. He limped toward the house as the bike backed up and roared away.

"Hey, Leslie," said her brother Fraser. "Been a while."

He had lucked out, Fraser told her. His old friend Wes Melnyk had sent him the cash to buy a plane ticket soon as he had heard that Donna was dead. Leslie remembered Wes? Leslie did. Fraser and Wes had been best buddies when they were kids. Got into trouble all summer long. Now Wes had cleaned up his act. He ran the farmers market on his family's land north of Fiskar Bay. Wes was doing okay. He'd picked Fraser up at the Winnipeg airport late last night, taken him to his place for the night, then dropped him off here, at the cottage, this morning.

It had to be six years since Leslie had last seen her brother. He looked like he hadn't fared well. Not that he ever did. He was still in his early fifties but he seemed older, stooped and grey. He must have slept in the clothes he was wearing, worn pants, a dingy shirt, a jacket.

She offered to help him with the backpack as he staggered up the veranda steps. "I'll manage," he insisted, then dropped the backpack in the doorway and wandered down the hallway, looking into all of the rooms. Her suitcase was already lying on the bed in the best bedroom. He joined her in the kitchen. Leslie was grinding coffee beans in a hand grinder that had belonged to her mother. She'd failed to discover an electric one.

"You're planning on staying here?" he asked.

"I am," Leslie replied. "And that bedroom is mine. I'm having the cottage until the end of next week. Why don't you go stay with Wes?"

"Things are busy at Wes's," Fraser replied. Busy meant work and Fraser wasn't up for that. "Hey, Les." He leaned against the door jamb. "You can afford to pay for a room. Why don't you go find somewhere else and let me stay here?"

"It was Donna's turn. I got here first and I am staying."

Leslie's bottom lip jutted out. He'd known that stubborn look since childhood. Fraser took off his jacket and hung it on a hook at the back of the kitchen door. She got a whiff of body odour and wondered when he'd last washed. His cane looked old and came with a gilded handle. He hooked it on the back of a chair and sat down.

"See here," he said. "The deal is we each get four weeks each summer, right? And I've been gone for six years. Six years times four weeks equals twenty-four weeks, due to me. So, I should get to stay most of the summer."

"No." His sister poured boiling water on the coffee grounds. "It doesn't work like that."

"Sez who? And what's it matter to you? You live in Saskatoon most of the time."

"I still get to come here when it's my turn. And now Donna's gone I'll have to be the one who checks up on Mom."

"I could do that," said her brother. He didn't look like he could take care of himself, far less their ailing mother.

"What's with the cane?" she asked.

"RA. Rheumatoid arthritis. Bit of a bummer but I've got good meds. And this stuff helps." He pulled a baggie full of weed out of his pocket and a Zippo lighter.

"You're not smoking that stuff in here. That's a rule." That hadn't always been the case. When they were kids this kitchen had often been full of nicotine smoke. Lois had liked the odd cigarette but their dad had loved them. It was lung cancer that had taken him off.

"Okay, okay. I'll go outside." He stuffed the bag back into his pocket and pushed himself to his feet. Then he took the shiny handle of his cane in his hand and walked to the door, tall and gangly. Unstable, in more ways than one. She hoped he had good meds for that, too. "I take two spoonsful of sugar, no cream," he told her as he went. When she carried the coffee cups outside he was leaning on his cane, looking down at a wicker seat. "Where's the cushions for these?" he complained.

"No idea." The sun was high in the sky; it must almost be noon. And it was hot. "That's where Donna died." Leslie lifted her pointed little chin in the direction of the pier. She felt tears coming again and forced them back.

"I was told," was all Fraser said. He didn't even look in that direction. He still seemed more concerned with problems of his own. "Y'know, I could still stay here. It's just you that's here, right? There's loads of room," he persisted. "You don't need to hog the whole place."

He was right. There were four bedrooms, after all. He'd have to sleep in the other one downstairs, though. It didn't look like he could manage the stairs. Could she put up with him for a week and a half, she wondered?

"Maybe," she said. "But I've got work to do. I can't be spending time taking care of you." Nevertheless, she went and fetched a chair for him from the kitchen.

"Nobody asked you to, Les." Fraser smirked. He sat down and began to roll a joint. "I talked to Gord Palmer this morning. Got an ashtray?" He looked around.

"Lucky you." The ashtrays were on a shelf in full view, but out of Fraser's reach. Leslie sighed and fetched one. "He just sends me messages via the lovely Maria."

"Yeah, well, to hell with that. I phoned the house, this morning, before I came here. You've got to be persistent." He grinned. Yellow teeth, like a mad coyote. It had taken three tries before that smug little jerk, Graeme, answered. Fraser lit up.

"Not so small," said Leslie "He's a big boy now. You should see the muscles on him."

"Ain't tough, though." said Fraser. "I yelled at him and he went and got his dad."

"And?"

"Gord's talking like he's sure it really was suicide."

"That's what the police say, too." Leslie flapped her hand to drive away the smoke.

"Yeah, well, that's all bullshit, isn't it? He's trying to tell me Donna 'wasn't herself.' That the pandemic had 'taken a toll on her mental health.' Who's he trying to kid? When did you last talk to Donna?"

"It's been a month, maybe. We texted. She sounded fine. Was excited about how the business was doing and having Graeme home for the summer. You know that Amelia had started working with her at Bricks and Sugar? Everything was going okay, I thought."

"Except with her and Gordon?"

"You figure?"

"Sure, I figure."

"You haven't seen them in years, Fraser."

"Yeah, but I could tell, just from the way he talked. Too damn smooth, y'know?" He pinched out what was left of the joint. "Maybe he's the one who did her in. Made it look like suicide."

"No," Leslie said. "He can't have. He was in Ottawa when she died."

"He was? Well, bugger that."

"Bugger what?" said a third voice and their little brother, Jay, walked around the side of the house. "Fraser!" he said, spreading both arms wide. "You made it! It's been too long, man!"

Fraser staggered to his feet. Jay ran up the stairs and Leslie watched them hug, both skinny, Fraser almost a foot taller, wrapped around his smaller brother like he needed him for support.

"I guess I'd better make more coffee," she said.

"Coffee be damned." Fraser lifted his head. "Donna must have brought some booze. And is there anything in this house to eat? It must be lunchtime already."

Jay took over the kitchen. He washed the lettuce. Most of it was salvageable. Fraser sniffed out Donna's box of wine like an old hound dog. Jay talked while he whisked and stirred. He'd driven up to Cullen Village because he had to be at the village office for a meeting at two. He and Jennifer, his girlfriend, had this great idea: they were going to start a café, out of the Rec Centre, for the summer. Maybe they'd run it year-round if it worked out. The place had been used as a canteen before, so it had a commercial kitchen. They'd talked to the mayor already and he was in support. They just had to convince a committee now. They'd have to do takeout to begin with but as soon as people were allowed to dine inside again, they would be ready.

"You two won't be staying long, will you?" he asked as they sat down to mushroom omelettes. Salad. Warmed-up buns. "We were thinking we could stay here until we get the business on its feet."

Fraser was pouring himself a second glass of wine. He stopped and put down the bottle "Not so sure about that," he said. "I'd planned on staying myself."

"You can't stay here all summer," his sister told him. "Fraser thinks he can bank all the weeks he's not been here. Six years so he's entitled to twenty-four of them," she explained to Jay. "I've already told him it doesn't work like that."

"No, you can't do that, Fraser," Jay agreed.

"So how come you think you can stay here yourself all summer long?" asked his brother. "You've been here how many weeks, already?"

"Six, on and off," Jay replied. "But I did a lot of work. Took down the shutters. Paid the plumber to turn on the water. Raked up last year's leaves."

"Yes, but Fraser's got a point," said Leslie. "If he can't have it all summer long, why should you?"

"Because Jennifer and I will do some repairs," said Jay. "We'll pay for them, in lieu of rent. Paint the place. It needs it or the wood's going to rot. It sure needs looking after, now that we're keeping it. Donna's not going to be knocking it down after all."

"Donna was going to do what?" Fraser asked, confused. Leslie wondered how his meds reacted with marijuana and now alcohol. He wasn't eating. His omelette was growing cold on his plate.

"You know all about it, Fraser! She wrote us last year. Wanted us to sell our shares to her. So she could demolish this old cottage and build some big monstrosity in its place. You got the letter, didn't you? She told me that you did." Jay pushed the salad bowl toward his brother while he spoke. "She needed to buy us all out but I said no, so that wasn't going to happen. Eat some salad. That's a great vinaigrette." It was, but Fraser ignored it. He chewed his bottom lip while he tried to remember.

"She wanted to build another house here?" he finally asked.

"No!" Jay explained again, slowly. "She was going to tear this one down. Hazeldean. Cut down the trees. Everything."

"And then she was going to build a beach house. A big one. Sell it once it was finished. It would have made a nice profit. Donna told me prices had jumped up here already," Leslie explained, quite calmly.

"She wasn't! Over my dead body!" Fraser protested.

"That's an unfortunate choice of words, given the circumstances, Fraser," his sister remarked. "Think about it. It wasn't a bad idea," she told them, methodically eating her way through her salad. "You're never here, Fraser, and I'd as soon go on a trip to Europe as have to come back every summer. I know that means you get to be around more than us, Jay, but that's not exactly fair, is it. And who are we going to pass this place on to when we're gone? Your kids are in B.C. They've hardly ever been here. They're not going to want it. I've got no kids and Fraser here... Do you have any that we don't know about, Fraser?"

"Not telling." Her brother grinned. Then he nudged Jay. "I'll bet she was in on it!" He pointed a finger, nubbed with swollen joints, at Leslie. "You and Donna were working in cahoots, right? Were you going to help pay to build that new house then share the profit when it got sold?" Leslie's mouth opened and closed. "See!" he clapped his hands together, triumphant. "Got it right, first time, didn't I?"

"You just made that up, Fraser." Leslie dismissed what he had said, but Fraser was having none of it.

"Gotcha, Les. It's all about the cash, isn't it? You and Donna. Pair of money grabbers, the two of you. Just like Dad. Well, Donna's gone and that big house isn't going to get built here after all, so you can say goodbye to that little scheme." He yawned. "You know what, I need a nap." He pushed himself upright, lifted his cane, and hobbled off down the hallway to the second bedroom. Within minutes he was lying on the bed, sound asleep, still in his old clothes, his boots still on his feet.

"You really thought that was a good idea?" Jay accused his sister. They were both on their feet by now. He wasn't much taller than her. They stood almost eyeball to eyeball.

"Really what?" asked Leslie, arms akimbo.

"Tear down Hazeldean?" asked Jay. "You can't do that! This place has always belonged to us."

"It's a dump, Jay. It's time to let it go. The place is an old wreck, look at it. An eyesore. It's time it was gone, it's a tear-down. Don't you have a meeting to get to?"

He did. It was almost two.

"I have to go check on Mom," Leslie said. "Then I'm going to find somewhere else to stay. I don't need this hassle and I'm not staying here, having to put up with Fraser. I've got old school friends in Winnipeg. I'll call around and see if any one of them can put me up. If not, I'll find an Airbnb."

She strutted off down the hallway, took the suitcase off the bed and hauled it back to her car. She left her little ginger-haired brother to clean up the debris of their lunch, in the tacky old cottage that he loved so much. She didn't care if she ever saw the place again. Not now that Donna had died here. She and her sister had had such a good plan for offloading Hazeldean. Now that wasn't going to happen. It was too bad she had to stick around and put up with both of her brothers for a while. And she supposed she'd have to keep coming back to the Interlake to check up on their old mother, once a year, for sure. If it wasn't for that she would have been able to stay away for good.

8

JAY BORTHWICK'S MEETING with the mayor and a couple of councillors at the Cullen Village office went well. They were sorry about his sister's death but enthused at his plan to open up the kitchen at their Rec Centre.

"The Cullen Village Café?" the mayor suggested. Jay and his partner Jennifer had thought of calling it The Laughing Coyote as a nod to his city restaurant, once successful, now defunct.

"You can't be too adventurous out here," one of the councillors cautioned him. "We're used to burgers and hot dogs." Jay understood that. They'd keep the menu simple to begin with but they'd like to introduce some more interesting menu choices on the side.

"My partner's a pastry chef," he said. "We were thinking about offering some baked goods. Butter tarts? Cinnamon buns? She can do special cakes to order. Birthdays, weddings, you name it. And we're talking to an ice cream supplier."

Cullen Village had lost its ice cream shop to the pandemic. Going for a walk and buying a cone on a summer night was a long-held tradition. Reinstating that was a clincher.

"And you'll be staying at Hazeldean?" Freya Halliday sat across the table from him. Jay had recognized her as soon as he walked in the door. She lived right opposite the cottage. He'd met her several times already, when he had been out raking leaves, earlier this year.

"We hoped so," he said. "But it might not work out now, given what's just happened to my sister. My brother and my sister are both here and we all have shares in the cottage. Do you know if anyone has a cottage to rent? Reasonably priced?"

They doubted if that was possible. Airbnb had made it easy for cottage owners who didn't stay here all summer to rent out week by week, which had turned out to be profitable and popular. Cottages were booked weeks in advance, but they would put out the word.

Jay returned to his home in the city, to tell his partner the good news. The café was a go, they could start as soon as they liked. The sooner they could get going the better, since the summer season was short, he and the village committee had agreed.

Freya Halliday had taken the opportunity to have a long chat before Jay drove off. As soon as she got home, she told her husband, Doug, what she had heard.

"He'd like to winterize Hazeldean. Live there, all year round."

She looked out the window at the old cottage. Leslie Borthwick's car had been parked there earlier but it was gone now. Was she the reason Jay and his family couldn't stay there? If one of the Borthwicks was going to be a permanent neighbour, she'd as soon it was Jay. He was by far the most likeable of the family that she had met. He'd made an effort to take care of Hazeldean, and this café he was planning to set up would be an asset to the village.

The Hallidays needed to make sure he could get that up and running. If that meant finding Jay and his new family somewhere else to stay, temporarily, they would help. Didn't Doug's friend, Sandy Ferguson, have a mobile home that he wasn't driving anywhere this year, because he was waiting for a knee replacement?

"I'll go talk to him," said Freya's accommodating husband and took his car keys down off a hook.

Inside Hazeldean, across the road, Fraser Borthwick had found the gin and a bottle of Glenmorangie in a bag beside all that wine. And cheese in the fridge. He called his good buddy, Wes Melnyk.

"Come over tonight," he said. "Bring some of the gang. We'll have a party."

Herb Appleby's wife, June, was paying a long overdue visit to her old friend and neighbour, Lois Borthwick, at Harbourfront House, the care home in Fiskar Bay, when Leslie Borthwick appeared at the door of her mother's room. Leslie walked in and pecked her mother on the cheek. The old lady smiled sweetly but her eyes remained blank. She sat in a chair, wrapped in a blanket even although the room was warm. Lois had once been athletic. She and June battled it out on the tennis courts many times when they were younger but now she was frail, skin and bone. Lois was younger than June, but you would never know it. She looked ten years older.

"This is Leslie, your daughter," June told Lois, since Leslie hadn't mentioned her name. She offered to go so mother and daughter could have this time together but Leslie said she needed to have a word with the manager of Harbourfront House, right now. June could stay and visit as long as she pleased. Off she went down the polished corridor, her heels clicking on the tiled floor, a briefcase in her hand, like she was going to attend a business meeting. She disappeared into an office a few doors down.

June had brought flowers, a bunch of gerbera daisies that she'd picked up at the grocery store. A nurse came by and offered to go put them in a vase.

June talked to Lois about her family. How she'd seen Leslie arrive at Hazeldean that morning and then someone else that she thought might be Fraser, wasn't that exciting? Then Jay had driven up too. She didn't tell Lois that Fraser looked like he might be homeless, or that Donna had been found on the weekend, dead. There was no need to upset the old lady.

Another visitor arrived, a fair-haired, older woman in a summer dress. Lois's face lit up when she walked into the room.

"She doesn't know who I am anymore," said Sylvia Olafson, Lois's sister. "But I drop by most afternoons and she's always glad to see me. Aren't you, Lois?" she said and she gave her sister a proper hug. She'd brought her a fresh peach. "Lois loves these," she said. She'd stopped at the cafeteria on the way in and got a plate and a knife. Sylvia sliced up the peach while she was talking and then she pulled up a chair beside her sister and fed her, slice by slice, dropping each piece into her mouth like she was feeding a baby bird. She had a napkin ready, to wipe the juice off Lois's chin.

"Did you know that your niece Leslie just dropped by?" June asked. Sylvia stopped feeding Lois.

"She came to visit? When?" she asked.

"She's still here. In the manager's office," June told her.

Sylvia frowned. She looked toward the door then at the rest of the peach, still lying on a plate in her hand.

"I should go see what that's about," she said. June offered to give Lois the rest of the peach, if she liked.

"Would you? Thanks so much!" Sylvia handed her the plate and disappeared down the hallway. The nurse came back with the daisies in a vase.

"Look, Lois! Aren't these pretty colours?" She held them down so Lois could see them.

"No way!" A loud voice could be heard quite clearly from along the corridor. "You can't take her all that way."

"Oh no!"

The nurse sat down on the bed beside Lois's chair. She held a thin, bony hand in her own strong one. Sylvia must have left the door to the manager's office ajar. It was her voice they had heard. Leslie was speaking now. She was not so loud, saying something about it being closer to home. But they could hear every word that Sylvia said in reply.

"Saskatoon? That's not her home! She's been here for years. This is where she belongs." Then Leslie said something about it being more convenient and Sylvia really lost it.

"Convenient for Lois? No way. This is just like you, Leslie. You never come near her and now you say you're going to take care of her? She'll not last long if you take her away from here and that's what you really want, isn't it? You want her dead and gone. I know what this is all about. It's your mom's money you're after."

"That is a disgusting thing to say, Aunt Sylvia," Leslie enunciated quite clearly.

Someone must have noticed that the door was open at that point and closed it. They couldn't hear anything any longer. Lois ate the rest of her peach, quite unperturbed, but the nurse was visibly upset.

"That daughter, Leslie, never comes near her mother. She seems to think it's just a matter of paying the bills." She found some wet wipes on a shelf and cleaned Lois's face. She talked quietly to June, almost whispering. "Sylvia visits most days. She's the one that takes proper care of Lois. She rubs lotion on her hands and her feet. Wheels her out to the garden on days like this so she can feel the sun and listen to the birds. You know they both used to sing? Sylvia and Lois? Solos and duets with the Fiskar Bay Singers, years ago. They sang at my parents' wedding. Well, sometimes Sylvia will start singing one of those old songs and Lois joins in. She remembers some of the words. It brings tears to my eyes, listening to the two of them.

"It'll be a crying shame if Leslie takes her mother away from Harbourfront. I wonder if Sylvia can put a stop to it? Or Leslie's brothers. Do you think they know about it?"

"I'll make sure one of them does," June assured her.

The party that night at Hazeldean was a riot, literally. Trucks converged on the cottage, well into the evening. Some of them had Canadian flags emblazoned on their sides. Signs that featured the word "Freedom" hung in their windows.

There was a huge semi parked right outside the Applebys' house, another along the road in front of Susan Rice, the yoga teacher's, place. She would not be happy about that.

"Freedom truckers, right in our neighbourhood. Fraser Borthwick must be responsible for this." Herb Appleby peered out his bedroom window. Disobeying government advice would be just Fraser's style. And he must have friends who thought likewise. He had to have invited this rowdy crowd.

Herb had been told by the Hallidays that Jay Borthwick had gone back to Winnipeg and there was no sign of Leslie's car any longer. Fraser had been lounging on the veranda behind Hazeldean all that afternoon. Herb had gone over to say hello. Fraser's appearance, close up, had shocked him. "He looks down-and-out. I'd never have known him," Herb told his wife. He hadn't stayed long. There was a strong smell of marijuana hanging in the air. It was probably worse now.

There were at least two dozen people in the house, more outside. Crowds like that were against government regulations, because of the pandemic. They were yelling. Dancing. Playing loud music. They'd lit a fire, down on the beach. Some of them were way out in the water. Herb was sure they were stark naked. By midnight the noise hadn't abated.

It wasn't Herb who called 911 and reported the ruckus to the police. It was Susan Rice. This pandemic wasn't over. People could only gather in groups of ten, twelve or so. But there were dozens out there, and not one of them wearing a mask, she told the dispatcher, probably none of them were vaccinated against the virus, either. They were disturbing the peace. Susan's children couldn't sleep for the noise. She didn't mention that her boy and girl, one preteen, the other younger, were gleefully watching the goings-on behind Hazeldean out of an upstairs window while she talked.

Ravi Anand and Aimee Vermette showed up shortly after. They found the cottage full of truckers and their friends, tired of rules that made it difficult for them to do their work. They listened to the radio while they drove long distances, had done all through the pandemic. Conspiracy theories abounded on the airwaves, about how the virus had originated, how Big Pharma was poisoning people with these vaccines that the government told them they should get. You were supposed to wear masks all the time? Not them. There were folks making a fortune out of this and those people were out to control the world. The government was their puppet. Only guys like them knew the real truth.

One Sikh RCMP officer and a little French girl cop in uniform, both of them wearing face masks, didn't impress them one bit. They'd go home when this party was over and they would decide when that was, they said.

Ravi did a quick head count. Twenty-one of them in the house, a dozen on the veranda, more dancing around the fire down below and splashing about out in puddles along the edge of the lake. There were a few kids among them.

"Gatherings are restricted to a maximum of twelve people indoors. Whose party is this?" he demanded to know. A hand tried to yank the mask off his face. Someone tapped his head and asked if he'd like to go for a swim, since he'd brought his towel along.

"Aren't you the guy who runs the farmers market?" Aimee recognized Wes Melnyk.

That bothered Wes. He didn't want all of Fiskar Bay knowing he had friends like these and thinking that he might not be vaccinated. That might stop people from coming to his market. He put on a good face.

"I don't serve the public myself," he told her. "I just rent out the land. And I've had all my shots."

"You need to leave, now." Aimee barely reached his shoulder or that of the lanky man that stood beside him, leaning on a cane. He was bearded, unkempt, and quite drunk.

"No, no!" The man draped an arm around his friend's shoulder. "Wes can't go yet. The party's hardly started."

"Maybe I should, Fraser." Wes Melnyk peeled himself out from under his friend's arm. He didn't want to rub the local cops the wrong way.

"You're Fraser Borthwick? You're responsible for this gathering?" Aimee noticed Ravi at the door, his back to her. She might have to make an arrest. "There are almost twice the number of people in this house than are allowed," she declared. "That is a chargeable offence. So is disturbing the peace. I need you to come along with me, sir." She made sure she said it loudly enough for Ravi to hear her above all the noise.

"Come with me!" Someone mimicked her Franco-Manitoban accent and laughed. Fraser laughed too. She reached out for his left arm. He pulled it back and his expression changed.

"Don't touch me, bitch," he yelled. He raised the cane in his other hand and brought it down, hard.

Ravi Anand turned when he heard Aimee cry out and moved closer. He saw Fraser raise the stick again, pulled out his taser and zapped him. Fraser fell to the ground.

"The bastard's killed him," a woman screamed. Aimee Vermette was holding her shoulder. She looked like she was going to be sick.

A siren shrieked close by.

"More cops on their way," someone called from outside.

"Everybody out!" Wes Melnyk hollered and he ran for the door.

9

FRASER BORTHWICK SMELLED of stale booze. He'd lain in a
cell all Tuesday night, courtesy of the Fiskar Bay RCMP. He'd be
taken in front of a magistrate that afternoon, Roxanne informed
him in the bleak confines of an interview room, while they waited
for a van from the sheriff's office to come and escort him to
Winnipeg. She wore a mask and had insisted he did so too. He
was charged with three offences, the first, of disturbing the peace:
Fraser shrugged that off. The second, of assembling more than
twelve people in one place, contrary to current regulations.

"That'll just get me a fine." He dismissed that with a yawn.
That was true, and his trucker friends would probably pay it for
him. But assaulting a police officer in the line of duty was another
matter. Aimee Vermette had sustained a broken collarbone. "Not
my fault. She attacked me first."

Fraser's friends backed him up, but Ravi Anand said otherwise.
"Him? The guy that tasered me? Who's going to believe him? I'll
promise to appear in court like a good boy and then they'll let me
out, you'll see." He grinned his old wolfdog smile, confident, or
pretending to be. "How's about you let me go outside for a smoke
before they take me for a drive?" The police had confiscated all
his belongings, including his supply of weed. He'd been given his
prescribed pills, according to the dose, but that was all.

Roxanne didn't think that the magistrate would release him.
There was no guarantee he wouldn't vanish back to Ontario, where
he'd be out of the Manitoba provincial court's jurisdiction as soon
as he was free.

"How did you get here from Toronto?" she asked him.

"On a plane."

"How did you pay for the ticket?"

"Got it from a friend."

"You need proof of vaccination to travel and you don't have it."

"Sure I do. I've had the shots. You think I'm stupid?"

"Where is it?"

"That vaccine card? It wasn't in my pocket? Maybe it's in my backpack."

"What backpack?"

"It's at the cottage. You'll need to go look." His sly grin appeared once more.

"Maybe you got a ride from one of your trucker friends instead?"

"What trucker friends?"

She got up to go, tired of the game. She didn't believe a word he said.

"You're entitled to a lawyer," she reminded him before she left.

"Who? That old geezer that works out here? No, thanks. I'll get my own." The trucker crowd had good connections. If he needed legal advice, he would get it.

Roxanne allowed him his smoke. One cigarette. Constable Sam Mendes escorted him to the fenced scrap of grass out back of the building, in the blazing sunshine. The sheriff's van arrived before he was done and took him away.

Leslie Borthwick had been lucky. An old school friend from Winnipeg, one she'd known since elementary school, owned a cottage out on Bulrush Island, just south of Fiskar Bay, a strip of land that jutted out into the lake, connected to the mainland by a causeway. The friend was in Winnipeg most of the time and Leslie was welcome to stay there for the next day or two. Awful news about Donna, her friend said. Donna had been younger than them but she remembered her well. Was there any other way she could help?

Having a place to stay where the Wi-Fi worked was all that Leslie needed. The fact that she had the house all to herself was a bonus. She FaceTimed her husband Mark in Saskatoon and set him the task of finding a spot in a care home for her mother, soon as he could. Then she checked the current state of Lois's financial accounts. She'd taken care of that portfolio ever since her dad died. It had fallen to Leslie to sell the family home and her father's business, all those years ago, and to get her mother safely housed. Her brothers had no idea how much work she had done on their behalf and how she had taken good care of the money. It was worth more than three million now. Donna had known its value but their brothers didn't. They'd never asked her and she'd never told them. She sent them a report every year, but she kept the information in it minimal. They never asked her any questions. Leslie expected that they didn't understand what it said and she had never chosen to enlighten them.

She called the office of McVicar Law. Old Derek McVicar wasn't available but a new guy who was working there could see her at ten. That would have to do. Donna and Leslie had held joint power of attorney. Now Leslie needed to find how to get full authority over her mother's affairs.

Amelia, her niece, Donna's daughter, texted her: *Fraser arrested re: party last night Hazeldean. Call me?*

Leslie did so.

Some local MLA had let Gord, Amelia's father, know about the arrest and Gord had passed the news on to his daughter, since she now owned half of her mother's share in Hazeldean

"That's for sure?" asked Leslie.

Donna had left her share in the cottage to her children, Amelia and Graeme, in an even split. Amelia was planning to come up to the cottage today. She was leaving right now. Leslie wasn't to worry if there was a mess. Amelia would take care of it. She intended to stay over. It looked like she might inherit her mother's business and she was going to have a look at some properties out in the Interlake while she was there. Donna had signed contracts with the owners of three houses. Those needed to be taken care of right away. This would be a good way for Amelia to get first-hand experience of how her mother had managed things.

"Come and have dinner with me tonight and tell me all about it. I'm staying on Bulrush Island," Leslie said. She looked out the window. The house next door was old. It could use an upgrade. She would introduce Amelia to the owners. If Amelia was getting into the real estate business like her mom had done, she might find that useful.

A large mobile home had been driven to the parking lot at Cullen Village Rec Centre. Doug Halliday had manned the wheel, supervised by Sandy Ferguson, the owner. Now it was parked near the back door to the building, hooked up to power and water. Jay arrived, back from Winnipeg. The Rec Centre parking lot was not as pretty as the lakeshore at Hazeldean, but it would do, and the lake itself was only a five-minute walk away. The RV was as big as a house when the walls slid out. It came with three TV sets, one for each room. The old guys made sure that the satellite disc worked. Those would help keep Jennifer's boy, Carter, happy.

Jay's family could stay there all summer if they needed to, Sandy Ferguson told him. And he wasn't going to charge much for the rent.

"My contribution to the village," he said, as they shook hands on it. He and Doug both hoped the café would be a big success. How soon could Jay and Jennifer open?

"Tomorrow," Jay announced. He hadn't been able to work for months and he couldn't wait to get started. The Rec Centre's kitchen came with pots and pans, all set up and ready to go. Jennifer was driving up later with a vanload of supplies. They'd cook something small to start with. A lunch menu. "Come by and I'll give you some soup to try," he said.

"You should call it 'J & J's'," Sandy Ferguson suggested. "For Jay and Jennifer."

Cute. It seemed everyone had suggestions about the name of the café and what should be on the menu, but he and Jennifer were in agreement: The Laughing Coyote would be the name and they'd do the basics—bacon, eggs and pancakes for breakfast, burgers at lunchtime, fish and chips once they talked to a fisherman who might be able to keep them supplied with pickerel, the local favourite—but with some additional offerings that showed what they were capable of cooking. Jennifer had given in her notice at the bakery in Winnipeg. Soon she'd be baking out here, in Cullen Village.

Had he heard about the goings-on at Hazeldean last night? He had not. Sandy and Doug were happy to tell him all that they knew. He'd better got himself over to there and find out how badly Fraser's mob had trashed the place, Jay said.

A beige Ford truck with a camper van hitched behind was parked on the road outside the cottage. So was a little red Kia hatchback. A van sat in the driveway, CLEAN WHEELS printed on its sides. A woman wearing a mask and rubber gloves was carrying a blue bag full of empty bottles to the sidewalk and a man in brown work clothes was down on the beach cleaning up what was left of a large bonfire. He'd filled two garbage bags already.

Someone had hung white ribbons out on the pier. They were trailing down from the railing, where Donna had gone over. Maybe there had been had some kind of ceremony.

Jay's niece, Amelia, sat at the kitchen table, tapping at a laptop. Another cleaning woman was in the living room, polishing the fire irons beside the big stone fireplace.

"I am so sorry about your mom," Jay said as he hugged Amelia. He hadn't seen her for a while. She was an interesting blend of both parents. She had Donna's curls but hers were black. Amelia had inherited Gord's dark colouring. Her skin was smooth and tanned and her eyes were brown, but the rest was Donna, the small, slim build, the same nose, the same jawline, her mom's mouth. It was kind of spooky when she smiled, as she did now.

What had happened here was awful, she shuddered, but she wasn't going to sit around and mope. Her mom would want her to make sure that Bricks and Sugar survived, so that was what she, Amelia, intended to do. She had the same stubborn look as her mother. Her Aunt Leslie too.

She'd intended to come before she heard the news about Fraser and his big party, she told him. She needed to get on top of this job right away. Her mom had said she'd bring Amelia out here to show her how to upgrade a house but now Amelia was going to have to do that by herself. She'd asked Charlie Cain, the contractor who worked for her mom, to come along so he could show her the ropes. That's who was outside cleaning up the beach. Soon as they'd seen the mess they'd got the cleaning company to send out Amara and her sister, Meera. They were the best.

"I'm going to take over Bricks and Sugar," she said. "Dad thinks it's a good idea and Graeme's not interested. So it's all going to be mine. Mom told me what she had planned. She always said she'd hand it on to me. This is what she would have wanted me to do."

The kitchen was too shabby to sparkle but it was clean. "It's the only room that's been sanitized so far," said Amelia. "Don't go into any of the others until Amara and Meera are done."

Jay told her about his plans for the café and how he and Jennifer were moving into a mobile home. "But maybe we don't need it now. If Fraser's not going to be here maybe we can use this place after all."

"It's not available right now, Uncle Jay." Amelia snapped her laptop shut. "Mom had the cottage until the end of next week and it's still her turn. I'll be staying here until then. There are three houses around here that Mom had planned to fix up and sell. I've got all her notes for them. And the estimates. Charlie Cain's going to be staying out here too, until the work's done. That's his camper outside."

"Okay," said Jay, being reasonable. "No big deal. Jennifer and I can stay in the RV until you're finished, then we'll move in. Leslie will be back in Saskatoon, she won't want it. And it sounds like Fraser's going to end up in jail."

"I might have to be here a while longer." Amelia stuffed the laptop into a bag, stood up and slung it over her shoulder. "There are other houses that could use our services and this area is a hot market. People haven't been spending money these last two years and interest rates are low. Houses at the lake are being snapped up as soon as they're listed, way above the asking price. We can talk more about this later, if you like. Charlie and I have to leave soon to go look at a house. Amara and Meera still have a lot of cleaning to do."

She made it clear that sticking around wasn't convenient. Jay left. He needed to get back to the Rec Centre, anyway. Jennifer would be arriving soon and they had work of their own to do.

Leslie Borthwick was not thrilled with how her meeting with the lawyer had gone. The new man at McVicar Law was efficient, she had to admit, but it seemed that having sole power of attorney over her mother's affairs was far from being a done deal. Her brothers could insist on two signees. Would either of them think of it? She was pretty sure it wouldn't occur to Fraser, but it might cross Jay's mind. And there was the problem of Aunt Sylvia, who seemed to think she had a right to stick her nose into things. Leslie needed to act fast. Get her mom moved, as soon as possible. Maybe if the question of another signee came up, she could suggest her niece, Amelia, as a second person.

Leslie liked what she knew of Amelia. She was smart and ambitious and she had a good work ethic. Here she was already, getting work done, even although her mother had just died. Amelia was young, but with a bit of support she would go far, and as her aunt, with no children of her own, Leslie was inclined to offer some help.

Amelia would inherit some money from her mother as well as the business. Maybe the new house at Hazeldean that Donna had envisioned could go ahead after all. Leslie hadn't seen the plans but she knew all about them. Donna had told her how it would look. Spectacular. There was no reason why that couldn't happen. Leslie could invest enough cash in the project to pay for materials; Bricks and Sugar would provide the labour. When it sold, as it would, Leslie would pay back the money into the Borthwick account and split the profit between herself and her enterprising niece. A win-win.

Of course, it did mean that Jay and Fraser would have to sell their shares in Hazeldean to Amelia. Buying them out would be part of the cost of the project. Donna had tried to do that last year, but she'd offered them less than forty grand each. That was not enough. Leslie and Amelia could sweeten it. She didn't see why her brothers shouldn't be persuaded. Fraser didn't really care about keeping Hazeldean. He was just being contrary, as usual, and he was broke. Some ready cash would take care of that problem.

But Jay needed to be made to see reason. That idea he had about living permanently at the cottage needed to be aborted. He'd mentioned fixing it up but did he have any idea how much that would cost? Thirty to forty thousand, at least, to winterize the place and that was just the basics. Jay didn't have that kind of money. Leslie could suggest that she might invest in a new restaurant for him. He wasn't going to want to serve burgers out of Cullen Village Rec Centre for long. He could resurrect The Sleepy Fox in Winnipeg. That might swing it.

She'd fill Amelia in on what she was thinking over dinner. Leslie wasn't going to cook. Amelia had said she would pick up pizza on the way. All Leslie had to do was stop at the liquor store and pick up a decent bottle of wine. She should have brought more of those good bottles that were in the kitchen at Hazeldean when she left, before Fraser and his friends had got their hands on them and drunk everything in sight. There had been a bottle of Glenmorangie. What a waste.

She should talk to Amelia about sharing the power of attorney tonight and get that taken care of. Amelia would let her do what she wanted as far as her mother's, Lois's, affairs were concerned. Leslie was sure of that, especially if Amelia knew she would benefit. Leslie had always liked her niece far more than her brother, Graeme. He was good-looking enough but all muscle and no brains. She couldn't begin to have a conversation with him. She might make Amelia her only heir. She'd make sure to hint at that too, over pizza tonight.

Much to Roxanne's surprise, Fraser Borthwick was released later that afternoon. A lawyer had acted on his behalf, sure enough. He'd insisted that his client be allowed to have a shower and a change of clothes before he met the magistrate. He'd even been allowed to trim his beard, watched over, of course, in case he did something stupid with the scissors. He'd leaned on his cane before the judge and managed to look meek. Harmless. Talked quietly. He'd invited a few friends over and it had got out of hand. It hadn't been his fault. And he'd panicked when the policewoman had grabbed him. He was sick, in constant pain, easily thrown off balance. He'd reacted without thinking. His sister had died recently, taken her own life, his lawyer reminded her ladyship. That had caused Mr. Borthwick considerable distress. The jails were full and the magistrate saw no reason for him to want to return to Ontario. She set a later court date and let Fraser go on a promise to appear, just as he had predicted.

Wes Melnyk had come to listen, then he drove Fraser back to his farm. He felt bad about the whole episode. He was the guy who'd got the word out about the party. There was an old motorbike in the back of his barn, he said. Fraser had once known a bit about bikes, hadn't he? Maybe they could get it going, then Fraser would have wheels of his own. And the guys who'd been at the party had had a whip-round, since Fraser had got into this bit of trouble because of them. There was some cash, in a bag, back at the house, to help Fraser out for now. He could stay at Wes's for a while, as long as he took a shower now and then—Wes's wife was a stickler for that. And he could eat with them. They were vegetarians but it was good, healthy food.

Fraser said that was fine by him.

10

THE OLD HARLEY in Wes's barn still worked. All it needed was a clean and a tune-up. Wes had called their old friend, Mike McBain, and he had come over first thing in the morning and got it running just fine. Fraser had tried to pay him but Mike had only charged him for the materials and that wasn't much. Fraser could buy him a beer, later, if he liked, he'd said. He and Fraser's cousin, Sig Olafson, would be in the bar any time after five, as usual.

It had been a while since Fraser had driven a bike by himself. He took a back road from Wes's farm, one with hardtop, not gravel, which ran straight south. Then he could cut to the east, across to Cullen Village. He spied a farm truck up ahead, hauling a trailer full of hay bales. There was no pasture growing in the fields this dry summer and farmers were having to buy feed for their animals. It was costing them a fortune, Wes had told him. Fraser should offer to pay for his room and board, he thought. He could afford to. His friends from the party had been generous. He zoomed past the trailer, his walking cane propped up behind him with its golden handle on top, like a flagpole. He was getting the hang of this just fine.

Leslie had refused to say why they were supposed to meet today, at Hazeldean. With Amelia, Donna's kid. She was all grown up now, Leslie had said. Fraser supposed she must be. She'd been a gawky teenager last time he'd seen her. But she was at the cottage, he had been told, taking over her mom's business, all by herself. She'd cleaned up all the mess that he and his friends had made. What was he supposed to say? Thank you and sorry? No way. He hadn't asked her to do that. He and the guys would have got round to it eventually.

What he wanted to know was what plan Leslie and Amelia were cooking up between them. They had to be up to something. Why else would they want to see him at Hazeldean, together? He'd bet that they wanted him to offload his share of the house. Donna had offered him forty grand or something for it, about a year ago. He wasn't going to let it go that easily. He'd make them work for it. Wes said he shouldn't sell for less than sixty-five.

And Big Sig had told him that Leslie was trying to get their mom moved to Saskatoon. What was that about? Wouldn't that be kind of hard on the old girl? He should stop by the care home and visit Mom later, see how she really was. Meantime he could hassle Leslie about that. Get her riled up. This visit might be kind of fun. He was making good time. He'd be at Cullen Village in no time at all. He was going to be a bit early at this rate. Not his style at all.

Leslie Borthwick was also on her way to Hazeldean. She and Amelia had talked until long after dark the night before. They got along very well and they had made a plan.

This morning her husband had called to tell her about a couple of prospective homes for her mother in Saskatoon. The one Leslie preferred had a wait list. The other was more expensive but could accommodate Mom fairly soon. Did she want to move Mom in there, then shift her over when a space opened up in the other? Her husband wondered if the old lady needed to be transported by ambulance. Leslie didn't think so. It wasn't like she was sick or anything, she was just old and forgetful. Leslie could make her comfortable in the back of her car and drive to Saskatoon in one day. Maybe she could get some drugs to help her mother sleep on the way.

She'd called Jay to find out if he could join them but he wasn't going to be available to talk until the evening. He and his partner were serving lunches out of their café today. He was all excited about that and didn't want to talk about anything else. Maybe he could bring Jennifer and her boy over to visit tonight, he'd managed to say. He'd like them to meet his new partner and stepson. That wasn't what she and Amelia had wanted but she could hardly say no.

"Don't worry, Aunt Les," Amelia had said, when Leslie had reported in. "Jennifer will maybe be more sensible than Uncle Jay. She won't be as attached to the cottage as he is and they are bound to need the money. Look where they're living right now, in a rented motor home in an empty parking lot. And starting up the café must be costing them." Amelia was probably right.

Fraser was available and he'd said he would make it. "One o'clock sharp, yes, ma'am!" he'd said, and hung up. So, it would be Fraser up first if he didn't get sidetracked before he got to Cullen Village.

Leslie was surprised to see that he'd arrived before her. There was an ancient Harley Davidson sitting in the driveway, behind Amelia's little red Kia. She parked at the roadside, took her briefcase out of the back seat, locked her car and strutted up the driveway.

Fraser was at the back of the house, throwing up behind an overgrown shrub. Disgusting.

"You drink far too much!" she said as she walked past him. He reached out a hand to block her way.

"Don't go in there, Leslie," he croaked. She pushed his hand aside and walked straight up the steps onto the veranda and into the house, calling for Amelia. There was no answer. Her niece wasn't in the kitchen. Leslie reached the living room. Amelia was sprawled, face down, in front of the big fireplace. She was wearing a soft pink nightdress, her feet were bare, one arm stretched above her head. The hair at the back of her skull was a matted mass of clotted blood. Her face was turned toward the doorway where Leslie stood. Flies buzzed around her bloody head. They congregated at the corners of her eyes and her open mouth, filthy things.

She staggered back down the hallway and outside, gasping for air. "We have to call the police," she said to her brother. He stood below her, rocking back and forth, hanging onto the veranda railing, as if he didn't have the strength to stand up.

"They've just had me in jail, Les," he said. What did he want her to do? Let him drive off on his beat-up old motorbike and pretend he hadn't been here? "Come up here and sit, Fraser," she ordered him. "You're not going anywhere," and she dialled 911.

Roxanne Calloway drove to Cullen Village as soon as Ravi Anand and Sam Mendes reported in from Hazeldean.

"It's a mess, Sarge," Ravi's voice rang out over the car phone as she blared her way along the lakeshore, ignoring the fifty-kilometres-per-hour speed limit imposed during cottage season. "It looks like she's been bludgeoned. We've got the aunt and the uncle here. She's holding up but he's in poor shape."

She called Inspector Schultz as soon as she had seen the body.

"Gordon Palmer's kid?" he had asked. "And it looks like someone's killed her?" He'd get McBain back up there, today. Meantime, Roxanne would be able to take care of things at that end? Do the preliminaries? She could, she told him. Roxanne had attended several scenes like this during her days with the Major Crimes Unit and she knew what needed to be done.

It was just as well she hadn't yet made it into Winnipeg, hadn't done that pregnancy test, hadn't said a word to Matt or to anyone else about maybe being pregnant. Here she was, now, in charge of a murder scene, doing the job she used to do even if it was only for a day. She felt an old, familiar adrenaline rush. This situation was temporary, she reminded herself. Izzy McBain would be here before the end of the afternoon, and Izzy would take over. But for now, the case was in Roxanne's hands and she got to work. Called Ident, got the site retaped and guarded. The usual. Then there were interviews that needed to be done.

Fraser Borthwick was still pale and shaky, sitting on the edge of a chair on the veranda, smoking. A cigarette, Roxanne was glad to see, not a joint. She needed him clear-headed. Meantime, his sister Leslie explained how they had planned to meet with Amelia at one. Fraser had arrived first and found her dead. She, herself, had reached the cottage minutes later.

"She had dinner with me last night," she said. "Out on Bulrush Island. I'm staying at a friend's house there. She was with me until after eleven. I asked her if she'd like to stay the night but she insisted that she wanted to get back here and off she went, across the causeway in her little red car." Her face screwed up at the memory and her eyes filled with tears. She hadn't realized that she'd never see her niece alive again.

"What were you going to meet about, today?" asked Roxanne.

"This cottage." They were sitting on the veranda, away from the sight in the living room. Leslie looked bleakly at her surroundings and blew her nose. "I used to love this place. Now I think I hate it. First my sister and now Amelia, both dead here. You see those ribbons, out on the pier? Amelia must have put them there, for her mother. And now she's gone, too."

"Why would someone want to kill them?"

"Donna as well as Amelia? You think that they've both been murdered?"

"We'll have to revisit how your sister died."

Leslie thought that over. It had to be something to do with the business, she said. Amelia was going to inherit it from her mother. She was planning to carry on doing the same kind of work, that was why she had come out here. Donna had been going to refurbish and sell some houses nearby. Maybe it had something to do with that?

Maybe the police should talk to her brother-in-law, Gord Palmer, she suggested. Have a close look at that marriage, because Leslie knew for a fact that it was over as far as Donna was concerned and Gord was keen to act as if nothing was wrong.

He'd built up a public image as a family man and he didn't want that reputation tainted by a divorce.

"That might explain why Donna is dead, but not Amelia," said Roxanne.

"I know. I don't understand that at all," Leslie admitted.

They were interrupted by the arrival of old Dr. Gaul.

"Another one, Roxanne?" he wheezed, all of eighty years old but still unwilling to hang up his shingle. He had a loyal following of patients in the Interlake, as reluctant to let him go as he was to give up his life's work. He went inside to look at the body. "She's been dead six hours at least." Rigor mortis had set in already. Two blows had been delivered to the left side of the head, from the back, by a right-handed person, using some kind of weapon. "What a waste," he said before he left. "She's so young."

Ravi took down Leslie Borthwick's statement, then told her she could go. "You're not planning to leave the vicinity immediately?" Roxanne asked. Her sister's cremation was scheduled for the next week, she replied. After that, she would have to go home.

"The cremation might have to wait," said Roxanne.

"But I need to get back to Saskatoon!" Leslie protested. "Why can't I leave?"

"We'll let you know," was all that Roxanne was prepared to say.

Once she had gone, Fraser replaced his sister in the chair on the veranda. He hadn't seen Amelia in years. He hadn't known she'd grow to look the spitting image of her mother, a dark-haired version. He was inclined to babble, still shaken up by the shock of what he had discovered. Did he know what Amelia was doing out here? He thought so. He'd bet that she wanted to buy this cottage from him and his brother, Jay. They all had shares in it. Him and his brother and his sisters.

What had happened to Donna's share? Fraser wasn't sure but Amelia must have got it. Her and her brother, Graeme. He wouldn't be surprised if Leslie and Amelia had figured out some kind of a plan last night. To do what? Well, Donna had wanted to rip this old place down and build something big and shiny in its place. Tear down the trees. Jay had told him so. He would bet that Leslie and Amelia were planning to do the same thing and sell it after. Make some money off of it. The problem was that Jay had said he wanted the cottage too, so he could live here all year round with his new family. Winterize it.

"Who's going to want it now?" he said. "First Donna ends up hanging off the pier, and now Amelia's lying in there with her head smashed in. I wish I'd sold my share when Donna asked me, last year. I'd be glad to see the back of it."

The forensic team arrived just as he was preparing to leave.

"Are you going to be okay on that?" Roxanne had asked as he wobbled off on the back of his old bike but he'd just waved and driven off in a blast of exhaust fumes.

Dave Kovak and his crew were going to be at Hazeldean for some time. They'd have to check for blood spatter and bone fragments, among other things, and try to find the weapon. The fire irons were of interest. They were metal, and there was a poker. It was past 3:00 pm and there was still no word from Izzy. Lunch service at The Laughing Coyote must be wrapped up by now and Roxanne was about to spoil Jay Borthwick's opening day.

Lunch had gone well. The gazpacho that they had added to the menu had sold right out and the butter tarts were a hit. Jay was cleaning up and Jennifer was throwing together a batch of pastry for tomorrow's chicken pot pie, but news of the active police presence at Hazeldean had buzzed through the village and Roxanne's arrival was half expected.

"What's happened?" Jay opened the door to her. They sat at a Formica-topped table while she described the scene in the living room at the cottage. Jennifer covered her dough, wiped her hands clean and came to join them. She was a tall, capable-looking woman in chef's whites, brown hair in a single braid behind her, under a round cap. She squeezed Jay's shoulder before she sat down.

"This is such a shock," she said. "Another death at that beautiful old cottage?"

When had they last seen Amelia? They hadn't. They'd been too busy getting set up and started here. The plan was for them to go over there tonight. Jennifer had been looking forward to meeting some of Jay's family.

Leslie would have been there, too and they were going to take Jennifer's son, Carter, along.

Where was Carter? At summer day camp in Fiskar Bay.

"Ah," said Roxanne. "My son goes there too." Talking about the everyday helped blunt the horror of what she had to describe to them. "So, it would have been a family visit?"

"Well, yeah."

"You wanted sole possession of the cottage?"

They did. Jay had spent the best days of his childhood there and Jennifer had fallen in love with it the minute she saw it. They couldn't think of anywhere else they would rather live.

"Amelia wanted to have it, too," said Roxanne.

"She did?" Jay's blue eyes met Roxanne's across the table, guileless. "I didn't know that."

"But you knew that she was restarting her mother's company?"

"Not until this morning when Leslie called. And I was too busy to pay much attention."

He hadn't seen Amelia since before the pandemic, when she was in her first year at university. The Palmers had come to his old restaurant for dinner. He had some photos. He thumbed through his phone, looking. There they were, Donna and her daughter, side by side, laughing, wineglasses in hand, in happier days. They looked almost identical, one dark haired, one fair.

"Can you send me that?" He did so.

"I can't believe they're both dead." He looked back at her again, bewildered. She left him in his partner's capable hands. Everything he said rang true. Either Jay Borthwick was a really good actor, or he knew nothing about his niece's death.

11

GORD PALMER HAD barely been informed of his daughter's unexpected death when the story leaked. She had been brutally slain at the family's summer cottage in peaceful Cullen Village, in the Interlake. Palmer's wife had died there too, less than a week ago, an alleged suicide. Within minutes, speculation was rife on the internet. Were the police wrong? Had Donna Palmer also been killed? Was Gordon Palmer's family being targeted?

Palmer had his enemies. What politician did not? There had been death threats before. But then some troll had posted "You'll be next," from an untraceable URL and precautions had needed to be taken. Gordon was to be whisked off to a safe hiding place along with his son. The Conservative Party wanted him to be in Ottawa but that was not going to happen. He needed to stay in Manitoba, within the provincial court's jurisdiction. He was, after all, a suspect as well as a potential victim.

"I need to talk to him in person before they move him," Izzy said. Inspector Schultz agreed, and he knew where she would find him—at his constituency office, with police protection. Palmer's staff and his committee insisted that they meet with him before he was driven to the airport. His destination was only accessible by plane.

Things were under control for now out at Cullen Village, Schultz assured her. Roxanne Calloway was covering the basics for them. She would inform the relatives living out there of the death. Schultz had also talked to Dr. Farooq at the Provincial Medical Examiner's office. They'd have to take a second look at

Donna Palmer's body, since suicide might not be the cause of death after all. This case was now a priority. They needed to have autopsy results sooner rather than later.

Izzy would need to get a team together. That was a bummer. Resources were stretched but there was a guy called Trent Weiss, new to the MCU. He'd be okay as her file coordinator, Schultz told her. Weiss was summoned, a skinny guy, not much taller than she. His job was to sit at a desk and deal with communications, data, stuff like that, but right now Izzy needed someone at her side.

"You're with me, for now," she told him. She wanted an extra pair of eyes and ears around if she was talking with the slippery Mr. Palmer.

She wished Trent had a bit more height and muscle when she saw the press gathered outside Gord Palmer's constituency office. It was located in a strip mall at the south end of the city. Palmer's face beamed out from photographs six feet high, pasted to the windows, his name spelled out in Tory blue. The pavement outside teemed with cameras. Gord Palmer's present location was certainly no secret.

Trent doggedly pushed a path through the crowd. Izzy followed, ignoring the questions being fired at her. "Was his wife killed too?" seemed to be the main one. "Have there been more threats?" was another. The glass door was opened by a uniformed constable, just wide enough to let the two of them squeeze through.

Gordon Palmer was in the back office strategizing with his team, Maria Smith, his assistant, informed them, a clipboard on her arm, her high heels making her look taller than she was. Must he be disturbed? Hadn't Sergeant McBain talked to him already? Time was of the essence right now.

"They'll need to take a break," Izzy informed her. "The situation's changed."

Maria Smith rolled her eyes then disappeared through a door. Izzy caught a glimpse of men in dark suits, a couple of women in blue jackets and skirts, gathered around a table. The heat outside didn't matter to them. They spent their working days in air-conditioned rooms like these. She waited. It took ten minutes for the door to open again. They trooped out past her, looking alternately irritated or reproachful at the two RCMP officers standing there, then Maria held the door open so Izzy and Trent could enter.

"Can you please keep it to half an hour?" she asked. "Max?"

The table had been cleared of papers. Gord Palmer sat at the far end, shaved, dressed as immaculately as ever, but there were bags under his eyes and his hands were fastened around a coffee mug. Trent Weiss took up a stance inside the door. Another uniformed constable stood guard outside.

"Sorry for your loss, Mr. Palmer," said Izzy. She pulled out the chair closest to him.

"Thank you." She remembered how unaffected he had seemed by his wife's death. It looked like Amelia's had hit him harder. "It's a great shock. First my wife, now my daughter. And these death threats are a concern."

"Those happen, don't they?"

They did, but this seemed more…he searched for the right word. "Pertinent."

"You're well protected," she assured him. "You're going to be safe. Meantime I am investigating the deaths of your wife and your daughter. I need to ask you some more questions."

He understood that, he said and pulled at his cuffs. His gold cufflinks caught the light. As he did so, his demeanour changed. The targeted victim vanished. He straightened his back and focused a level gaze at her, a practised politician, ready to field whatever questions she threw his way.

"Where were you last night?" she began.

"I worked late. Until ten. Maria can verify that. Then I went home."

"Was anyone else at the house? Your son?"

"No one," he said. "What time did Amelia die?"

"After eleven last night and before seven this morning."

"Are you suggesting I could have driven up to Cullen Village and back any time during the night? Why would I want to kill my own daughter?"

"I don't know," said Izzy. "But you should know we are going to be looking into your personal finances. Your computer files. We will search your house and your car if we have to. Everything. So, if there's anything you would like to tell me and save us all that trouble, now's your chance."

"Absolutely nothing, Sergeant," he assured her. "Go right ahead." He smiled, as though the idea that he might have anything to hide was absurd. "To return to your first question. The premier had left a message for me, yesterday. I called her back after I got home. We talked at some length. Then I wrote some work memos. I retired for the night around midnight. Today's schedule was busy. That, of course has been disrupted. I can assure you I was nowhere near Cullen Village."

"Your daughter had just inherited money from her mother. She'd planned to take over the company."

"She had. It made sense. Donna had been grooming Amelia to play an active role in Bricks and Sugar and my daughter was keen to take on the challenge. Getting to work right away, doing what her mother would have wanted her to do seemed to help her cope with her grief."

"Is there anyone who might have resented that she was taking possession of it?"

"I have no idea. I don't know much about the people who were involved in Donna's business."

"Do you know if Amelia had any enemies? Someone who resented her personally?"

He did not. His daughter had lived away from home these past three years. She shared an apartment with a friend. He'd barely seen her during the pandemic. Amelia had always been independent; he'd been proud of that. She was smart and capable. If she had disagreed with anyone, he had no idea who that might be. He had last seen her when they'd got together on Tuesday, at the lawyer's office, with Graeme, to make sure she could take over the running of Bricks and Sugar. Get started right away, as she wanted. The actual changeover of the title into her name hadn't happened yet, wasn't even close. This was going to be a mess, and here he was, having to leave town when he should be here, taking care of things.

"The business will belong to Graeme now?"

He supposed it would.

"And her share of the cottage at Cullen Village?"

"That too."

Where was Graeme right now? He was at the Rowing Club, meeting with his coach and collecting his gear before he flew off with his father into this enforced seclusion.

"We are having your wife's body re-examined," said Izzy. "When we last talked, you sounded pretty sure it was suicide."

"And I have not changed my mind about that," said Gordon Palmer. "May I also remind you that I was in Ottawa when Donna died. There is no way I could be responsible for her death." She couldn't argue with that. "Are we done here?" Gord Palmer tapped his wristwatch, a Rolex. "I am more than busy. And we are keeping important people waiting."

She took her leave, Trent following in her wake. Maria Smith waited outside with the party members who had been meeting with Gord Palmer earlier. They hurried past Izzy to rejoin him without looking her way.

"Well then, Trent," she said, "let's go visit the Rowing Club."

"You really think he could have done it?" Trent asked, taking the passenger seat. He already understood that Izzy McBain liked to drive herself.

"He couldn't have killed his wife," she said. "But he's the only person in that family that thinks she might have been suicidal.

Everyone else has said it's out of character." She dodged her way around a patch of road works. Those occurred every summer in Winnipeg, snarling up traffic. "I wonder why he wants us to think that."

Trent had his phone out and was scrolling through messages. "That troll's made another threat," he said. "They haven't managed to shut him down yet. And a few copycats have sprung up."

They reached a road that led through a leafy suburb. The Rowing Club occupied a prime spot on a bend in the river.

Graeme Palmer was also under police protection. Another uniformed RCMP constable stood at the top of a flight of steps outside the clubhouse. Graeme was one of a group of young people sitting talking on a deck that ran the full length of the building. Izzy and Trent watched him detach himself, his hands in the pockets of his khaki shorts, freshly showered, tanned and lean. Donna and Gordon Palmer's son was a good-looking young man.

"The law," they overheard him tell his friends. "Come to talk to me about my ma and my sister." That earned him sympathetic looks, especially from a couple of girls at his table. He looked down at Izzy and Trent from the top of the steps, ignoring the presence of the uniformed Mountie nearby. The club secretary might let them use his office, he said, and led them inside without a backward glance.

They walked through a large clubroom. Rowing machines lined one end. Big windows looked out over the deck to the river. The office was small, windowless in comparison. Graeme took the comfortable desk chair and left a wooden hard-backed one for Izzy. Trent Weiss closed the door and stood inside. He took out his phone again and tapped, half listening while he did so. He should be paying more attention to what was going on. Izzy was beginning to figure out why Trent had been accepted into the MCU. He was a techno guy, destined for a career in surveillance, unable to leave his phone alone. She would have to talk to him about that. But meantime, she had to deal with Donna and Gordon Palmer's handsome son.

"Sorry about your mother and your sister," she said. Graeme nodded his head. He didn't seem to be grief-stricken but he was young, all of nineteen years old, and a jock. Maybe he wanted to look cool or had been trained to mask his emotions. "How come you're not ready to leave here? Aren't you getting picked up soon? To go to the airport?"

"I can't afford to stop proper training." Graeme Palmer pushed the wheely chair back and hoisted one foot, in a white deck shoe, onto his knee. There wasn't an ounce of fat on his sculpted body, but Izzy noticed a muscle twitch beside his left ear. The relaxed, unaffected attitude was a pose. Graeme was more perturbed than he seemed. "My coach is negotiating so I can stay at his place instead of going up north. I can't work out, where my dad's going. They can't even fly a rowing machine up there for me to use."

"It's for your protection."

"I can take care of myself," said Graeme. "I'll be with my buddies. Nothing's going to happen to me here."

"We need to make sure you are safe."

"My people and yours are talking," he informed her, looking across the desk at her like she was stupid. Izzy got that reaction sometimes. She was young, a woman; she dressed casually, but she seldom experienced it from someone so young. Being a sergeant in the Major Crimes Unit usually afforded her some clout.

"When did you last see Amelia?" she asked.

He ran his fingers over the top of his head. His hair was blond, would be curly like his mother's had been if he let it grow. On Tuesday, he told her. They'd stopped by the lawyer's office. Financial stuff, to do with his mother's money. Otherwise, he never saw his sister much. His father's birthday, maybe? February?

And his mother? The tick twitched again and the corners of his mouth tightened. Early, the morning before she left for the cottage. He wasn't at their house in Winnipeg much. Usually just slept there. He spent most of his days here, at the club. He didn't just train. He helped coach young rowers. And most of his friends were here.

"You don't eat at home?" Not unless he had to.

"You'll have inherited money from your mother's estate?"

So he'd been told. That was still in the works. He had no idea how much he would get.

"You'll receive quite a bit more, now that Amelia's gone?"

He supposed so.

"Your mother's business will be yours, now, too?"

He wasn't sure about that. The fingers of one hand began to tap on a muscled, tanned thigh. He would sell it, soon as he could, if it did belong to him. Graeme had no wish to be in the house-selling business. One lip curled in distaste at the question.

"Rowing's an expensive sport, Graeme." Izzy leaned back in her chair as far as she could, mirroring his position. "All that money's going to come in useful."

"That's not an issue. I've got a scholarship for university in Calgary in September and my coach is confident I'll start to attract sponsors. If I train right." Graeme dispatched that suggestion without a moment's pause.

"Where were you on Saturday night?"

"Here, with friends."

"And last night?"

"The same."

"All night?"

"How do you mean?"

"You have a car?" asked Izzy.

Of course, he had. Graeme drove a BMW. His parents had given it to him when he graduated from school.

"That's interesting," said Izzy. "Amelia only got a little red Rio."

"Amelia was a rotten driver," he commented, dismissive. "They gave her something small enough that she could park it. I'll be driving to Calgary end of the summer."

"I'll bet you can drive real good, Graeme," she said. "How long would it take you to get up to Cullen Village and back, on a quiet night?"

"I wouldn't know, officer. I've never tried it. I haven't been near that crappy cottage for a couple of years."

Izzy stood up and took her leave. Graeme might still be around, should she need to speak with him again. She certainly knew where to find him.

"Where's your coach?" she asked. He unfurled himself from the chair in one smooth move.

"In a meeting," he said. "Like I told you. Getting everything arranged so I'll be staying in Winnipeg. He's having to sign all kinds of papers." He remained at the office door, reaching into his pocket for his phone as they left. They found their own way out.

"Who do you think he's going to call?" Trent asked as they walked down the deck steps. Graeme Palmer's friends still sat at the table, watching them go. The uniformed RCMP that guarded Graeme waited patiently by the door.

"The coach? His father? He's been thrown more by these deaths than he'd like us to think."

"Gord Palmer's bank account's overstretched," said Trent, once they reached the car. "His credit cards are maxed out and he has a car loan."

"You've been busy," Izzy said. "How did you find that out?"

"Someone at Ident's working on it," said Trent. "I checked in. While you were talking."

"How serious is it?" she asked.

"Bad enough that he could use a lot of cash right now."

"That so?" Another road sign loomed ahead, and a traffic lineup. Izzy detoured down a side street. "You're really into computers? Stuff like that?"

He was, he told her. Had been since he was a kid. He'd worked in IT before he joined the force. Izzy revised her opinion of Trent.

Technology wasn't her strong suit. Having him work that end while he was on her team might be useful.

"Can you find out if Maria Smith is flying off with Palmer to wherever it is they are taking him?" she asked him.

"His assistant?"

"That's her. And if she was in Ottawa with him when his wife died? Or if she was here?"

"Shall do." He pulled out his phone again and clicked away once more.

12

THE LATEST EVENTS at Hazeldean had drawn the usual amount of interest among the residents of Cullen Village, and the fact that two bodies had now been found was disturbing. But both women who had died were members of the Borthwick family. The threat had to be specific to them, so although the villagers were curious, they were not as alarmed as they had been on a previous occasion when their neighbourhood had been visited by a series of murders. Then, the killings seemed random and they had thought that they might be in danger. This time they did not sense the same threat.

They also knew from past experience what to expect from the police. Forensic technicians would swarm the cottage, a big van would take the body away, zippered into a body bag, the cottage would be taped off and placed off-limits. That was a nuisance since it meant they couldn't walk all the way along the path at the top of the berm or wander the beach as they liked to do, and in a hot summer like this, that was something that they missed, but the tape wouldn't be up forever. The police might ask questions of them. Word was that Sergeant Calloway had already interrogated Jay Borthwick at his new café. They hoped he wasn't involved. Word was out that Jay and Jennifer served good food.

Their usual routines continued. Herb Appleby, Doug Halliday and Sandy Ferguson were all active members of the Cullen Village Heritage Society. Before the pandemic an historic train travelled from Winnipeg every weekend during the summer months, driven and maintained by volunteers like themselves. It had carried a full load of tourists and the Cullen Village Railway Museum had been one of the main stops on its route. That activity was still on hold. Cramming people into railcars was not permitted. Nevertheless, they dressed up in railway hats and vests every Saturday and Sunday just in case visitors dropped by who wanted to know the history of the station. The general store next door was part of their exhibit, well stocked with old-fashioned candy and souvenirs. They did a decent trade and the money that they raised went to support the endeavours of the society. This was Thursday, the day when they always got things ready.

They sat at a table in the wooden station building, polishing their collection of antique railway lamps. On the walls hung photographs of days past when Winnipeggers arrived in their hundreds to enjoy a day at the beach. A train called the Moonlight Special brought young people to dance a Saturday night away in the large dancehall that had once existed. There had been a "Daddy Train," too, that ferried working fathers to and from the city each weekend.

Sandy had brought along a cake, a chocolate torte with raspberry filling. Jennifer Boychuk had made it as a thank-you gift for their help in finding her family a temporary home. She had decorated it with a drawing, in chocolate icing, of an old steam engine. Doug lifted the shiny lamps up onto a shelf, out of the way of any stickiness. They found plates and a sharp knife.

"She said she was sorry she didn't have time to make a model of a train in real chocolate," Sandy said as he cut three generous slices. "I hope what's happened today doesn't put her and Jay off moving here. That café is exactly what we need now that the pandemic's easing up."

Herb Appleby agreed. He was look forward to having Jay and his family as neighbours.

"What's going on at Hazeldean is shocking," he said. "I'll bet Fraser Borthwick's got something to do with it. He's always been trouble."

Fraser had been arrested for selling drugs when he was in his teens. Sandy and Herb had come to the beach every summer since they were children. They remembered when Fraser had tried to sell pills and marijuana to their own kids. They'd had to have words with Will about it. Fraser had gone to university not long after that but he hadn't lasted. He'd dropped out, then drifted off. At least they hadn't seen much of him since. The girls, now, they had been dynamos, both of them. Bright, smart. Donna had been good fun and Leslie had been okay too. She'd been good at getting things organized. Tennis games. Boating trips. Parties. Things like that.

"Just like their dad," said Herb. He'd finished his slice of cake. He didn't get to eat anything like that at home. June was a stickler for healthy eating.

"I always thought Leslie was a bit bossy." Sandy cut one slice more, thinner this time, and slid it to Herb, without asking.

"She was." Herb happily picked up his fork again. "And Will was always a bit hard on Fraser."

Doug and Freya Halliday had only lived in Cullen Village for twelve years. They were virtual newcomers. They didn't know as much about the Borthwick family history.

"What about Jay?" Doug asked.

"Years younger," Sandy replied. "The surprise child. Lois was close to forty when she had him and she adored him, right from the start. Maybe she protected him a bit more, or Will was too busy by then to pay him the same kind of attention as he had to the rest of them. Plus, Jay wasn't the oldest boy, so there weren't the same expectations. He grew up just fine."

"You know that Donna Borthwick planned to rip down that cottage? Demolish it, entirely? Put up a two-storey monster house in its place?" Doug reported, indignant. The mayor had told Freya about it. Donna had called the village office to inquire about a building permit less than a month ago. "Can you believe it? That would have blocked our view of the lake completely." It was true

SING A SONG OF SUMMER   105

that the Hallidays could only see a patch of lakeshore from across the street, but that little glimpse was precious.

"They can't tear it down, can they?" asked Herb. "Hazeldean's one of our designated historic cottages."

"Yes, they can. This village has no bylaw that states they can't. Get that wife of yours to check. If someone owns the place, they can do whatever they want." Sandy had brought cold Cokes over from the fridge in the general store, one for each of them. They came in traditional bottles. He passed them around.

"The fireplace in that cottage is unique," Herb protested. "Bulldozing it would be a sacrilege." He had kept a close watch on the comings and goings at Hazeldean all morning and seen one of the white-suited forensic people carrying out the long metal poker that usually sat on the hearthstone by that big stone fireplace. Perhaps that was the murder weapon. They uncapped their bottles.

"What we need to do is get Freya to push through a bylaw to protect our heritage sites. You know, the way things stand, some council could decide to do away with our museum if they wanted to." Sandy looked around, at the framed photos, the railway artifacts they had collected, carefully cleaned and labelled. The station and the store next door were original buildings, going back to 1910. It was unthinkable. He limped to the drawer where they kept paper and pens. "We should draft a letter to council and get the ball rolling. Begin a campaign."

They put their heads together, drank their cold drinks and talked about a plan.

Fraser and his cousin, Big Sig Olafson, made it to Harbourfront House in time to take his mother for a walk before bedtime. The residents of the care home were tucked in early at night but it was still warm outside. They were given permission to take her out, as long as she was back by 7:30. He wouldn't say a word to her about her granddaughter, Amelia, being dead, he told the nurse who was getting Lois ready.

"No point in getting her all worked up. She probably doesn't remember that the kid ever existed."

He wasn't up to pushing his mom in a wheelchair but Big Sig could. They'd stopped at the grocery store on their way and bought cherries, in a plastic bag with a zipper top. Sylvia, Sig's mother, had told him that they were Lois's favourite. "Just make sure she doesn't choke on a stone," warned the nurse as they left.

They pushed Lois along a path by the lake, looking at the red-winged blackbirds and the purple martins that flew near the shore, all the way to the harbour so she could see the boats. The harbour wall was lined with roosting seagulls. She held the bag of cherries like they were treasure and munched her way through them. Cherry pits were tossed to right and left as Sig pushed her along and Fraser did his best to keep up, hobbling along on his cane. It was still hot but a breath of wind coming off the water made walking bearable. They stopped at a bench so Fraser could have a breather. It was hard to make conversation with Lois, but Sig had inherited the family singing voice, and everyone in his family knew that the old lady still knew a few songs, so they warbled their way through a couple of old favourites.

"Those lazy, hazy, crazy days of summer," Lois sang and laughed, her mouth stained with cherry juice. Dog walkers and bike riders grinned broadly as they passed. Even a couple of serious joggers, running purposefully for their health, deigned to smile.

"There's no way Leslie should move her to Saskatoon. Look at her. She's like a sparrow," said Fraser. Lois was a tiny, bony thing, nested in a blanket in spite of the heat.

"Mom's gonna put a stop to that. You should talk to her," said Big Sig, helping himself to a handful of cherries. "How about we get her back to the home. It's time we met Mike at the bar, and you owe him a drink."

Finn Calloway had a new best friend called Carter, who had just moved to Cullen Village. Maybe he could come to Finn's place to play after summer camp tomorrow, he asked?

"Let me talk to his mom," said Roxanne, stalling.

"What do I say to him?" she asked Matt once her boy was off to bed. "That Carter's stepdad is a suspect in a murder case that I'm investigating and getting too friendly might not be a good idea?"

They'd gone out onto their west-facing veranda. The sun still had a little way to go before setting, but the shadows were long and the air had cooled slightly.

"It won't be your case for long," Matt reminded her. He was right. Izzy had texted saying she'd be in the Interlake tomorrow, as soon as she'd cleaned up a couple of loose ends in town.

Roxanne needed to get back to her regular work. Canada Day—July 1—was at the end of next week and there would be a big parade in town. Meetings were scheduled so that all would go smoothly. The RCMP would be providing a motorized escort for the dignitaries and monitoring the crowd as well as performing their regular duties.

"You don't really think that Jay Borthwick's a killer?" Matt wondered. He hadn't met the guy, but everything he'd heard about him was good. And he'd run into Carter and his mom when he'd picked up Finn from day camp. Carter seemed like a nice kid.

Roxanne kicked off her sandals and settled onto a lounger.

"No, I don't," she admitted. "But he wants to take over Hazeldean for himself and fix it up so he and Carter and his mom can live there year-round. Donna and Amelia Palmer wanted it for themselves, too, but they had an entirely different idea. They were going to rip it down and build a big, new house in its place, then maybe sell it on. So Jay had a reason to want them gone and right now he's living within walking distance of the cottage. He could have gone over there any time during the night. There wouldn't have been a soul around to see him."

Matt had worked in the RCMP before he'd gone to law school. He knew how the police thought. Motive, means, opportunity: Jay Borthwick had them all. Being able to talk to Matt about what she was thinking was helpful. And she wasn't telling him anything that was confidential.

"If they want to live in the house, why would Jay kill someone there?" Matt had a good point. He sat down on the top step. Maisie, the Lab, his constant companion when he was at home, snuggled up to him. His terrier, Joshua, was under the veranda, where it was cool and shady. "And isn't that cottage in bad shape? Is it worth fixing up?"

"He seems to think so. How do you know about that? About Hazeldean being in a bit of a mess?"

"Because I've had some contact of my own with the Borthwick family." Matt grinned a knowing smile. Roxanne tucked her feet up under her.

"Tell me more?" she asked.

Leslie Borthwick, he told her, had dropped by his office. She and her sister had had joint power of attorney for their mother. Now there was only Leslie and she wanted to be in sole charge of her mother's affairs.

"You should check out how much Lois Borthwick is worth," he suggested. "Her husband owned a string of insurance offices when he died and they had a big, riverside house in the city. Those were all sold. Leslie works in finance. She'll have invested the money. Get your guys to go look."

"Fraser and Jay and Leslie all benefit when Lois goes?"

"I expect so." He squinted into the setting sun, a golden ball in a blaze of red and orange. Bright pink light filled the western sky. "They all got some money when their father, Will, died, and a quarter share each in Hazeldean. But all the rest is still with Lois."

"Donna has to have had money of her own. Amelia was promised the business, so there must have been enough cash left to give an equal amount to Graeme. It's only been days since

Donna died." Roxanne thought it through. "Nothing can have been transferred over to Amelia yet, and she was only twenty-two. She probably wouldn't have written a will. It's hard to figure out why anyone would want her dead. Maybe she found something out about why her mother died and that's why she was killed."

"You think that Donna was murdered?"

"'Course I do," said Roxanne. "Both of them dead, in the same place, and less than a week apart? It's too much of a coincidence."

"There's someone else you should talk to." Maisie's blond head lay on Matt's thigh. He rubbed her ear. "Have you met Lois Borthwick's sister, Sylvia Olafson?"

"Derek McVicar mentioned her. That's Sylvia, who used to work at the clothes shop?" asked Roxanne. "Tall? Icelandic blond? Used to model every year at their fashion show?"

That had been an annual fundraising event for the local Women's Resource Centre. There hadn't been one for a couple of years but one was planned for the fall if larger groups were allowed to gather by then. Roxanne made a point of putting in an appearance at local fundraisers. It made for good relationships between the RCMP and the community.

"The word is that Leslie Borthwick wants to move her old mother to Saskatoon. Sylvia's trying to put a stop to it. You could go talk to her and find out what she has to say about the Borthwick family," said Matt.

"Interesting," said Roxanne. "I might just do that."

"We still haven't decided what to do about Finn and his new buddy, Carter," Matt reminded her. "Why can't he come over here with Finn after camp? It'll save Jay and Jennifer the trip to Fiskar Bay. They're trying hard to get that café up and running. Jennifer told me they want to start dinner takeout at the café soon as they can."

"That's all happening very soon, after those deaths in the family," Roxanne commented.

"Jay's been out of work for over a year. It sounds like he can't wait to get started. They can come and pick Carter up after, or we can drop him off. Izzy will be taking over this case soon, won't she? If anyone is going to be arresting Jay Borthwick it's not going to be you. So that really isn't your problem."

He was right. Finn could use someone to play with in the evening and it was the neighbourly thing to do. In a small town, close relationships were sometimes unavoidable. It meant that police tended to stick together; Roxanne knew that from past experience. But that could isolate you. She did not want that to happen to her, or her child. She also knew that Matt liked to play an active role in the community.

"Sure, he can come over and play," she said.

She got up from the lounger. "Look at that sunset," she said. "We're going to have another scorcher tomorrow. There's some salt and vinegar chips in the kitchen." She walked, barefoot, towards the door to the house. "Do you want some?"

Now would be the perfect time to tell him their news. She was fairly sure that she really was pregnant. He'd be happy about a baby. It would be his first. But he'd also be concerned about her. He'd agree with the RCMP, that she should protect herself and their unborn child. Like them, he'd want her safely tucked away behind her desk, in her office.

She would only manage the case from this end a day or so longer. Izzy would arrive tomorrow, Friday. She could tell Matt about the baby after that, on the weekend.

13

ROXANNE DROVE TO work early again the following morning. Her route took her past the bungalow with the long stone wall, the house that Donna Palmer had intended to fix up and sell. There was a beige truck parked at the far end of the driveway, a camper behind it. There was still plenty of room for her to tuck her own car in as well.

Charlie Cain was sitting on the edge of a deck at the back of the house, a mug of coffee in his hand. The steps to the deck were gone and a toolbox lay beside him. He stood when he saw Roxanne and shook her hand with his strong workman's grip.

"I heard about Amelia," he said. "Can't believe it. She was just a kid." Did the sergeant want some coffee? The glass doors behind him, into the house, were open. He could go inside and get her some, no trouble. No, she said. She was fine. But she had some questions. He pointed to an upended log, set in the gap where the steps had been. They could talk on the deck if she liked. Did she need a hand getting up there?

Roxanne stepped on the log and hopped up, no problem. The deck ran the width of the house and was furnished with wicker outdoor chairs, a sofa, comfortable cushions. She looked across a wide lawn, patchy brown from a lack of water, shaded by mature trees. The lake gleamed in the sunlight. The air was warming up.

"What are you doing still working here?" she asked. "Amelia and Donna were your bosses and they're both gone."

"This job needs doing." He indicated one of the chairs where she could sit. "And the owners want the work done." Roxanne sank into a creaky armchair. He took another. "Those steps were beginning to rot. There's things to do in the bathroom and the kitchen. Nothing major. Then I'll scrape off the old paint and give the whole place a fresh coat. This place is going to look really good. A couple of weeks and I'll be finished."

"So the owners are paying you directly?"

He was wearing a beige ball cap. Everything about him was brown, his shirt, his shorts, his boots, his weathered skin.

"No. Donna set up a contract for Bricks and Sugar with them. There's two more houses out here that are at about the same stage. I'm working on getting those done. The money they bring in will cover the bills for now."

"So you're taking over where Donna left off?"

"I'm just doing what I can to keep things going for now, Sarge."

"Do you think that Amelia was ready to take over Bricks and Sugar?" Roxanne asked. "Could she have made a go of it?"

"We'll never know. She didn't get the chance to try, did she?"

"But you worked with her, didn't you?"

"Not much. Donna hired her on a student grant last summer but we were still in lockdown. Amelia worked from home, as Donna's assistant. She'd just graduated from business school. This would have been her first real job."

"If she had failed and Bricks and Sugar had gone under, you really would have been out of a job."

Charlie frowned. "There's always work for a guy like me. Just what are you getting at, Sarge? Are you saying that I had a reason to bump her off? To get rid of her so I could take over the business?" He took in a deep breath. "I was in Winnipeg the night before last. That's when Amelia was killed, right? I share custody of my kids and I'd promised to take them to a ball game. I don't want you asking my boys but my ex will confirm that I was there. And I was still in Winnipeg yesterday morning. I was at the office for Bricks and Sugar when the word came in. It was a shock to all of us."

"Okay," said Roxanne.

"You still think Donna killed herself?"

"It hasn't been ruled out yet. But there's no doubt that someone murdered Amelia. We're having another look at Donna's death, in case we got that wrong."

"That's maybe not a bad idea."

"Why do you think that?"

"Well, Donna and I got along," he said. "Once the lockdown eased up we were able to start going out to places like this, looking at houses again. Then we'd eat. She liked a glass of wine." He hesitated as if reluctant to tell her this. "She'd talk. She told her about her and Gord. That things weren't all that great between them and she'd hated being stuck at home during the pandemic. She was thinking about leaving him but he wasn't keen on that. He was short of cash. She wasn't. He wanted to keep that big house they lived in. She wanted to sell it."

"Are you saying that Gordon Palmer had a reason to kill his wife?"

"No!" He shook his head, vigorously, then backtracked. "I don't mean that at all. Maybe she did kill herself. She'd had two tough years. The business got stuck during the pandemic; she was having to work hard to get it back on its feet; she didn't much like the guy she was married to anymore. The boy didn't help much either, he's an Olympic hopeful, you know, and he was stuck in the house too, not getting the level of training he wanted, complaining all the time."

"But that was all sorting itself out. The business was getting back on track," Roxanne reminded him.

"Well, I don't know. All I'm saying is that something was bugging Donna. She was drinking too much. She couldn't get things sorted out with Palmer."

"She could have just left him."

"Yeah, but she wanted to make sure he couldn't blame her for the split. And she didn't want him coming after her for some of her money. She just wasn't very happy. Enough to kill herself? I dunno. It just doesn't seem like her. Donna could get down sometimes, y'know, but it never lasted very long. She'd always bounce back." He placed his calloused hands on his knees and leaned forward. "I've no idea what happened to Amelia, either, and like I said, I wasn't here when she died so don't put me on your list of suspects."

"Just how friendly were you and Donna?" asked Roxanne.

"I told you. We worked together. We got along."

"You didn't have a trailer with you, first time you showed up at Hazeldean. You have one now. You need somewhere to stay when you're out here. You didn't, back then. Were you planning to stay with Donna at the cottage?"

He took in another breath and blew it out through his lips.

"You've got that all wrong," he said. "I was going back to Winnipeg that night. I just came out here to check what work needed doing, so I'd know what stuff to bring out with me. So no, Sergeant, I was not having it off with Donna Palmer. I've got work to do. Is there anything else you want to ask me?"

He couldn't hide his annoyance. She'd managed to rub him the wrong way. She left. As soon as she parked the car outside the detachment at Fiskar Bay, she texted Izzy McBain: *Call me. Just talked to C Cain.* Then she went inside to her office to find out how plans for the Canada Day celebrations were progressing. Her regular job.

Izzy had another call to make in the city. Amelia and her boyfriend Karim had rented an apartment in a tall building near the university. Karim was slim and dark, still a student, working on an MBA. He and Amelia had lived together for more than a year, he told them. He showed Izzy and Trent Weiss into a rectangular room with a kitchen at the end. It was sparsely furnished, from IKEA and second-hand stores, judging by the style and condition. A computer desk filled one corner. The window provided a bird's eye view of the campus from fifteen stories up, through slatted blinds. There was no balcony but the apartment was air-conditioned and cool. Karim had an IT job on the side and worked from home.

Were they looking for Amelia, he asked? She was out at the lake. Was this something to do with how her mother had died? That had been bad, real bad. Amelia had been upset about it. Karim had met her mother, nice woman. Amelia was a lot like her. He had Amelia's contact information, did they need it?

"No one in the family's spoken to you?" Izzy asked. He'd heard from no one. He'd been busy working during the day and had an assignment that he needed to work on at night. He'd turned off all his devices, everything, so he wouldn't be distracted. He wanted to get it done, so he could join Amelia at the lake on the weekend. He'd never been there before. "We should sit down," Izzy said.

She and Trent shared a small sofa. Karim took the office chair at his desk and swivelled it round to face them. Izzy told him how Amelia's body had been discovered, the previous day. He gripped the sides of his chair as if he were afraid he'd fall off, stunned by the news.

"You haven't heard from Amelia's father or her brother?"

"They don't know about me," he said, his voice barely audible.

"Do you have a friend or a relative we can call?"

He did. He had a sister. He gave them a name and a phone number. Trent made the call. Izzy brewed some hot tea and took the chance to look around the kitchen and peep into the bedroom while the kettle boiled. There was a bed, not much else. A second room, barely more than a closet, held a desk, bookshelves with folders. Most of them seemed to contain Amelia's old class assignments. Her computer was gone. Chances were she had taken it to the lake. The apartment looked exactly like a place where two students lived together. Amelia may have come into money when her mother died, but it looked as if she and Karim had lived on basic student incomes prior to that.

Karim was talking nonstop about Amelia, about how smart she was, about her plans to take over her mother's business.

"She was so clever. So sad that her mother had died, but excited because she was going to run Bricks and Sugar by herself. She had an aunt that she hoped would help her. The aunt is out there, at the cottage. Amelia was going to meet with her. She was going to introduce me to her."

"The aunt hasn't called you either?" asked Izzy. She hadn't found any sugar in the kitchen but there were some cookies. She handed one on a plate to Karim.

He held up a hand, palm out, he didn't want it. His fingers were shaking. "No," Izzy insisted. "Eat it." The guy was in shock. Something sweet would help steady him.

"Her auntie maybe doesn't know about me yet, either," said Karim.

His sister Leila lived close by. She arrived soon; she was older than her brother, in hijab, two preschool children hanging onto her skirts.

"What is going on with this family?" she asked Izzy and Trent. "First her mother dies? Now Amelia? And no one talks to anyone? No one thinks to tell Karim?" She had met Amelia. She'd rather Karim had wanted to marry someone from their own community, but that was who Karim had chosen. He had been happy with Amelia so it was okay with her.

"Look at him. His heart is broken." Karim had not moved from his chair. The plate that Izzy had handed him had been placed on the floor. A little boy was eating the cookie. "You will leave us, please. I need to take care of my brother."

Izzy and Trent let themselves out and took the long elevator down to ground level.

"So Amelia had a Muslim boyfriend that her mom knew about but her dad didn't?" said Trent. "Her brother neither? And they've been together for more than a year?"

"It seems like only Donna knew."

They stepped outside onto hot concrete and the smell of car exhaust. There were more road works outside the apartment building and traffic was backed up. They both put on sunglasses against the dazzling light. Trent was neat in a shirt and cotton pants. They looked like they had just been ironed.

"If Jay had known about Karim, he would have called and told him, surely." Izzy found her key fob and unlocked the car.

"Would Leslie have known about him? If he was going to meet her on the weekend?"

"Maybe she hadn't been told about him yet," said Izzy. "Too bad I didn't know about this before I talked to Gord Palmer and his son."

They climbed into the hot car. Izzy turned on the air full blast. They both checked their phones. Trent knew now where Palmer had been taken, to a secluded spot in a provincial park hundreds of kilometres north. As Izzy had predicted, Maria Smith had accompanied him. Izzy read a text from Roxanne Calloway before she drove out of the parking lot. Why was Roxanne interested in Charlie Cain and what was he doing, still working out there? Assuming that that was what he was doing?

Her car came equipped with emergency lights. She switched them on and watched the traffic in front of her peel aside as she nosed her way through. "I think we'd best go check out Donna Palmer's real estate business before I head up to the Interlake," she said.

14

LESLIE BORTHWICK HAD been asked to meet with Chris Olson, the manager of Harbourfront House, that same morning. That was all right, she told herself. Leslie needed to talk to the woman anyway. She put on a flowery dress and a sunhat with a wide brim and applied lipstick. Looking one's best was always a good idea. She'd met Mrs. Olson occasionally and knew her to be efficient. Whatever this was about, Leslie was more than prepared to hold her ground. She wanted to get back to Saskatoon as soon as she could, and she needed to take her mother with her.

Mrs. Olson had other ideas. She took her seat behind her desk at the care home, blond, blue-eyed and solid of build, looking like a latter-day Valkyrie, and informed Leslie that the family had requested that Lois's doctor examine Mrs. Borthwick to see if she was fit enough to be moved to another province. The doctor was busy today, working at the hospital, and since this was Friday, she would not be available until sometime next week.

"This has nothing to do with my aunt's family," Leslie objected. "I am the person responsible for my mother's care."

Mrs. Olson had a special smile she used when dealing with family disputes. It showed concern but was firm. It had stood her in good standing many times. Now she applied it and folded her hands in front of her.

"You have two brothers," she reminded Leslie.

"Neither of whom has shown the slightest interest in my mother's welfare," Leslie declared. "My sister and I have always made the decisions about our mother's well-being, and as you know, my sister recently passed."

"You have our condolences." The manager changed neither her position nor her demeanour. "You've been diligent about paying for your mother's expenses here, but there is more to elder care than—"

"Of which I am perfectly aware," Leslie cut her off. "That is exactly why I need to move my mother to Saskatoon, so she can be closer to me. That is my decision," she reminded this immoveable brick of a woman, "and my responsibility since I have power of attorney."

One blond eyebrow rose on the smiling face. "You should discuss that with other members of your family, Ms. Borthwick," said Chris Olson.

"How do you mean?" Leslie asked, taken aback.

"I am not at liberty to say." The big woman rose to her feet, intent on ending the meeting. "As I have said, the doctor will examine your mother as soon as possible, then we will wait for her report. We cannot release your mother from this home until we know that it is safe for us to do so." She stood at the side of her desk, her hands still clasped in front of her. "That process might take a week or two. Talk to your mother's sister, Sylvia Olafson," she advised. "She takes an active interest in your mother's welfare. Maybe, between the two of you, you can sort something out." She walked to the door and opened it. Leslie was dismissed.

Leslie walked out into the bright sunlight. That meeting had not gone as she had planned. She should have known that her Aunt Sylvia had something to do with this. She should go and find out what Sylvia thought she was doing but the Olafsons had moved house just before the pandemic. Leslie wasn't sure exactly where their new house was located. Fraser might know, but she wasn't going to ask him. Both he and Jay would want to know why she wanted to talk to their aunt. She googled the Olafson name and Canada 411 came up with the answer, an address in a new development on the edge of town. She entered it into her GPS.

Leslie turned into Sylvia's street just in time to see another car draw up into the driveway ahead of her and a uniformed policewoman get out. She drove slowly by, looked in her mirror when she got to the end of the road, and saw the cop being admitted to the house. A meeting with her Aunt Sylvia would have to be put on hold. Leslie reconsidered: Maybe she should invite Fraser to have lunch with her. If she got him on his own, when he didn't have an audience to play to, she might get something like the truth out of him and find out just what her mother's side of the family was up to.

Sylvia Olafson walked most mornings with a group of women who all lived close by. It kept her fit and the group was always up to date with what was going on around them. She had been about to set off, her sneakers on her feet, all laced up and ready to go, when Sergeant Calloway from the RCMP showed up at her door.

Sylvia resigned herself to missing her walk. She texted one of her friends to let them know she had unexpected company and wondered how long it would be before they all knew who was visiting. They would be dying to know what this was about. As was she. Being visited by the RCMP on a Saturday would make anyone curious.

The house was large—four bedrooms and three bathrooms, she boasted as she led Roxanne into an immaculate kitchen. A double garage, attached, came with a built-in workshop where her husband could keep himself amused, out of her hair, now that they were both retired. He was out in the backyard right now cutting grass on a riding mower. The throb of its engine passed the window as she spoke.

Everything about Sylvia was perfect. She liked to dress well and was aware of her image. She'd inherited a fine, Nordic bone structure, straight blonde hair that looked like it might still be natural, pale blue-grey eyes. She'd be modelling at this fall's fashion show, she said, proud to be asked. She had to be well into her seventies.

"I plan to be there," said Roxanne. "If it happens." She sat on a stool at a granite-topped kitchen counter while Sylvia set out cream in a small jug and a bowl of sugar. Then she broached the subject she had come to discuss. "I want to ask you about your sister. She has dementia?"

Sylvia poured the coffee. Lois was indeed sick. It was early onset Alzheimer's. So sad. Lois was younger than her sister by a couple of years.

Sylvia perched on another stool. "She's not long turned seventy-two and she's been in Harbourfront these past eight years. I go to see her most days." It was so hard not being able to visit her during the big shutdown. But now things were improving. Sylvia and Art liked to travel. If they went on a trip, she could rely on her kids to go in and make sure their aunt was all right. She had three of them, a girl and two boys.

"One of them is Sigurd?" Sylvia and Lois had both been Sigurdson before they'd married and taken their husband's names. Sigurd Olafson had been named for his forefathers.

"Sig's always getting himself into a mess, but he's good at heart. You should hear him singing with his Aunt Lois," Sylvia said, sticking up for her son. Her other two were no trouble at all.

And Lois's children, Roxanne asked?

"The boys are all right," Sylvia said. "Fraser's a bit of a lost soul, but look at him, back here right now, taking an interest in what happens to his mom. And Jay's a gem, always has been." She couldn't say the same for the Borthwick daughters.

"I don't want to speak ill of the dead, Sergeant, but that Donna was a piece of work, I can tell you. And as for Leslie!" Her Icelandic eyes turned icy as she mentioned the name. "She's trouble and she needs to be stopped. Have you heard that she wants to move my sister to Saskatchewan? Lois is far too fragile for that. A trip like that's going to kill her. I've had a word with that nice husband of yours, Mr. Stavros, and he says that if we think that Leslie is not acting in my sister's best interests, we can stop her having power of attorney for Lois.

"Or since two people were appointed in the first place—Donna had joint power of attorney with Leslie, you know—we can insist that there should be two of them again. And I could be that second person. Leslie cannot be the only person making decisions about what happens to my sister. So we've talked to the manager at Harbourfront, and she's talking to the doctor. We're going to make sure Lois doesn't get shipped off to Saskatoon, for starters." She stopped to sip a mouthful of coffee then continued, barely stopping for breath.

"Leslie's never come near her mom, not in years. Hardly crosses the door, even when she's staying at Hazeldean and she's only there for a week or two, most summers. Donna neither. If you ask me, all they've ever been interested in is the money. There's lots of it, Sergeant. And don't you go thinking that that's why I want to keep Lois here, because it's not like that at all. Art and I have more than enough." She looked around her suburban palace, justifiably proud of what she and her husband had achieved. "My kids, too, they don't need it And we all look out for Sig. We don't need any of that Borthwick money."

Roxanne was not sure if that was true. Sylvia and Art Olafson had worked all their lives. They understood the value of a hard-earned buck, and what a small fortune could provide in the way of comfort, security and expensive trips to faraway places.

"I've always looked out for Lois," Sylvia continued. "Even when we were little. All those years when she was married to Will Borthwick. People say that the girls took after her, but that's not true. Lois was always kind. It's her boys that take after her. Leslie and Donna look a bit like her, but that's all. They're tough, both of them, like their dad. And selfish."

"Tell me about him," Roxanne asked. Sylvia topped up their mugs, needing no encouragement.

"Will was a jerk," she informed Roxanne. "He always had cash to spare. He was working in his dad's insurance business when he met Lois. Used to come up here in the summer, to stay at Hazeldean. They met at a Saturday night dance. He was seven years older than her. Lois was straight out of high school, pretty as they come. Was going to go into nursing. She took one look at him and that was it. I saw it happen. Totally smitten.

"He showed up at the house the next afternoon with a picnic basket in the back of the car. The next day, he took her out on his dad's boat. They were engaged by the end of the summer. She did less than a year of nursing training, then she got married, all of nineteen years old.

"Will was always the boss in that household. She stayed home and took care of the kids. Never went out to work. Just kept everything clean and did what she was told. In the summers, she got some time to herself, though. She brought the family out to that old cottage at Cullen Village, soon as school was done, and they stayed until the September long weekend. I saw lots of Lois then. She loved being at Hazeldean. Will drove up sometimes but he never stayed long. He was busy, building up his business. He had different branch offices by then. Donna and Leslie got their business heads from him. And they learned to work hard, I'll say that for them."

"He died young?"

"All of fifty-seven years old. It was cigarettes that got him. He smoked. Well, we all did back then but Will never had a cigarette out of his mouth. Lung cancer. Lois was left a widow, just before her fiftieth birthday. That was twenty-three years ago. She was sad for a while, but some good things happened. We went on some trips together. Mexico. New York. A Caribbean cruise. She always paid. Art and I still didn't have much spare cash back then. I tell you, Lois was kind. Generous.

"She started getting forgetful before she was sixty. It took a few years but she knew she was losing her mind. She said she wanted to go into Harbourfront when that time came, to be near to me and my family. Close to home. Fraser was gone, doing drugs in Toronto. Leslie was living in Saskatoon, and Donna wasn't long married to Gordon Palmer. Jay was just a kid. He was still in university by the time she needed to move. She knew her children wouldn't have much time for their mom, and she was right. She had a beautiful house in Winnipeg. It was sold and cleaned right out, lickety-split, Leslie made sure of that. All she was left with was a dresser and a few photographs." Sylvia looked around her own accumulation of things—her appliances and knickknacks and the many photographs scattered on walls and every available surface. She shuddered at the thought.

"Was Will Borthwick abusive?" asked Roxanne.

"Nothing physical, but he had a bad mouth on him. And he always had to be in control. That's what destroyed Fraser, if you ask me. He couldn't do a thing right as far as his dad was concerned. He was the oldest, and a boy. He wasn't like his dad at all, that was the problem. Jay came along a lot later, when Will was out working almost all of the time. Jay was still a kid when Will got sick. Will had a bit of a temper on him. Donna and Leslie got it from him. I've seen both of them lose their cool, screaming and yelling, just to get their own way.

"Maybe that's what happened to Donna. She went too far with someone. Said the wrong thing and that's why she's dead, Sergeant. And maybe Leslie had something to do with it. She's always loved money, even when she was a little girl. She never spent her pocket money if she could help it. Little Miss Scrooge, she was. It's Donna who always made sure Lois's bills at Harbourfront get paid on time, up until now. And she always just covered what's necessary. It's me and my daughter that Lois relies on for treats or if she needs new slippers or something. We're the ones that have always taken real care of her. Not those girls of hers, not ever."

"And Jay? He's grown up now."

"Jay's okay. He comes to see Lois when he can. He was busy with that restaurant he had before the virus shut it down. Then he couldn't visit when we were in lockdown. Maybe if he moves into Hazeldean like he wants to, he'll be able to see his mom more often."

Everyone always made excuses for Jay, Roxanne noticed. Everyone in his family was on his side. "You know about that?" she asked.

"How he wants to fix the cottage up and live there? Of course we do. It would be the best thing that could happen. Lois used to call Hazeldean her happy place. She would be so pleased if he did that. Move in with that nice woman he's found. She loves that old cottage too. She wants to make it into a real home and raise her kid out here."

"Even if it's the place where Jay's sister and his niece have died?"

"Well, I hear it needs a lot of fixing up. Maybe if it looks a bit better that'll make things okay." Sylvia Olafson believed in the healing power of cleanliness.

The conversation had taken longer than Roxanne had expected. She left Sylvia standing in her doorway, flanked by baskets of flowering begonias. Her husband, Art Olafson, stopped his mower beside the garage, climbed out of the seat and joined her. They disappeared inside and closed their glossy black door behind them. Two streets over, Roxanne passed some women walking on their way back home. They gave her a cheery wave.

She drove slowly, thinking about what she'd heard. Sylvia Olafson must be in touch with Jay Borthwick, as well as his brother, Fraser. How else would she know about his plans to renovate and winterize Hazeldean? And that Jay had found himself a nice woman who shared his interest in the house, if she hadn't met Jennifer in person?

Was one half of the Borthwick clan working against the other? Had Jay and Fraser and their aunt and her family joined forces to make sure that Jay got to live in the cottage, that Lois stayed in Manitoba, and her money was controlled by them, and not by Leslie? Was that why Donna and Amelia's plan to tear down Hazeldean needed to be stopped? Was that why they had died?

15

LESLIE BORTHWICK CALLED her brother Fraser. "Come for lunch," she said.

"Why?"

"Because we need to talk."

He grudgingly agreed. Things were getting busy at the Melnyk farm because tomorrow was Saturday, farmers market day. Wes's wife had hinted more than once that they could use a hand. Saying that he needed to go and meet with his sister would get him off the hook, plus he wanted to have a word with Leslie about this plan she had to move their old mom to Saskatoon. He wasn't sure that was such a great idea.

He roared his bike across the causeway to Bulrush Island and pulled up in a cloud of dust outside the house where Leslie said she was staying. It was a big place, all shiny and new, air-conditioned inside, but Leslie had set up lunch on a patio table at the back, under an umbrella. He'd rather have been inside, out of the heat, but maybe he could smoke out there. You could see all the way down the south basin of the lake, to a water tower at Cullen Village, at the edge of the water, not far from where his other sister and his niece had died. He preferred not to think about that. This house had its own dock. A boat was moored there.

"Can we go out in that?" He pointed.

"No, we may not. Sit down," she ordered him. She must have stopped at the grocery store. Rotisserie chicken, potato salad and coleslaw from the deli counter were on the table. Leslie never was one for cooking but that didn't matter. Fraser wasn't hungry.

"Where's the wine, Les?" He found a spot in the shade of the umbrella and waited while she fetched a bottle and unscrewed the cap. A glass of cold white helped him feel more like himself. He and she had witnessed the same gory scene yesterday and that gave him an unusual sense of solidarity with his sister. He knew she couldn't have killed Amelia because he'd seen how she reacted. And she must believe the same about him.

"I think that Gord Palmer's responsible for what's happened to Donna and Amelia," she was saying while she carved up the chicken.

"How come? Wasn't he in Ottawa when Donna died?"

"I didn't say he did it himself. I said he was responsible. You know they weren't getting along?"

He hadn't, but he wasn't surprised.

"So, you're saying he got someone else to do the job for him? Don't be stupid, Leslie. You never liked Gord Palmer. You just want it to be him that did it. And y'know what, he might have wanted Donna out of the way, but how about Amelia?" He picked up a chicken leg and considered eating it. "She was his daughter. He wouldn't have wanted to kill her. You've got that wrong."

"How are you doing for cash, Fraser?" Leslie asked.

"Not great. You know how it is with me." The change of tack surprised Fraser, but he wasn't stupid. He wasn't going to let on about the wad of cash in his back pocket. He'd offered to pay some to Wes Melnyk's wife but she'd said to hang onto it, that he could help clean out the chicken coop instead. He'd said he would think about that.

"Maybe I can help you out," Leslie announced. She had never, ever, offered him money before. He wasn't going to say no, but he did wonder what his side of the deal was going to be. He put down his wineglass. Best not to drink too much. Stay alert. Leslie went into the house and came back with five brand new pink hundred-dollar bills, fresh from the ATM. It wasn't much, not half as good as his trucker buddies had been, but he pocketed it.

A couple with kids waved from the lawn next door. They were wearing life jackets. Must be going out on their own boat. They stared at Leslie's scruffy guest as they reached the dock. He waved at them. They did not wave back.

"I might not want to keep my share in Hazeldean after all," said Leslie.

"Do you think Jay will still want to have it, after what's happened there?" Fraser asked.

"He might. The pier will get taken down in the fall, as usual. They'll put up a new one in the spring so it won't be the same one. And the house can be scrubbed out and fixed up to look different."

"Donna offered me forty grand for my share," he said.

"Not enough," his sister told him and topped up his glass with more wine. He resisted drinking it.

"Got some water?" he asked. She went and found a cold bottle in the fridge. Leslie wasn't usually this obliging. She was definitely up to something. She'd been checking house prices out here, she told him. "It's worth way more than that. Even in the state it's in, the location's excellent, it's a huge lot, it comes with a stretch of beach. It should fetch at least $275,000 right now. Don't sell your share to Jay for less than sixty-five."

Leslie sat down again with her back to the sun, a hat on her head, sunglasses on her nose. It was hard to read the expression on her face now that it was all in the shade.

"How's Jay gonna find that kind of money?" he asked.

Leslie had thought about that as well. "He and Jennifer can't be entirely broke," she said. "They're finding enough cash to set up this café that they've started and they have a house in Winnipeg. I think it's maybe hers. I'd bet the divorce and the collapse of The Sleepy Fox wiped him out. So, she must have enough to buy us all out and do the repairs they want to do, if she doesn't have the house mortgaged to the hilt."

"Just how much money does Mom have, Les?" Fraser asked.

She studied her chicken, not keen to reply.

"I can't say offhand. How come you need to know? You've never asked before."

"I am now. See, Les, our Aunt Sylvia's been spelling it out for me. She says Dad owned at least six insurance offices when he died. They all got sold."

"You got some cash, then," said Leslie. "We all did."

"Fifty grand apiece." He hadn't remembered how much it had been but his aunt had reminded him. "All the rest of the money got stashed away. And then when Mom moved up here, the house got sold. There were cars. She had a grand piano. He had a billiard room. Everything went."

"It's all invested. We pay for Mom's keep out of it."

"Sylvia says that there's got to be a chunk left over."

"Does she now?"

"Yes, she does. And you've been in charge of it for all these years. And y'know what else? You can't move Mom away from here, Leslie. You've seen her. She's just skin and bone. Sylvia knows what it costs to keep her at Harbourfront. She's going to apply to be in charge of her care alongside you and she's going to make sure Mom spends the rest of her days here. I might stay here myself. Help keep an eye on her."

Leslie put down her fork and sat up straight. She laced her fingers on the tabletop. "You want to do that? The winter here's grim," she reminded him.

"Yeah, but I've got buddies. And it's cheaper to live here than in Toronto." Fraser and Big Sig had had a long talk about that, just last night.

"What would you do for income?" asked Leslie.

"Well, there would be the cash from Hazeldean."

"That won't last forever. I've got a suggestion," said Leslie. "How about we arrange for you to be Mom's other power of attorney, instead of Sylvia. We're her oldest children. It should be our job to look after her."

"And she gets to stay here?"

"I could reconsider that."

"You just want to keep control of the cash."

"I've always been in charge of it, Fraser, and I've taken very good care of it. You know, since Donna died before Mom did, the estate will be divided three ways when Mom finally goes, between you, me and Jay. There's no provision in Mom's will for Donna's share to be passed down to her kids.

"And since you have health issues that make it hard for you to make a living, there's no reason why I can't separate out the share that's going to belong to you. I could give you a monthly allowance from it to tide you over until Mom passes on, then you'll get whatever's left over. How much do you think you'd need, if you wanted to stay here?'

He didn't know. He'd have to think about that.

"Don't take too long." Leslie drank down some more of her wine. "If I decide not to move Mom after all, I still need to get back to Saskatoon soon as I can. We should see the lawyer and get the paperwork written up before I go."

Fraser's mouth widened into a leery smile. He could see what Leslie was up to, now. So that was why she had wanted to take her mother away—so that their Aunt Sylvia would never become a second power of attorney and find out what was going on with the money. He had to give it to her—she'd figured out this new game plan double quick, where she'd dole out some cash every month to keep him happy.

"You're funny, Leslie," he said. She frowned at him. She didn't get it.

Things might now go the way she wanted. She might not be allowed to go home to Saskatoon just yet. He was sure she wasn't the killer but the police didn't know that. He knew from experience way more than Leslie did about how they operated. They would probably insist she stick around a bit longer, but he wasn't going to tell her that. Meantime, he should have a word with his little brother and get him up to speed.

On the other hand, what she was suggesting wasn't a bad idea. He might go for it. Some regular cash coming in would be a good thing. If he was going to live here at Fiskar Bay full time, where would he stay? He should ask Wes, he would know. He needed to get going, he told his sister. He'd think about her offer and get back to her.

"Don't wait too long, Fraser." She saw him out.

Another pair of neighbours eyed him curiously as his motorbike sprang into life. He breezed off down the causeway and sent a flock of ducks flying.

Izzy and Trent Weiss found the Bricks and Sugar office in yet another Winnipeg strip mall, sandwiched between an East Indian food store and a hairdresser. A giant thrift store was the mall's main draw. The frontage of Bricks and Sugar was not that of your usual real estate office, an array of homes for sale, with little photographs and descriptions. Instead, two large photographs filled the front window, before and after interior shots of the same property, demonstrating how Bricks and Sugar could work magic on an old house, transforming it into a gleaming, streamlined living space, easy to maintain and very desirable. Although Donna Palmer had just died, two women were still at work inside.

"Madison Yanovsky," one of them introduced herself, a short-haired woman with glasses, in her forties, round of face and body. "I was Donna's office manager. You can call me Maddie." The younger of the two was Hannah, their receptionist.

"You're carrying on?" Izzy asked. "Keeping the business going? You haven't stopped since Donna and Amelia have both died?"

"We have to. There are house sales in progress and staff need to be paid. We are so busy we can't afford to take time off. We need to make sure the money keeps coming in." She showed them around, pleasant, seemingly eager to help. Nothing in her manner or in her surroundings hinted that the company's owners had just died. Everything at Bricks and Sugar was carrying on as usual.

The waiting area was furnished with comfortable chairs and fresh flowers. Catalogues lay on occasional tables, featuring specific properties. Virtual tours were available for interested house hunters, Maddie informed them.

"You use a videographer?" asked Trent. "And a professional photographer?" He nodded in the direction of more large, framed photos on the walls.

"We do. Everything here was created according to Donna's vision," Maddie explained, "and it works. We want the business to carry on exactly as Donna set it up. Provide personalized, top-quality service. Make sure people get the best price for their house and find a new home that's just right for them."

"For a fee," said Izzy.

"Well, of course."

Bricks and Sugar employed four realtors and a contractor. He was currently in the Interlake, upgrading some houses. A company was subcontracted to clean for them and they had a working partnership with a garden centre when landscaping was required. They also supplied fresh flowers.

"Where did Donna work?"

That office was as pleasantly decorated as the rest. There was a desk, but pride of place was given to a conversation arrangement of sofa, table and chairs. Again, there were flowers, bright cheerful ones, even although Donna was gone.

"Where did Amelia work?" asked Izzy.

"She didn't have her own office yet," was the answer. "She worked from home last summer and she was just getting started again. She would probably have taken over this space. It's quite awful to think that anyone would want to do away with either of them. Donna was so talented and Amelia was only twenty-two years old."

"But she was going to inherit the business?"

"So we were told. She had no experience. She only graduated with a degree in business admin last year. But you know what new grads are like. Think they know it all. Our lawyer is checking everything out but he thinks that Bricks and Sugar will belong to Graeme, the brother, now. We're hoping he'll sell it to us."

"We being who?"

She and the contractor were forming a partnership. What was his name? C.H. Cain. He had all the funding that he needed. Maddie had an appointment to talk to the bank about raising a loan for her share. "We'll keep the name. People know and trust it."

"That's a quick decision," said Izzy.

"It has to be. We don't want Graeme Palmer offloading it onto someone else without us knowing," Maddie replied.

The police officers were welcome to look through Donna's office. Could she bring them some coffee? Hannah would make some, fresh. And she knew the password to Donna's desktop computer. She opened it up for them. They waited for her to leave, then closed the door.

It didn't take long for Trent to find something of interest. Donna had maintained a detailed calendar. Business appointments were entered in blue, personal ones, like a manicure appointment a couple of days before she had gone to Hazeldean, were in red.

"Look at this, Sarge," Trent pointed at the screen. The letters CC occurred in both colours. On June 21, the Monday after Donna Palmer had died, they appeared in red and blue and that ran right through until the following Friday.

"That's the handyman, Charlie Cain," said Izzy. "It looks like he was going to be out at Hazeldean for more than a week and it wasn't going to be entirely business. Roxanne Calloway, at the Fiskar Bay detachment, wants to talk to me about him."

She should try to get up to the Interlake today. Meantime, this computer needed to be taken into HQ for examination.

Dave Kovak called on his car phone; he was on his way to Cullen Village. Dr. Farooq from the Provincial Medical Examiner's office had talked to him. They were certain that Amelia Palmer had died from two blows to the head, but they still weren't sure what had happened to her mother. Donna had certainly been strangled, but had someone throttled her with their bare hands, then tied the cord from the bathrobe around her neck and hung her from the end of the pier to make it look like suicide? The bruising around the neck suggested that might be possible but was not conclusive. He was going out to take a closer look at the pier to find out if it was possible to have killed her first then faked the hanging.

"Can you meet me there?" Dave asked her.

"Sure," said Izzy. She'd drop Trent and the computer off, then she'd be on her way.

She texted Roxanne Calloway: *At Hazeldean @ 6. Meet there?*

16

HOW AMELIA PALMER had died was fairly clear.

There must have been a confrontation in the living room that had so escalated that her assailant had grabbed the poker from the set of fire irons on the stone hearth and swung it. The first blow had caught her on the left side of her head. They were looking for someone right-handed. As Amelia began to sway backwards she had taken a second blow to the other side of her skull.

"You're sure it was the poker?" Izzy asked Dave.

"There's a hook near the end for moving logs around and an indent on the side of her head, just above the eye, left side, matches it. The killer must have caught her with it on the second swing. It would have been a backhander."

Although the poker had been washed clean, it had soldered joints where some blood might be embedded, evidence that it had been the murder weapon. The poker was being scrutinized at the lab in Winnipeg.

"Can you tell if the attacker was taller than Amelia?" Roxanne tried to imagine the scenario.

Not really, Dave indicated. But the killer must have moved quickly. Whoever it was had a powerful swing and enough presence of mind to clean up afterwards. The cleaners that Amelia had brought to sort out the mess after Fraser's party had done a good job, but so had the intruder. The living room and the hallway leading to the veranda had been wiped clean. There were prints in the kitchen and the bathroom, but they were mainly Amelia's. They'd have to check who the other prints could have belonged to, but Amelia could have met other people here before she died, like the Cain guy.

"So someone else was here? Someone who only went into the living room?" asked Roxanne.

Somebody wanted to make sure that no one knew that they were in the room where she was attacked. But that could be anyone who visited here.

Obviously, Amelia had been murdered, but they still did not know exactly what had happened to Donna. Dave wanted to go out to the end of the pier, to find out if someone could have strangled her first then faked the hanging.

"Great that you're both here," he said. "We can act it out." And he strode off down the hallway and out in the direction of the pier.

"We can?" Roxanne knew how this enactment would work. She would get to play the victim. She looked over the brown, dry lawn to the pier outlined against the clear water. White ribbons marked the exact spot where the bathroom cord noosed around Donna's neck had been tied to the railing. Amelia must have fastened them there.

"Sure we can," said Izzy, and followed Dave across the grass.

"Do you think someone choked her with their bare hands?" asked Roxanne as they walked, one behind the other, along the narrow pier. She noticed June Appleby next door watching from her deck. Everything they did was going to be described later, in detail, on the Cullen Village grapevine.

"That's right. Someone strong enough to do it," said Dave. The medics hadn't seen anything resembling thumbprints on the throat, but the bruising and compression caused by the bathroom cord could be masking that. "What I need to know is whether someone could have lifted her over the railing, after they killed her. She wasn't big, only weighed about 110 pounds," he said, "but that's still a heavy weight to lift from the floorboards of the pier."

"So you want us to try?" asked Izzy. She looked at Roxanne. "You're skinnier than me. How much do you weigh?"

Roxanne wasn't sure. Maybe 125 pounds?

"So," said Izzy. "You lie down and Dave or I can try to lift you over." This was happening exactly as Roxanne had expected.

"You're going to stop before you get me to the top," she said, looking over the railing. The ribbons were long, white, shiny satin. They stretched down to the rocks below. Stones were piled up in a small cairn on the ground below the spot where Donna's body had hung. Memorials always happened in scenes like these.

"Sure," said Izzy.

"You worried about this, Roxanne?" asked Dave.

"No. Not at all." But she was and she didn't know why. Was she feeling more vulnerable because she was pregnant? Roxanne knew she wasn't in any danger. Dave wouldn't let anything go wrong. He and Izzy were discussing how to lift her up off the floor onto the bench that ran along the inside of the railing. After that, they would have to get her upper torso over the rail until gravity took over and pulled her down toward the lakebed on the other side.

Roxanne lay down on the wooden floorboards of the pier. She breathed deeply as Dave made the first attempt. He raised her up into a sitting position, wrapped his arms round her from behind and heaved. It took some effort, but within seconds he had hoisted her body onto the bench and lifted her legs.

The pier railings were simply built, of horizontal planks, one at the top, one at the middle. Single posts formed the supports, which were about four feet apart. Only one bar prevented Roxanne from simply rolling over and falling off the other side. The bunch of ribbons was right above her, the ends trailing past her shoulder. She sat up.

"Donna didn't have to go over the top," she said. "They just had to lift her this far, attach the cord to the upper railing and push her through the gap in the railing. She was smaller than me. It would have been easier than you think."

Donna's suicide could have been faked by a man as big and as strong as Dave, but could it be done by a woman?

"You need to try it," he said to Izzy.

Roxanne sighed. She was going to have to submit to this whole procedure again. She lay down. Izzy repeated what Dave had done. It took a lot of hauling and grunting but eventually Roxanne was lying back up on the bench. It was hot work, this summer's evening.

They sat afterwards, in a row, the water a metallic shimmer behind them, a flock of pelicans swooping in to land on the water. June Appleby had watched every move they had made. She disappeared into her house.

"Donna Palmer was shorter than you by at least three inches. Someone my size could have done it. But it was hard going and I'm fit," said Izzy. She was. She didn't play hockey often but she worked out in the gym regularly.

"So. A man or a healthy woman," said Dave.

"Or someone with an accomplice. It would be easy if there was a second person," Roxanne remarked.

They sat for a moment in silence. Hazeldean was in shadow, the sun behind it, a large, unnaturally scarlet ball suspended in streaks of grey and purple.

"I don't like the look of that," said Dave.

"Forest fires, out west, Roxanne replied. The red colour of the sun was caused by the light filtering through ash suspended in the atmosphere. She had been receiving reports all day: Woodlands were burning in the western Canadian provinces. There were a couple of fires smouldering in northwest Manitoba. It was inevitable that the smoke would blow their way soon, maybe sometime tomorrow. The air would become thick with it, unhealthy and foul.

"Donna Palmer had money of her own," said Izzy. "She stashed it in a private account, out of reach of her husband. Just over $400,000. She left it to her children."

"So now Graeme will get it all?" Roxanne asked her. "He's an athlete, isn't he? He must be fit and strong."

"He is. As arrogant as they come, but he twitched a bit when I mentioned how his mother died. I don't think he can have killed her, but it's a lot of money to inherit."

"We haven't ruled out suicide yet," Dave reminded them. "We just have to consider the option of murder. It still might have been only Amelia that's been killed. How did Graeme get along with his sister?"

"Hardly spoke to her. I think Amelia just got along with her mother. She's the only one who knew about the boyfriend. We keep running into dead ends." Izzy jumped to her feet. "I'm going to have to stay over here tonight and sort this out tomorrow. Send me whatever you've got, soon as, Dave? Can we talk this through in the morning, Roxanne? You'll be coming into the office? Guess I'd best go visit my mom. I'll have to go and scrounge a bed."

"Good luck with this one, you guys." Dave locked up the house and the three of them took off, each in a separate direction. Roxanne was halfway home when she realized that she hadn't mentioned her meeting with Charlie Cain to Izzy. That could wait until they met tomorrow.

Fraser Borthwick had decided he would go visit his brother. Jay and his partner, Jennifer, were busy when he reached the Cullen Village Rec Centre, hauling heavy wooden picnic tables from a storage shed behind the building. A couple of old guys were helping them.

Fraser took his cane from the back of his bike and limped toward them. They were setting up the tables, spaced several feet apart as regulations dictated they must, under the shade of some trees. Dining outside was permitted as long as diners were distanced. They'd serve up barbecued chicken and ribs tonight, Jay told him. He was all excited about it, like a little kid.

Fraser hadn't met Jennifer before. She realized right away that Fraser couldn't help them move tables around.

"Go wait in the trailer until we're done. We won't be long," she told him. "There's wine in the fridge in the kitchen. Help yourself." Fraser appreciated that. Jennifer might be okay.

A kid called Carter was watching TV inside. He'd been at day camp, kayaking. It had been great, he said, but his eyes didn't leave the screen. Fraser didn't mind. He unscrewed the cap on a bottle of white and found a glass in a high cupboard in the tiny kitchen. There wasn't any food around. Jay and Jennifer must do all their cooking in the Rec Centre, he thought. That was okay. As usual, food didn't interest him.

It wasn't long before Jay walked in the door. Jennifer and the old guys were going to finish setting up the tables, he said.

"What's going on at Hazeldean?" he asked, pouring himself a large glass of water. It was hot, working outside. "First Donna, then Amelia?" He sat down beside his older brother. "Should we be worried? Is it going to be one of us next?" He looked anxious as he swallowed down half the glassful.

Fraser shrugged. Why would anyone want to bump him off? But then he remembered how much he stood to gain when his mother died, plus there was his share of Hazeldean. That was worth way more than he had thought. He'd gone from being a man with nothing to being one of worth. Jay, too. They would each inherit the same amount of money.

"Maybe we should," he admitted. "Do you know how much cash Mom's got stashed away? How much we'll both get when she pops off? Have you seen what she looks like lately? She's failing, Jay. She might not have much longer. It might happen sooner than we think."

"You sure? I should go see her again." Jay knew that there was money but he'd never asked how much. He'd always thought he would wait, he told his brother, and get what was coming to him when the time came. The only thing he really wanted was the cottage.

"Still?" asked Fraser. "In spite of what's happened there?"

Sure he did. It had always been a great place. Hadn't they had the best times there when they were kids? And Jennifer liked it as much as he did. She said they'd clean it up. Burn some smudge, light candles, make it okay.

"It's kind of spooky," said Fraser, not convinced.

"Yeah, but people have done things like this before. You know that Stavros guy? The lawyer? He built that house that he and Roxanne Calloway, the cop, live in, right on the spot where his aunt and her girlfriend died. Planted trees there or something to remember them by."

Fraser hadn't heard about that and he wasn't really interested.

"So you'd buy me out?" he asked.

The door banged open. Jennifer came in, pink from exertion in the heat, her braid hanging down her back.

"You guys carry on talking," she said. "I've got menus to print. And I'm going to have to send out notices. This is going to be our real opening. We might have a band! Isn't that exciting?" She disappeared into another room.

"Seventy thousand," said Fraser.

"I'll need to check with Jennifer about that. It's her money."

"You don't have any of your own?"

"No." Jay shrugged. "The Sleepy Fox cleaned me out and I haven't worked since. But we're okay. Jennifer's husband died and she got a pile from the insurance."

"She's willing to sink it all into a house that belongs to you?"

"Sure she is. It'll be ours once we get married. Soon as my divorce comes through." The lines across Fraser's forehead deepened. It sounded like it would take a while before Jay would have enough money to pay him.

"Can you get the cash now, so you can pay me?" he asked.

He'd have to wait, said Jay, until the house in Winnipeg sold, but if he and Jennifer were sure of getting Hazeldean for themselves they would get that house onto the market right away. It was all fixed up, ready to go, so it should sell fast enough. They would need to find out if Leslie would sell her share, too, though, to be sure.

No problem, Fraser assured him. She had told him so herself. She didn't want the place either. She wanted to get back to Saskatoon as soon as she could but that might be on hold again now that Amelia had died. She'd decided she didn't want to move Mom after all.

"She's changed her mind about that? That's good. What made that happen?"

"You know Les. She just wanted to make sure she was in charge of the money or something," Fraser said, vaguely. He didn't want to tell his brother that he, himself, might become their mother's other power of attorney, alongside Leslie. There was no need to complicate things.

"I haven't seen Mom since April," Jay was saying. "Jennifer and I have just been so busy." He'd completely missed what Fraser had said about Leslie and the money. Jay was definitely not the brightest of the Borthwick clan, Fraser reminded himself. Nice guy but not the swiftest.

"Do you think Leslie did it? Killed Donna and Amelia?" Jay said in a quiet voice, so the kid wouldn't hear.

"No way," said Fraser. "My money's on Graeme. Maybe Gord's behind it all. Leslie says he and Donna were going to split up. Now the two of them will get whatever Donna had salted away and Gord will get to play the bereaved widower. That'll maybe win him some votes."

"Graeme will have all of Donna's share in Hazeldean now," said Jay. "I suppose I'll need to talk to him, too. But I can't imagine he's going to want to keep it, do you? I'll bet he'll be glad to get rid of it."

Jennifer reappeared in the doorway. It was time to get Carter to bed. He was going to go over to his friend Finn's house tomorrow so that she and Jay could get everything ready for tomorrow night's big barbecue. Maybe Fraser would like to drop by any time after five? He could bring that couple that he was staying with? Ribs, on the house?

He'd let them know. Cozy family barbecues weren't his thing but he might put up with it this time to keep on their good side. Just until Jay and Jennifer came up with the cash to buy him out of that cottage. He couldn't wait to be shot of that place.

17

"NOTHING EVER CHANGES around here." Izzy put two paper coffee containers down on the table in the room where she and Roxanne had first worked five years ago. That had been when she was a rookie constable who Roxanne had seconded into a Major Crimes team, which had led her into the MCU as an investigator. Izzy had moved on. She dragged a whiteboard away from a wall. Markers were still stored in the same drawer where she had left them years before. "How old are these? Do they still work?"

"Try them and see." Roxanne lifted the lid on a coffee. Black. It was hers. At least Izzy had not brought doughnuts, as she would have done not so long ago. Her mother must have fed her breakfast. Roxanne did not have to cope with the smell of sugar and deep-fried dough making her feel nauseous.

"Matt's at home with your boy?" Izzy had laid aside two markers that didn't work. A green one did. She tacked photos to the board, Donna and Amelia Palmer, smiling identical smiles and looking very much alive.

"Finn's made friends with Jay Borthwick's boy, Carter. He's there for the day. They're going to build a skateboard ramp." It was Saturday. There was no summer camp and Matt did not have to go to work.

"You and Matt haven't had any kids of your own yet?" The question caught Roxanne off guard. She felt her face turn pink.

"No. Not yet."

Izzy had her back to her, writing names below the photographs. She hadn't noticed. "That's one of the things that made me run," she commented. "Matt was always set on becoming some kind of superdad."

"You don't want to have any?"

"No. Not ever." Izzy turned to pick up more photos from a file on the table. "I watched my mom raise four of us. Not my thing." She lifted a shot of Jay Borthwick from the pile, one taken when he was a successful chef, holding one of his signature pasta dishes out to the camera to be admired.

"I hope we don't have to get tough on him," said Roxanne. "Carter and Finn are becoming best friends."

"The kid's not his son though, is he?" Izzy reached for pictures of the other two Borthwick siblings. They had checked Jay's background, she said as she pinned up the photos. He had started his Winnipeg restaurant with a business partner, and his first marriage had ended a year later. His wife had taken off for B.C. with their two children. He'd hooked up with Jennifer a few months later. She had worked for him as a pastry chef. She had been married but her husband had died, leaving her with a small son to raise.

"Kind of like you." Izzy reminded Roxanne that she was also a widow with a child. It was eight long years since RCMP Constable Jake Calloway had been shot in the line of duty. She, like Jennifer Boychuk, had moved on. "They got together and he moved into a house that Jennifer owns in Winnipeg."

"Do you know why they want Hazeldean?" asked Roxanne. "The Sleepy Fox was a success until the pandemic happened. Why would they not want to stay in Winnipeg and reopen it?"

"Don't know." Izzy sat and lifted the lid on her coffee. "Maybe they don't want to repeat themselves. Or they want to raise the kid out here. Like you and Matt are doing." She picked up an old mugshot of Fraser Borthwick, taken when he was much younger. He'd still had long hair and a beard then but they were brown. He didn't look quite so worn.

Izzy's favourite brother, Mike, had dropped by the McBain family farm last night. The two of them had gone out back to visit their dad's horses, standing out in a field close to a pile of smouldering hay, left so the smoke would keep the flies and the mosquitoes away. Fires were disapproved of. They were going to be banned soon in this dry weather but no one was going to tell Farmer McBain not to smudge his horses. Mike had seen Fraser Borthwick earlier that evening and Fraser had been bragging that Jay was going to pay him seventy grand for his share in Hazeldean.

"Jay and Jennifer must have some cash," Roxanne said to Izzy.

"Once she sells the Winnipeg house, she will. It belongs to her and it's not mortgaged."

"Fraser isn't really a suspect, is he?" Roxanne looked at Fraser's photo. "He was still in Toronto when Donna died."

"We can't rule him out," said Izzy. "It's still possible that Donna hanged herself. He could have killed Amelia. He was pissed off that they wanted to rip down the cottage. It's not much of a motive, but he's an odd kind of guy."

"He looks arthritic. Would he have the strength or the speed to do that?"

"Don't be fooled. Mike says he fakes it. Wants people to think he's helpless because it works for him. He's a con, Roxanne. Talks bullshit. He's a lot craftier than he looks. He manages to get by without ever having to do a solid day's work. You know his cousin, Sig Olafson?"

"Big Sig?" Roxanne had come into contact with Sig a few times during her time at Fiskar Bay. He'd featured in a few bar brawls.

"Best buds since they were little, according to Mike. Did you ever see Sig play hockey? He was the enforcer on Mike's team growing up. When Big Sig's gloves came off things always got interesting."

"Are you saying that he could be killing on Fraser's behalf?"

"Not really," Izzy admitted. "But it's a possibility. He could be helping Fraser out. There's the money, too. Fraser's going to inherit quite a chunk more from his mother's estate now that Donna's gone."

"Do they all know how much cash there is?" Roxanne looked at the row of pictures, Fraser, Leslie and Jay.

"Leslie certainly did."

Leslie's photograph was from her website, taken to show her as a person you could trust, reliable, smart and confident. She had met her husband Mark at university. He was from Saskatoon and had gone back there to run the family business, a successful furniture store that served everywhere north of Regina. Leslie had married when she was twenty-two and they had lived there ever since.

"She's an accountant and she knows everything about the Borthwick fortune. She's been taking care of it for years."

"No children?"

"No, not her. Or Fraser."

"So Amelia's brother, Graeme, benefits the most from his sister being dead?'

"He sure does." The shot Izzy had of Graeme was one of him in shorts, a golden boy, bronzed by the sun, hair bleached, wide shouldered, lean hipped, every muscle defined. He would not inherit any of the money that Lois would leave when she died, but his mother had bequeathed him some. Now he'd receive Amelia's portion of that estate. He'd have an income to support his rowing habit, for now.

"You think this is all about inheritance?" asked Roxanne.

"Got to be," Izzy replied. "The thing is, they all benefit in some way. It gives every single one of them a motive. And they could all get to Hazeldean at night. You know how quiet it is at Cullen Village, once everyone crashes. Anybody could drop by that cottage in the dark and no one would be any the wiser. There's not a single house nearby with camera surveillance and it's an easy drive from Winnipeg. So they all had the opportunity, too."

"Gordon Palmer?" His photograph was in the pile. So was one of Maria Smith, his assistant.

"She's been working with him for four years, since before the pandemic," said Izzy. "He was in Ottawa when Donna died but she stayed here. Amelia had a Muslim boyfriend that she kept hidden from her father. She'd been living with him for more than a year. Donna knew about him, Gordon didn't. It sounds like he barely ever saw his daughter. There's that whole business of how Donna wanted a divorce and he didn't. That family was all screwed up."

"And there's Charlie Cain," said Roxanne.

They compared what they knew about him. Roxanne was sure he'd been more involved with Donna Palmer than he'd let on, and he'd avoided telling her that he and Maddie Yanovsky intended to buy Bricks and Sugar.

"I guess I should talk to this guy," said Izzy.

It had been a quiet Saturday so far. Aimee Vermette was working the front desk, her arm still in a sling, but she could handle a phone and a computer with one hand. Ravi Anand was out on a call, an attempted break-in that had happened overnight, but would be back soon. Things in the detachment were under control for now.

"Why don't you bring Cain in here?" asked Roxanne. "I could sit in while you interview him."

"Okay." Izzy grinned. "That'll be fun. Never thought I'd have you as my sidekick."

Charlie Cain was far from pleased to be picked up, just as he was installing the new steps behind the summer bungalow, but he cooperated. He drove himself to Fiskar Bay in his beige Ford truck.

He sat in the confines of the grey interview room, the stark fluorescent light overhead, the recorder whirring, looking a bit like one of the turtles that lived by the local creeks, his head pulled defensively down into his collar as if it was a carapace, his eyes watchful, swivelling from one policewoman to the other.

He hadn't lied, he said. He had not been in a relationship with Donna Palmer. They'd worked together, they got along. That was as close as it got. Izzy laid a printout in front of him, the page from Donna's calendar, the initials CC in red and also in blue.

"She wrote her personal appointments in blue," she said. "And look at this. She booked you in for five days while she was at Cullen Village, all in blue."

"She must've made a mistake," he replied without missing a beat. "Forgot to change the colour. Those are the days we were supposed to work out here."

"You show up twice some days, in red and in blue." He couldn't say what that was about. Donna was sometimes careless when it came to paperwork. Maddie was always having to clean things up for her.

He was guarded and he had answers for everything. He didn't know what to do with his hands, though, without anything to occupy them. He scratched his head, rubbed the edge of the table. Tucked his thumbs up into his armpits. Untucked them and stroked his thighs, nervous, uneasy. His mouth was fixed in a stretched smile. It made him look even more reptilian.

Why would Donna have bought sexy lingerie and massage oil, good wines and gourmet food if she had only intended to work?

"Because she liked to indulge herself?" he replied, snappy, like one of those turtles again.

"You said she confided in you. About her failing marriage."

"Only when she'd drunk some. She never said she was seeing someone else and I never saw her with anyone. I would have been busy working all that week; I like to get the job done as soon as I can. Donna would have had time to herself. She could have had anyone visit that cottage and I would never have known."

"Did it scare you that Amelia was going to take over the business?" Izzy asked him. "She was young and she had no experience. Were you worried that she would let Bricks and Sugar go under?"

"We didn't know that. She was a smart kid and there was enough work to get her through the first few months, so she had time to find her feet."

"She wanted to build a big house from scratch out at Hazeldean, like her mother before her. Would that have overstretched her?"

"Don't think so. The plans were all drawn up and it had been costed out. There was money coming in from somewhere to back the build. It would have been a great learning project for her."

"Money coming in from where?"

"I don't know. Donna set it up."

"I talked to Maddie Yanovsky yesterday," Izzy said. "She says the pair of you are going to buy Bricks and Sugar."

"That's just an idea," he said. "There's nothing definite."

"Really? Maddie seems to think it'll go ahead. She's going to the bank to raise a loan to cover her end of the deal. She says you have enough money yourself for your half. Amelia died Wednesday night and you two decided to buy by Friday? That's pretty quick."

"We had to move fast," he responded. "We don't want Amelia's brother selling it off to someone else, right from under us. It's a good business and we know how it works. We talked on Thursday. Knew we needed to get going on it right away."

"You never said anything about it to me," Roxanne commented.

"You didn't ask. And there was nothing definite to talk about."

"So," Izzy mused. "It's possible that we've got this all backwards. That you and Maddie Yanovsky figured out ages ago that the two of you could run Bricks and Sugar yourselves. I've got a guy checking out the accounts and he says they're good. The business is showing a decent profit. All you needed to do was get rid of Donna, and you had the perfect opportunity out here at the beach. A strong guy like you could have killed her and tossed the body off Hazeldean pier, no trouble at all. The only problem was that Donna's daughter took over Bricks and Sugar after that. So then she needed to be got rid of, too."

"Good story, Sergeant, but it didn't happen like that. What's your question?" Cain knew that they had nothing on him except those notes in Donna's calendar and he'd dodged those. They might guess he'd been Donna's lover as well as her handyman, but they couldn't prove a thing. His head emerged from his collar, making him look more like his usual competent self. They let him go. He whistled as he drove back to the house where he was doing repairs.

Aimee Vermette had had a quiet morning, enough time to find a photograph online. It had been taken in the office at Bricks and Sugar earlier in the year. Donna Palmer stood in the middle, all smiles, her pretty daughter beside her. Charlie Cain was on her other side, more than a head taller than she was. Maddie Yanovsky stood beside Amelia. They all held wineglasses, celebrating something.

"I'll have that." Izzy took the printout upstairs to add to her picture gallery.

"I don't believe him," Roxanne said.

"Me neither." Izzy leaned back against the table. "I think the real story's somewhere in the middle, that he and Maddie had talked about how well they could run the business themselves, then the opportunity came up so they grabbed it. But it doesn't mean they carried out the killings in order to make it happen. I'd almost bet he was having it off with Donna but it doesn't mean he throttled her. Who do you think gave Donna Palmer the money to build that new house at Hazeldean?"

"We should go talk to Leslie." Roxanne pointed at her photo. "She might know something about that. She's staying out on Bulrush Island."

Izzy didn't miss that Roxanne had said, "We." She was planning to come, too.

"Let's go find her," she said.

18

BULRUSH ISLAND WAS a busy place on summer weekends, even when a faint, smoky haze dimmed the sun. It did cool the air so it was tolerably warm after all the hot days and there wasn't enough smog yet to keep anyone inside, unless they had respiratory problems. People trimmed their gardens and tidied their almost perfect cottages, messed about in boats, walked their designer dogs. Children ran amok, given a freedom to roam that they were never allowed in the city. They could paddle by themselves but never swim without an adult present and there were limits as to how far they could wander. They all knew that the causeway was off limits. The island contained them.

Large cars, trucks and SUVs filled every driveway, including the one where Leslie Borthwick was staying. A black Mazda was parked beside her Lexus. She was no longer living alone in the house. The woman who opened the door to Roxanne and Izzy widened her eyes in alarm when she saw a woman in an RCMP uniform standing on her doorstep. The other one said that she was a sergeant, too, in the Major Crimes Unit.

"I'm Jenn Wilson. Leslie and I went to school together, in Winnipeg. This is not more bad news, surely?" she asked. No, Izzy told her. They just needed to ask Ms. Borthwick a few questions. Jenn welcomed them in, told them that she herself was just leaving to take the boat to town so she could gas up and get some supplies. There was no one else in the house to disturb them. She'd just tell Leslie that they were here, then she'd be gone.

Leslie, like her friend, was dressed casually, in cropped pants and a summer top. She hadn't planned to go anywhere today. She was still working while away from home and she needed to catch up. Would this take long, she asked?

"We hope not," Izzy replied.

Leslie showed them into a spacious living room. Chairs and sofas were covered in tan-coloured leather. The laminate floor was made to look like blond wood. A low glass and steel table stood in front of an unlit woodstove. Above it hung a framed, nautical map of the south end of the lake. Bulrush Island was clearly identifiable, a long finger of land stretching into the water, a red dot marking the spot where this house stood. The map predated the house, though. A small rectangle showed the roof of an earlier, tiny cottage that took only a quarter of the available space. The replacement—the new beach house—almost filled the width of the lot.

Large windows overlooked the lake, but a windowless wooden façade faced the street, broken only by the entranceway. Cottagers who built expensive houses like these appreciated their privacy.

"This house must be like the one that Donna wanted to build," Izzy remarked. She folded one tanned leg over the other. She wore long shorts today, dressy for her.

"I suppose so. This style is all the rage right now. Donna's might have been bigger. There's more room to build at Hazeldean. The lot there is way wider than this." Leslie took the chair opposite and also crossed her legs. The two of them faced one another across the glass tabletop, like two chess queens about to go into play.

"How much would it have cost to build?" Roxanne watched and listened from the middle of a sofa, at right angles to the two chairs.

"I wouldn't know. That was Donna's business," said Leslie.

"But you were going to finance it."

Leslie looked at Izzy. Her mouth opened then shut.

"We'd talked about it, no more than that," she conceded. She knew they would find out if they wanted to. Maybe someone had told them already.

"It would have been worth a lot. How much does a big lakefront house like that go for these days?"

"I wouldn't know," said Leslie.

"Yes, you would," Izzy retorted.

Leslie looked at her over the top of her glasses. "I live in Saskatoon," she reminded this young policewoman. "I don't keep up with the cost of housing out here."

"Six hundred and twenty-five thousand." Roxanne knew exactly how much. She sometimes thought she and Matt should move into a place like this, with lots of room, easy to look after, a lake view, close to town, if only he could be persuaded to move. She kept an eye on local house sales, just in case he ever showed a sign of changing his mind.

"Wow," Izzy acted surprised. "That much? Charlie Cain would have built it in no time, as part of Donna's business. And she would have sold it, easy. She'd have used the loan she got from you to cover the costs. Then she'd have split the profit with you? Was that the deal? Did you set something up the same way with Amelia?"

"If I had, there would be no reason for me to kill either of them," Leslie replied irritably, her sandalled foot tapping against the steel frame of the table.

"I'm not so sure about that." Izzy dismissed the suggestion. "You could have got Charlie Cain to go ahead and build it for you and pocketed the lot yourself. Had he ordered the materials already?"

"Except that was never the plan." Leslie's tone turned condescending. "Not then, not now. I don't want to have anything to do with Hazeldean, not anymore. Not after what's happened there. I loved my sister. She was my best friend." She stuck her chin out, defying Izzy to disagree. "I was looking forward to helping Amelia. I liked what she was trying to do. It took courage to take on running that business right after her mother died. She was gutsy and so young. She shouldn't have died there. I can't believe that happened to her. I want to get rid of my share in the place as soon as I can. Hopefully, my brother will still want to buy it from me. I need to get home to Saskatoon. The woodsmoke is far thicker there and my husband is asthmatic."

"We may need you to stay here a little longer."

"What for? I'll have all the paperwork I need for my mother's care completed within the next day or two. You have no good reason to keep me here."

"Well, then," Izzy uncrossed her legs and stood up. "We'll check in with you in a couple of days and let you know. Meantime, can you send us an up-to-date statement of what's in your mother's accounts?"

"That is a private matter." Leslie rose and faced her.

"Not when one of the beneficiaries has died under suspicious circumstances," Izzy told her. "We can get a court order if we have to."

Leslie sighed.

"You were going to take your mother to Saskatoon with you." Roxanne had almost reached the door. "Has that plan changed?"

It had. Her mother was frail. Keeping her here, in Fiskar Bay, seemed a better solution.

"But you won't be here to see how she is doing? And you're still going to be the person who makes all the decisions about what happens to her?"

Jay might go ahead with his plan to live here and Fraser was also talking about it. Between them they could keep Leslie informed about their mother.

"Fraser?" asked Roxanne. "How's he going to do that? He's got no money and no way of making any." The last thing she needed was Fraser Borthwick living in the neighbourhood, setting up shop as a drug dealer.

"I wouldn't know," said Leslie. "It might not happen. It's maybe just talk. You can't count on anything when it comes to Fraser. But it looks like Jay will be around." Roxanne noted that she didn't mention her Aunt Sylvia, the person who was most likely to look out for Lois Borthwick. Did she think the police didn't know about that?

They took their leave and drove to the causeway. A couple of cars driving toward them on the single track forced Izzy into a passing place. There were rushes in the marshland on either side, terns swooping above the water.

"I don't think Leslie's our murderer," Izzy said as a large Mercedes squeezed past on the narrow track. "She sounded totally genuine when she talked about her sister and her niece. I think she really did care for them, so why would she have killed them?"

Doug Halliday and Herb Appleby had welcomed one or two visitors to the Cullen Village Station Museum that morning. It was quiet for a Saturday. Sandy Ferguson always took care of sales at the General Store next door, where he could sit behind the counter all afternoon. He sold tea towels and fridge magnets printed with photographs taken when the station was first built, more than a hundred years ago. T-shirts, all blue, with a puffer train printed on the front along with the station's logo, were available in different sizes, and the selection of old-fashioned candies included liquorice pipes, fat wads of pink bubblegum, stretchy taffy and suckers in different shapes and colours.

At lunchtime, he locked the door and limped his painful way to the station building. It was hazy but the temperature had fallen below thirty degrees for the first day this month, and that was welcome. He took care to make sure his protective mask fitted properly. The air was becoming contaminated with smoke and it was making him wheeze. He needed a new knee but the pandemic had played havoc with the health system and it would take months before he could have the necessary surgery. He needed cataract surgery too, but he could still see to count change. Doug and Herb would be sure to notice if any new visitors arrived.

It was too bad the train still could not load up with visitors and make the trip. Some villagers had worried that the recent murders would put people off visiting Cullen Village, but it seemed they were doing the opposite. Doug Halliday had already told them about cars driving slowly past Hazeldean, people pointing at the police tape that had been put up again, stopping at the corner so they could get a glimpse of the pier.

"Tell me about it," Herb had grouched. "I could hardly back out of my driveway."

Someone from the Manitoba Railway Enthusiasts Society, of which they were all members, had suggested that they should organize a murder mystery train trip, once the train was running once more, with a stopover so they could describe exactly where and how the events had occurred. "The police should have solved this and put the murderer safely behind bars by then," a member from Winnipeg had suggested. Maybe a local theatre group could stage enactments?

"Just like what happened last night," Herb said. "For real."

He told them in detail what his wife had seen on Hazeldean pier—Sergeant Calloway lying down at the end of the pier, pretending to be dead, and two people, must be detectives from the RCMP, taking turns tying to hoist her onto the bench singlehandedly.

"Did they manage to lift her?" Doug asked.

They had. The man had had no trouble doing it. A younger woman had struggled but she had managed it in the end.

"They must be wondering if that's what happened to Donna Borthwick. If someone killed her then threw her off the end of the pier," Sandy said. "So, they mustn't believe it was suicide after all."

"Of course, it wasn't," Herb assured them. "I knew that from the start. There's no way Donna would have killed herself. And now it seems that her daughter's been murdered as well." He swallowed a mouthful of root beer from a can. He liked it better than Coke, even if it didn't come in a fancy old-fashioned bottle.

Sandy looked sadly in the direction of Hazeldean. "Who is going to want that place after all this?" he asked. "Maybe it should be torn down after all. They could build a new house. Start fresh."

The silence that followed was leaden. "No one"—Herb put down his can—"is going to tear down that cottage. It's historic. Part of this village's heritage."

They nodded their heads in agreement, remembering that their own precious station was vulnerable also.

"You still think that Fraser is responsible?" Sandy asked.

"I'm not so sure about that any longer," Herb responded. "From what June described, he would have had to pick up a dead body by himself and he doesn't look capable of lifting a cat. But he has friends. One of them might have helped him."

"You live right next door," said Doug. "You haven't heard a thing out there at night?"

"I have not."

Sandy received a text. He read it.

"How about this!" he announced. "The ice cream van is making a delivery right now at the Rec Centre."

This was very good news. They all planned to attend the barbecue this evening. They'd placed their orders already. Ribs all round. Jay had said that if the ice cream came in time they could have real cones again, just as they had every summer since the three of them had been boys.

Herb looked out the window. A family was approaching on bikes, parents and two children, all wearing protective masks. It was beginning to look foggier out.

They finished their drinks, dropped the empty cans into a recycling bag, tucked it out of sight into a cupboard and went to take up their places.

19

WHEN ROXANNE GOT home later that day, a newly built skateboard ramp blocked the driveway. Finn and his new friend, Carter Boychuk, dragged it aside to let her through then put it back and began skating again. Matt had insisted they wear their masks.

"They've been out there all afternoon," said Matt. "No trouble at all. Carter's a nice kid."

Roxanne went to change out of her uniform and put on a summer dress. They were going over to the Rec Centre at Cullen Village, as soon as she was ready, for Jay and Jennifer's barbecue. They would drop Carter off at the same time.

All the picnic tables were taken by the time they got there. Matt had known it would be busy. He'd brought along folding chairs and set them up on the grass beside the parking lot. Other people had had the same idea and brought chairs or blankets so they could picnic.

Jennifer was inside the centre at the counter handing out takeout packages and taking in cash. There was a lineup. Jay was outside, turning meat on a large barbecue, chicken and ribs, burgers and hot dogs. He sent more smoke up into the sky, but this smelled of well-seasoned food.

"You can stay and eat with us if you like," Matt told Carter. "Your mom's real busy right now."

The boys ran off to join a couple of kids they recognized from summer camp. Finn did not go to the school at Cullen Village. He attended one in Fiskar Bay, close to Roxanne and Matt's workplaces, so he didn't get to hang out with the local kids very much. Roxanne was glad to see him running around in a group. Mostly he met school friends for organized sports. He didn't get free time very often when he could relax and play like this.

Coloured lights had been strung in the trees, brightening up the grey sky. A group of musicians had set up a mic and loudspeakers at the edge of the tarmac and were tuning up. This looked like it might become a party. It was hard to imagine that anything sinister could happen in this cheerful and friendly village.

Roxanne noticed her friend Margo Wishart at a table with two other women, Roberta Axelsson and Sasha Rosenberg. Three elderly couples occupied the next table, Freya Halliday and her husband, the pair who lived next door to Hazeldean, and a smaller man and his wife that Roxanne did not recognize.

A man, dressed to look like Elvis Presley, walked out the door of the Rec Centre. His yellow polyester body suit had a metallic sheen and the legs flared; his black hair was greased and he wore long sideburns. He waved to the crowd. Some of them cheered. They all knew who he was. He worked as a plumber when he wasn't pretending to be Elvis. He took up his place in front of the band, the drums rolled and they launched into a rendition of "Whole Lotta Shakin' Goin' On." They weren't bad.

Matt came back with their food. Roxanne might not be able to eat in the morning but these days she became ravenous in the evening. She'd taken to raiding the fridge when Matt wasn't looking. She resisted tearing into her rack of ribs and made herself eat slowly. There was homemade coleslaw and a baked potato. Jennifer and Jay were following local advice and offering traditional fare tonight. Nothing adventurous.

The boys joined them, hungry too. The lineup for food had diminished. Two or three couples were dancing to the music.

"You ain't nothin' but a hound dog," sang the wannabe Elvis.

Roxanne noticed that the three older couples were listening to Herb Appleby, who was holding forth. Their heads were close together, so they could hear what he was saying above the sound of the music. Margo Wishart sat at the end of her table. She looked like she might be listening in, too.

Matt tapped Roxanne's arm. "You're off duty tonight, Sarge," he reminded her. She was. And all of tomorrow, if she was lucky. "We'll have the house to ourselves for a while. Jay Borthwick says he'll take the boys for the afternoon. Says it's his turn."

Maybe they could take the dogs for a walk at the dog beach. That might be a good time to tell him about the baby.

A truck with large wheels rolled into the far end of the parking lot and stopped in front of a lineup of cars. Sig Olafson jumped out of the driver's side. The other door opened and a cane emerged, followed by the gaunt figure of Fraser Borthwick. Big Sig crossed the carpark and waved to the band. The bassist waved back and Elvis nodded his dark head in Sig's direction. They must all know each other. They'd probably gone to school together.

Fraser lurched over to the barbecue and talked to his brother. Jay shook his head slowly while he brushed sauce on pieces of chicken. Fraser looked around him but he didn't react. The party didn't seem to interest him at all. He turned to his brother and said something else. Jay shook his head again, more forcefully this time. Fraser turned away and went toward the Rec Centre door.

Big Sig was now standing beside the Elvis lookalike with the mic in his hand. He clutched it to his chin and spread his feet wide apart; the band struck a chord and he launched into "Love Me Tender." His voice throbbed. The crowd roared approval.

Fraser emerged from the Rec Centre carrying a large paper bag full of food in one arm. He waited, leaning on his cane, for Sig to reach the end of his song. Elvis raised Sig's arm high. "Big Sig Olafson, folks!" he yelled and the crowd stood up and applauded. So did Matt and Roxanne.

Sig grinned and waved as he left. Fraser was already halfway to the truck. They climbed aboard and drove off. Roxanne glanced around the crowd once more.

"I wonder why Leslie Borthwick's not here," she said to Matt. "Why would she not show up for her brother's party?"

"Maybe she didn't think it would be this big of an event." Matt watched Jay turn off the barbecue and close the lid. Garbage cans lined with bags had been set up at corners. Cottagers were dumping bones and other scraps into them. They had progressed to eating ice cream. Jennifer was serving cones inside. Jay Borthwick called the boys over.

"Dad says there's six flavours," Carter told them. "We get to choose two," and they scooted off to get their pick.

"I think I might like strawberry," said Roxanne.

"You would?" Matt was surprised. Roxanne rarely ate a sweet dessert.

"A single cone will do. What do you want? I'll go pick them up." Roxanne looked to the west as she walked to the Rec Centre door. The sun was a large red globe hanging in a solid band of charcoal. She knew what that meant; she'd read the latest weather reports coming from Saskatchewan before she left the office. The wind was predicted to pick up tonight, blow in from the northwest and bring a thicker blanket of woodsmoke with it.

Finn and Carter met her inside the door, double cones in their hands.

"Carter's dad's going to take us canoeing tomorrow!" They had kayaked for the first time yesterday at summer camp and they'd loved it. Neither of them had ever been out on the water before.

"We'll be done serving brunches by one," Jennifer told her, scooping up Roxanne's order. "Monday's our day off and we don't have to prep, so Jay's got the time to do it."

"Matt will bring Finn over," Roxanne promised. "Thanks for taking him."

"It's the least we can do. You've had Carter over at your place all day today."

The party wasn't over. The band was thumping out "Jailhouse Rock." People were still dancing but some were going home. The three elderly couples had left already. Margo and her friends were walking toward an old brown Buick. Roberta must have driven from her house and was going to drop the other two off.

Matt had already loaded their chairs into the car. Once they had eaten the ice cream they dragged a reluctant but tired Finn home.

"It's been a great evening," Roxanne told him. "But you need to get a good night's sleep if you're going to go out in a canoe tomorrow."

She hoped he wasn't going to be disappointed, that the smoke wouldn't arrive until evening and stop them from going paddling in the afternoon.

The road to Margo's house passed by Hazeldean. The cottage was in darkness, a crescent moon hanging over the lake behind it, its glow dimmed by a thin veil of soot.

"Such a shame." Roberta had slowed down to look. She hadn't driven this way since the deaths had occurred. "Someone should have taken better care of that old place. And now these two deaths."

"Maybe it would be best if they did just rip it down, said Sasha from the front passenger seat. "It's like it's got a curse on it."

"Don't go saying that to Herb Appleby." Margo sat in the back. She'd be the first person to be dropped off. "He's got a thing for heritage cottages. Believes they should all be preserved for posterity."

"Oh, right, Hazeldean's got one of those fancy signs, hasn't it?" Roberta had noticed it as they drove past in the dark. "Doesn't that mean it's protected?"

"No, it doesn't." Margo unbuckled her seatbelt as Roberta parked outside her house. "Herb and Freya Halliday were arguing about that over dinner tonight. Herb wants Freya to put through a law that says those old cottages can't be demolished."

"That right?" Sasha swivelled round in her seat. Her little house was almost as old as Hazeldean. She loved her cottage. It had character, unlike these boxy slabs that people were building these days, huge ones that filled their lots. Every time one of them went up, trees had to be cut down. She didn't want to see that happen at her place. "Is it only the ones with that special designation that would be covered?" The motion-sensitive light at the end of Margo's driveway illuminated their faces as they talked.

"I don't know. There's only about twenty cottages on the list." Margo had been asked to serve on the heritage committee when she first arrived in Cullen Village. "I've seen a brochure that described them. I don't think there's many copies around but the village office will have one. Maybe there's another in the library at Fiskar Bay." She noticed a black furry head at her window, watching for her to come home. "Do you want to come inside? We could have a glass of wine?"

Jay Borthwick and his partner hadn't secured a liquor licence for their pop-up café. Maybe some people had brought drinks to the barbecue but they had not. A nightcap might be welcome. Bob the dog gave them an enthusiastic welcome.

"Hazeldean has a fireplace that's unlike anything else around here," Margo said as she let him outside into her fenced yard then opened a bottle of Shiraz. "I've seen it. It's built of local stone, with nooks in the sides, and goes all the way up to the ceiling." Sasha rolled her eyes. Her house had nothing as special as that. "Freya's been finding out what happens when heritage houses in the city need upgrading and she's not sure that they should make it a rule that a cottage can't be replaced. She said maybe someone could rebuild at Hazeldean and incorporate the fireplace into the design and wouldn't that do? Herb got quite angry about that.

"He says it's a matter of lifestyle. That the cottages were built so that kids could get fresh air and sunshine, all summer long, away from the city. That mothers could come out here and spend real time with their children. That this was where they got to explore and bike and swim, away from TV and distractions like those. They grew up strong and self-reliant because of it."

"What planet is he on?" snorted Sasha. "They all bring their smartphones and their iPads out here now." That was true to some extent. The past few weeks, kids had still been homeschooling because of the pandemic and they had been glued to their devices for hours at a time, but now school was over. A bunch of them had been playing at the barbecue this evening.

"It's a long time since mothers could spend all summer long out here with the kids," Roberta agreed. "They're too busy with their own jobs now. They're here this year because of the pandemic, but that won't last."

"Which is what Freya and another woman at the table told him. June just kept quiet. I guess she's heard it all before." Bob scratched to get back in. When Margo opened the door she could hear coyotes yipping, not far away. They must be out hunting. "Herb just kept insisting that Hazeldean's special. That they had good times there."

"And now that's done and over. Someone should tell him that. What's he thinking of? Two people have been killed there already." Roberta emptied her glass. She'd have liked a refill but she needed to drive home and she lived outside the village, on the other side of the highway. Some drivers were crazy on Saturday nights. Sasha needed to get home to her own dog as well.

"Maybe Herb's the one that needed to get rid of Donna Palmer and her daughter," Sasha said as the two of them made their way to the front door. "If he's a fanatic for the old house and those two women wanted to tear it down."

"It's not a very good reason to kill anyone," Margo reasoned. "I don't think so. He's a good neighbour." But once they had gone, she poured herself another glass and considered that.

The Borthwicks and the Applebys had summered here, side by side, for all those years. Was that why Herb Appleby was so adamant that Hazeldean must remain as it was and not be torn down? Nostalgia? Sentimental attachment? Herb didn't seem the sentimental sort. She needed to find out more. Maybe she could do some quiet investigating of her own. If she discovered anything, she'd pass it on to her friend, RCMP Sergeant Roxanne Calloway.

20

THE SUN ROSE next morning like a blood orange in a dull grey
sky. A distinct smell of burned wood hung in the air and it was
going to get worse as the day progressed. This was not a good day
for Jay Borthwick to take two small boys out on the lake for hours,
paddling in a canoe.

Roxanne called him. He was busy in the kitchen at the Rec
Centre already, prepping brunches.

"Don't worry, it'll be okay," he assured her. "Bring Finn over,
just like we planned." He didn't want to disappoint the boys and
he'd promised. They were looking forward to it. He wouldn't take
them out on the lake; he'd take them to the creek for an hour or
so instead and wouldn't keep them outside more than that. If they
wore masks it would be okay. They'd get a taste of what it was like
to handle a canoe have some fun. She could hear him bustling
around, whisking and measuring as he spoke.

"Okay," she said. "We'll be there by one."

"Good," said Matt, when she told him. "I need to take the
mower in to get fixed. We can drop it off then go to the garden
centre and pick up stuff we need."

That wasn't how Roxanne had thought they would spend their
afternoon alone together, but errands did need doing. Maybe it
wouldn't take long and they'd still find time to walk and talk.

Doug Halliday, Herb Appleby and Sandy Ferguson arrived outside
the Cullen Village Railway Museum just before noon. They only
opened for the afternoon on Sundays. Doug and Herb had walked

over together, but Sandy needed to drive. He'd stopped off on the way at the Rec Centre café and picked up cinnamon buns, a treat to share at the end of the afternoon.

Sandy liked to park at the far end of the parking lot in front of the station, so that any visitors that arrived by car had easy access to the front door, but his usual spot was taken by a silver-coloured Lexus.

"Doesn't Leslie Borthwick drive one of those?" asked Doug. It had to be hers. It had Saskatchewan licence plates. Why would it be here, they pondered?

"I thought she was staying with friends," said Herb, "but not in the village. Somewhere up closer to Fiskar Bay."

"Maybe she has another friend that's here visiting for the weekend and she's staying with them instead." The station lay at a corner where two streets lined with cottages converged. Cars filled the driveways this busy summer weekend, some parked on the grassy verge. "Maybe she didn't want to leave an expensive car like that out on the road." Sandy locked his own vehicle. Doug took the bag of buns from him so he could hobble along, supported by his cane. "But she shouldn't be parked there. We might need the space. She might have asked."

"That's Leslie for you." Herb held the keys to the station door. "She's always done exactly as she pleases. I've known her since she was a little thing. Bossy as they come, even back then."

"Maybe one of us should have a word with her, when she comes to pick it up," wheezed Sandy, but he didn't volunteer to be the one to tackle Leslie Borthwick in person. Neither did either of his friends. They went into their beloved station, put the buns away for later, donned their railroad hats and jackets, made sure there wasn't a speck of dust on their displays and countertops and forgot all about Leslie Borthwick's car for now.

Carter Boychuk came running out of the Rec Centre to meet Finn when Matt drove up. Finn grabbed his mask and his water bottle.

"Dad's just finishing up. Come on inside." The two of them disappeared through the door of the building without a backward glance. Roxanne followed them. Jennifer passed a bag over to her. Quiche, for later.

"Don't worry about them. They'll be fine. Jay will text you when they're done." Jay was in the back kitchen, cleaning off pans. Roxanne went back to the truck, the broken riding mower stowed in the back, and off she and Matt went, like many other couples, to do errands.

Jay had not been able to pick up the canoe the day before. They'd been so busy getting ready for the barbecue, he hadn't had the time. This was tricky since the canoe was at Hazeldean, but he knew exactly where to find it, under a tarp beside the garage. He did notice Finn look questioningly at the yellow police tape that was strung across the driveway when they arrived. There had been just enough space for Jay to park in the driveway in front of it. "POLICE: DO NOT ENTER" Finn read aloud.

"No worries!" Jay told the boys. "We're not going inside the house. That's what that tape's really about." He should leave the kids in the van but he could use a hand carrying the canoe. He led them to the garage at the side of the cottage—"Don't worry about the masks, we won't be long"—and watched their eyes light up as they saw the red canoe. It was old but it was reliable. Jay had paddled it himself when he was their age. They were thrilled to be asked to lift one end and help him lug it to the van. He'd hoist it up, tie it to the roof rack and then they would be off, he told them.

Then he led them to the shed behind the garage to find life jackets. There were several stashed in a box on a shelf. Jay knew where they were. He and his sisters had worn them when they were kids. "Try these on for size," he said, passing over two of the smallest. The paddles for the canoe were propped in a corner. Now all he needed was a couple of pieces of rope to tie the canoe to the rack on his SUV. There used to be hanks hanging on nails on the wall of the shed but the nails were empty. There was no rope. The people who cleaned up after Fraser's party must have tidied up in here as well. They must have put the ropes away. Where could they be?

Carter and Finn were busy figuring out how to fasten the life jackets, almost ready to go.

"Here, boys." He gave them the paddles and told them to take them to the car. He was sure bungee cords used to be in the garage. Maybe the ropes had been put with them. He flung open the door. Like the shed, it had been cleaned up and tidied. Half the stuff that used to be there was gone. He looked everywhere but couldn't find the cords. No rope. Nothing.

The boys were hovering, wondering when they'd be ready to go.

"Not long now," he assured them. Would there be anything inside the house that would work? There was a broom cupboard under the stairs. Something might be there. He could go inside, couldn't he, if he went by himself? It wasn't like he was going to disturb anything.

Finn looked anxious when Jay told them that he was going to go into the house after all. "I need to find a bit of rope. It'll only take a minute," he said. "You two stay outside. It's just me that'll get heck from your mom if she finds out." And he winked at Finn. They tried winking, too, and laughed.

"You just stay out front. I'll be right back." He strode to the back of the house and waved to Finn and Carter before he turned the corner.

Then he stopped.

Leslie was face down on the dry, grassy ground at his feet, her head among the shattered remains of one of the deck's big flowerpots. There was dirt scattered everywhere, shards of broken clay and a lot of blood. Her glasses lay among the debris. Her clothing was spattered with blood and dry soil.

Jay had no idea what to do.

The two boys raced around the corner behind him and slid to a halt, Carter first. Finn almost crashed into him. Like Jay, they stopped and stared.

"What's going on, Dad?" Carter looked up at his stepdad.

"Is she dead?" Finn asked in a quiet, awestruck voice.

Jay sprang into action. "Let's get you two back to the car." He stood between them and the body so they wouldn't see the dead figure on the ground. "Don't look at this."

"I need to call my mom." Finn rummaged in a pocket.

"That's okay, I'll call the police." Jay reached out a hand to turn each of them around and began walking them to the driveway. They kept turning back to look, like they couldn't tear their eyes away. The woman who lived next door had left her deck and was walking along the path on the top of the berm toward them.

"Has something happened? Do you need some help?" she called to him.

Finn had his phone. He shrugged Jay's hand away. His thumb found his mother's name.

"Mom!" he said. "You've got to come here, right now. There's a dead body."

Matt had a cart full of gardening supplies. He wanted peat moss and sheep manure. Roxanne reached out to stop him adding a weed whacker to the pile.

"We have to go," she told him. "Something's happened." She continued talking to her son. Where exactly was he? Who was with him? He told her. Could she talk to her?

"They've had a big shock," June Appleby told her. She had taken them to the front steps of Hazeldean and would stay with them until Roxanne arrived. And yes, Jay had called 911. He was still talking to the dispatcher. He looked pretty shaken too.

Roxanne asked June to pass the phone back to her son. Matt was talking to a garden centre employee, apologizing for leaving the full cart behind. They had to go. It was urgent. Half of the people in the store knew who Roxanne was, even when she was dressed for a day off, in skinny jeans and a shirt. They watched her and her partner run out to their truck and roar off down the hazy road to Cullen Village.

"Wonder who's dead now?" a customer said to the employee, who was just about to push away the cart for unloading. And they both laughed.

Ravi Anand and Sam Mendes had been patrolling near Cullen Village. They reached Hazeldean first. Ravi had gone to the back of the house by the time Roxanne and Matt arrived. A Jeep SUV with a roof rack stood at the end of the driveway, an old red canoe and its paddles lying beside it. Finn and Carter sat either side of June Appleby on the front step of the cottage. She had helped them take off their life jackets and had a protective arm around each of them. Both boys were big-eyed and serious. Sam was standing at the driveway, by the SUV, talking to Jay.

"I'm sorry that they had to see that," June said. "It's upset both of them."

Roxanne squatted down in front of the steps, eyes level with the boys.

"You're going to be okay," she told them. "I'm going to need you to tell me what you saw but that can happen later. Right now, Matt's going to take you home."

"I want to see my mom," Carter whimpered.

"That's exactly where you're going. Let's get both of you into our truck."

Matt led the boys away. Roxanne thanked June and turned her attention on Jay. She was angry.

"You!" She pointed a finger at him as she marched across the baked grass. "What did you think you were doing, bringing those boys over here?" Jay flinched. He'd had a shock himself. It was his sister lying out back with her head in a pool of blood and dirt.

His normally pale, freckled skin was drained of colour. He was shivering.

"I didn't think," he stammered.

"That is police tape!" Roxanne's pointed finger shifted in that direction. "Don't you know what that means? Can't you read?"

"Roxanne!" Matt called to her. Roxanne realized she had been yelling. Sam was watching, his mouth open. He'd never seen his boss lose her cool like this before. "Over here!"

"You stay right there," she told Jay. "I'm not done with you."

"You need to get someone else to handle this," Matt told her as she got to the car. "You're far too close to this case now. This has become personal. Call Izzy right away and get her to take over." The boys were inside the truck but the passenger door was still open. They could hear everything. Roxanne knew that Matt was right. It wasn't just friendly advice that he was giving her, it was professional. But still … Right now, she was the officer in charge.

"Okay," she told Matt. "I get it." She stuck her head inside the door of the cab. "You've been brave," she told the two boys, "and you're not in any trouble. I'll see you back home," she said to Finn. She turned to Matt. "You go. I'll get a ride."

She walked back to where Sam Mendes was keeping an eye on Jay.

"Arrest him," she said. "For entering a crime scene. Take him in and lock him up until we have time to question him."

Jay slumped. Tears oozed out from under his straw-coloured lashes. Roxanne did not feel sorry. She was still furious with him for exposing Finn to this murder scene. The two boys watched from the back of the truck as Carter's dad was led to a police car, then Matt drove them away.

Roxanne went to the back of the house. She wanted to have a look at the body, then she would call Izzy.

21

WHAT HAD HAPPENED was fairly obvious. Leslie had left the cottage through the back door in a hurry, crossed the veranda, gone down the steps then across the lawn to the driveway at the side of the house. She had been killed by a heavy clay flowerpot full of dirt, which had been on the veranda and dropped onto her head.

Her suitcase was in the bedroom. She'd opened it, taken out a makeup bag and put it in the bathroom. A hairbrush and a tube of hand cream lay beside it. Nothing else appeared to have been removed from the case. There was an open wine bottle on the kitchen counter. A glass sat half full on the table, her open laptop and her phone beside it.

June Appleby reappeared on the deck of her house next door and waved to Roxanne.

"I need to tell you something!" she called. June knew where Leslie's car was. She had been on the phone with her husband, Herb, who was at the station taking care of visitors. The car was there, in the parking lot. He and his friends had found it when they arrived at lunchtime.

"She must have left it there so no one would suspect she was at the cottage," Roxanne said to Ravi Anand. "Then wheeled her suitcase over here in the dark."

"Why would she come here?" asked Ravi.

They had no idea. Nor did they know who else might have known that she was there.

Izzy texted to say she was about to leave the city. It would take at least an hour for her to arrive, driving in smog, but until then Roxanne was the sergeant in charge.

Roxanne took the police car Ravi had been driving, left him and Sam to guard the site and went to the station museum. There sat the silver Lexus, just as June had described. A few tourists were wandering around, all wearing their masks. Poor air quality was becoming more of a health hazard as the day wore on. People with respiratory problems were being advised to say indoors. Smoke now blanketed the village like a fog.

June had informed Herb about the new remains at Hazeldean, He shook his white head when Roxanne drew him aside.

"Dreadful business, this," he said.

"Someone from the Forensic Identification Unit will be by in about an hour to examine the car," she told him. "Can you make sure no one goes near it until they arrive?"

"Sure can, ma'am." Herb took up position beside it, his face grim. No one would get near.

Next, she made her way up the highway, frustrated at having to take her time, but poor visibility hadn't stopped tourists from being out and about. They puttered along, admiring the view, not that there was much to see today. She crawled the car across the causeway to Bulrush Island because of the haze. The smoke was dense, visibility reduced to a few feet. She was glad that no car was coming toward her. One of them would have to back up to the nearest passing place in this murk if they had. Eventually she reached the house where Leslie had been staying.

Leslie's friend, Jenn Wilson, was shocked at the news. "She's what? Dead?" She flopped into one of her tan-coloured armchairs. Tears welled up in her eyes.

"We had a late dinner together, and I asked her if she could find somewhere else to stay by Monday morning, since my husband was going to come out for the rest of the week. She got quite angry with me, insisted I'd said she could stay as long as she liked, but I didn't. I thought she'd only be here a day or two and I didn't know John was planning to come out, either. John doesn't like Leslie very much."

Roxanne looked around for a box of tissues. She spotted one in the kitchen and went to fetch it. She wasn't sure Jenn's husband was the real problem. She'd seen the expression on Jenn's face when she opened the door and saw the police car in her driveway. Having the RCMP come calling was not good for your reputation in an upscale neighbourhood like this, nor was having a house guest who had a close connection to an active murder investigation. It was more likely that Jenn or her husband had had second thoughts about having Leslie to stay.

"She said that she'd get out of my hair right away. I told her there was no rush but she left her dessert unfinished and went to fetch her suitcase. I tried to persuade her to stay the night, but Leslie can be like that. Once she makes up her mind, there's no changing it. She'd had a couple of glasses of wine and she'd have had to drive the causeway. It was getting dark and it was a bit smoky out, but she said she had somewhere to go where she would be bothering no one. And off she went." Jenn had not imagined that Leslie would go to Hazeldean cottage. Hadn't the police placed it off limits?

"And now she's dead? Somebody killed her? I should never have let her go. I should have tried harder to get her to stay." Jenn clutched her Kleenex.

"Don't blame yourself," said Roxanne. "None of this is your fault."

The woman blew her nose and wiped her eyes. "Just what happened to her?" she asked. Roxanne was not prepared to share the gory details.

"I can't tell you that," she told her. "But I do need you to keep this news to yourself for now." Jenn nodded, her eyes and the end of her nose all red.

It must have been close to ten when Leslie had driven away last night, and it would have taken her another fifteen or twenty minutes to reach Cullen Village. By the time Leslie parked the car it would have been completely dark, the air thick enough with smoke to hide moon or starlight. But that was not late for a Saturday night in cottage country. Backyard parties would have been going on at the village. Leslie had taken a risk, trundling a suitcase along the road past the Halliday house. Someone might have been seen her cross the police tape and enter the cottage she co-owned with her brothers.

By the time Roxanne returned, Hazeldean had been taken over by Ident personnel once more. They'd erected a tent over the body and were putting up lamps to combat the gloom. Everyone was well masked. The smell of wood ash hung in the air. The house was being scoured for any sign of Leslie Borthwick's late night visitor. They hoped they'd find a print but so far there was nothing.

"How can that be?" asked Dave Kovak. "It looks like an impulse killing. Whoever did this must have grabbed that pot as the nearest thing to hand. This is summer. No one wears gloves in the heat we've been having."

Leslie's phone and computer would need to go to Winnipeg for scrutiny. Dave would flag it as priority but the lab was backed up.

"Three deaths in a row? It has to be done right away." Izzy had arrived and taken charge. She had a better suggestion: Her file coordinator, Trent Weiss, was a tech whiz. He could be here in an hour or so and pick up all of Leslie's devices.

Two of Dave's team relieved Herb Appleby from his vigil and inspected Leslie's car. The station had closed early. Visitors were fewer because of the polluted air, but Doug Halliday had stayed to keep Herb company. Sandy had excused himself and left. He was wheezing badly. With all the disruption to their usual routines they forgot about the bag of buns. They were left to grow stale on a shelf where mice would probably get at them.

One of the men in white suits told them that the car would be towed in for examination. They saw him lift a box from the liquor store out of the trunk. Leslie must have stocked up. Perhaps she had a drinking problem, just like her dad and his dad before him, Herb said as he and Doug walked home, curious to see what was now happening at Hazeldean. A woman was talking to the head of forensics. From her red hair they recognized her as Sergeant Calloway, out of uniform.

"She was called in unexpectedly when they found the body, and then she arrested Jay Borthwick," Herb reported. June had told him what had happened at the cottage that morning and how angry the sergeant had been. "Not surprising. Her boy was right there. He must have seen the body."

Izzy was standing on the veranda when Roxanne walked around the back of the cottage. "Good you're here. We need that car," she said. "I need to send Ravi Anand over to get statements from both of the kids."

"I should be with Finn when you do that," said Roxanne.

Izzy had a different plan. "Matt's at home with him, isn't he?" She looked down at Roxanne from the top of the steps. "He'll be fine. Meantime, you and I need to talk."

Being told what to do by Izzy McBain was a new experience for Roxanne. Ravi had come to get the car keys. She could see him and a couple of Ident guys watching to see how she would react. She decided it was best to comply and went along when Izzy suggested that her car would be a good place to talk privately.

"You can't work this case any longer, Roxanne," Izzy said once the car door was firmly closed. She turned on the engine so she could run air. They both lowered their masks.

"Matt's already told me that." Roxanne watched the van from the Provincial Medical Examiner's office draw up. It had arrived quicker than expected, given the poor visibility on the highway. It couldn't get into the driveway because Jay's SUV and the canoe were still there.

"It hasn't stopped you going around interviewing people."

"I talked to Jenn Wilson, the woman that Leslie Borthwick was staying with. She's never had anything to do with Jay. There's no connection between them."

"You didn't know that. And you arrested Jay."

"I did not. I got Sam Mendes to do it." Roxanne said it jokingly, trying to lighten the conversation

Izzy tapped her fingers on the steering wheel. She wasn't smiling.

"There's no way he's our killer, Roxanne. He'd never have brought the boys over here if he'd known that body was lying out the back. Couldn't you just have taken a statement and let him go?"

"He should never have brought them here. He broke the law when my kid was in his care."

"Yeah, and you got mad as hell because he exposed Finn to this mess. But you're a cop, Roxanne. You know better. You got yourself emotionally involved. You overreacted. I don't blame you, but you have got to stay away from everything to do with this case from now on. So, tell me what you've found out since we last spoke, and then go home."

Roxanne did not know what to say. She had been Izzy's superior in the past. She'd spotted her potential, encouraged her to join the Major Crimes Unit. Now she was being chastised by that same Izzy. Not that Izzy wasn't right, but it still rankled.

"You'll be staying?" she asked. "Investigating the case from here?"

"Looks like it. I've been focused on the Palmer angle. Bricks and Sugar, that connection. But Leslie being dead doesn't fit with that at all, so I'll probably be around for a while."

"I'm in charge of the detachment for this area," Roxanne reminded Izzy.

"Yeah, and I'll keep you informed. But no active engagement. Okay?"

Roxanne had to agree.

"Do you know why Leslie came here? To this house?" Izzy asked.

Roxanne told her how, according to her friend, Leslie had left Bulrush Island in a snit, just at nightfall.

"She often acted on impulse like that?"

"It sounds like Leslie's always upped and done whatever she decided to do," said Roxanne. "But why come here? She knew this was still being treated as a crime scene."

"Where else would she have gone? The hotel's full and all the local Airbnbs are booked. I know. I've been looking for a room where I can stay and there's nothing. She'd drunk some wine and maybe didn't want to drive into the city. So she thought that she could move in because she co-owns the place and nothing much was happening here. I expect Jay thought the same thing. That it was his place so it was okay for him to drop by."

"That doesn't excuse him," said Roxanne.

Having dinner at Bulrush Island explained why Leslie hadn't shown up for her brother's big barbecue last night.

"But Fraser did," said Roxanne. "Something went wrong between him and Jay. Something was said that Fraser didn't want to hear. And you shouldn't write Jay off as a suspect. Maybe he brought the boys here because it helped make him look innocent. He just didn't expect them to run around the back and see the body."

"Do you really think Jay's devious enough to figure that out?" asked Izzy. "He seems a pretty straight-up kind of guy to me. I suppose I'd better go talk to him, then I'll let him go. These guys are going to want that SUV of his out of the driveway." Two of the technicians were moving the canoe and the paddles back to the garage.

"I'm going to need a ride home," said Roxanne.

"Guess you will. And I still need to find somewhere to stay. Being at my mom's doesn't cut it."

Izzy pulled the car out from the curb. Everything was under control here, for now. She'd drop Roxanne off home then go to Fiskar Bay and deal with Jay Borthwick.

22

JAY BORTHWICK WAS scared. He'd never been in trouble with the law and certainly never been locked in a cell before. He didn't know how long the RCMP would keep him here. He figured he should talk to a lawyer and find out how much trouble he was in. Aimee Vermette called Derek McVicar on his behalf.

"Perhaps you could ask my colleague, Mr. Stavros," McVicar said, trying to wiggle out of the job. It was, after all, a Sunday afternoon. But Matt, it seemed, was disallowed because his wife was involved with the case. Derek had planned to go sailing but that was cancelled. You could barely see the boats out in the harbour because of the ash hanging in the air. He had no good reason not to put in an appearance. So he arrived, met with Jay and heard his side of the story.

"My client has been placed under arrest for crossing a police line and entering a crime scene that he thought was inactive. That tape's been up for four days already. You've had him locked up for two hours. Isn't that excessive? Where is your sense of compassion? The man just witnessed a horrific scene. It was his own sister he found dead. He's traumatized, and you threw him into a cell?"

"He hasn't been charged." Izzy wasn't going to take the blame for Roxanne's decision. "I need to ask him some questions, though."

"Then he'll be free to go?"

"I hope so."

Jay looked a wreck, still pale, shadows like bruises under his eyes. He shifted uncomfortably in his chair and looked around at his new surroundings, the grey interview room, the blonde sergeant in jeans opposite him, the recording device.

"Are the boys okay?" he asked.

"They're both home with their moms," Izzy told him. "Tell me why you took them with you to Hazeldean. You knew you shouldn't be there, that you were doing something wrong. That you were setting a bad example."

Jay clutched the edges of his seat, avoiding making eye contact.

"I'd promised I would take them out canoeing. I should have picked up the boat yesterday. I meant to, but things got busy because of the barbecue that we had last night. There were tables to set up. People brought lights for us to hang. A band called to see if they could play. It all got way bigger than we expected. There just wasn't time.

"Then brunch this morning lasted until one and the boys were waiting, all excited. I took them along. I didn't know what else to do and I didn't think it would matter. You guys hadn't been around since Amelia died. I thought you'd maybe forgotten to take down the tape. I was just going to stop at the end of the driveway and get the canoe."

"And the paddles. And the life jackets."

"I couldn't find the rope I needed to tie the canoe to the car roof. It wasn't where it should be. The cleaners Amelia brought in must have moved it. I needed to go looking. I never thought the kids would follow me. I told them to stay beside the car."

"But they're boys and they didn't. They probably wanted to go look at the pier. Instead, what they saw was the bloody remains of your sister."

Jay looked stricken. Derek McVicar, sitting by his side, raised a reproachful eyebrow.

"Do you know why your sister was at the cottage?" Izzy asked.

Jay fixed watery blue eyes on her, like he needed her to know that he was telling the truth.

"No, I don't. Leslie always did whatever she wanted as far as Hazeldean was concerned. Maybe she thought she was allowed, that since it was days since you found Amelia's body the police tape didn't matter too much. Just like I did."

"She didn't go to your barbecue."

"Maybe she didn't know about it."

"You didn't invite her? Your sister?"

He paused in thought.

"We just didn't run into her," he said eventually. "If we had, we probably would have said something. I don't know Leslie all that well. She's fifteen years older than me. She was going into high school when I was born. I was only nine years old when she got married. Was the ring bearer at the wedding. And then she went to live with Mark in Saskatoon. I haven't seen much of her since then."

"She's been in charge of what happens to your mother and her money since your father died."

"I suppose. I was in my last year of school when that happened."

"You and Fraser will inherit all that cash now that both your sisters are dead."

"Eventually. It could be a while. My mom is still alive. She's not much over seventy. Sure, she has Alzheimer's. I dropped by to see her back in the spring, when I first came out to Hazeldean, before all this happened. Took her daffodils. She didn't know who I was but she seemed happy enough. They take good care of her in the home. She could still last for years."

"We'll need to talk about her affairs soon," Derek butted in. "The portfolio is substantial. You and Fraser will need to decide how it should be managed and also who will be making decisions on behalf of your mother."

It was Izzy who asked how much the portfolio was worth. More than three-and-a-half million, last time McVicar had seen a statement. Jay's jaw dropped.

"That much?" he asked. "And none of it goes to the grandkids?"

"No," said the lawyer. "Her will's quite clear on that. It was drawn up years ago, just after your father died, and she kept it simple. It was never updated. The money was to be split between the four of you. If any of you died before her, your portion was to be divided equally between the existing siblings."

"So, you see," said Izzy, "your sisters have conveniently died so you and Fraser will inherit all of it between you."

"I'd no idea," Jay protested. "We got a report from Leslie once a year, but it was all written in the kinds of words and figures that accountants use. I didn't know what any of it meant. Are you telling me that when Mom goes I will be a millionaire?" He turned those blue eyes on Izzy once more. He looked genuinely astonished.

"And you never wondered? I find that hard to believe," said Izzy. "It's a great motive, isn't it?"

He stared at her, open mouthed.

"Where were you last night, after the barbecue?"

"Nowhere!" he raised his hands, palms open, as if had nothing to hide. "People stayed until after eleven. We had to tell them to leave. The village has a noise bylaw and we didn't want to get into trouble. Then we still had to clean up. It was after one when we got to bed. We were tired out. I slept."

"Your brother Fraser came by last night."

"He did. I'd told him to stop in and have some ribs. He picked them up. Didn't stay."

"I'm told you had words."

"Who said that?"

Izzy didn't say. Roxanne had been present at the barbecue. He could figure it out for himself. "What was that about?" she asked.

He took his time replying again and rubbed his chin as he thought. "You know we've been talking about buying Hazeldean outright? Me and Jennifer?"

"We've heard that."

"And it means we'd have to buy out Fraser's share?"

"Was he willing to sell it to you?'

"He said so. Came by and told me he wanted $70,000 for it. Jennifer's had the place appraised. It's not worth that much, it's a fixer-upper, the state it's in these days. So we offered him $55,000 max. He said he'd go think about it."

"And he wasn't pleased?"

"I guess not."

"You don't have to worry about having to buy Leslie's share any longer." He supposed not. "And one of these days you'll have even more money of your own." He slumped in his chair, as if he realized how that added to his motive. "Why are you so keen on owning the place?"

"Because I've always been happy there." Jay drooped further, the picture of dejection. "I love that cottage. Jennifer spent her summers out here too, when she was little. Her mom and dad rented a trailer out by the creek. She loves Hazeldean as much as I do. We've been talking for months about what we'll do to upgrade it and still keep the character of the place. We want to live here. Raise our kids in the village. Send them to school there."

"You're planning to have more?"

"For sure."

"And you still want to make that cottage your home, after both of your sisters and your niece have died there?"

"Maybe not now. I'll have to talk to Jennifer about that." The memory of Leslie lying on the ground with her head smashed in was fresh in Jay's mind.

"Could you have afforded to pay Fraser $55,000 before this happened?"

They could, but they'd rather hang onto the cash they had until the house in Winnipeg sold. They might need it for other expenses. They'd like a better site for the café than the Rec Centre, and winterizing the cottage would cost, if they still decided to do that. It was Jennifer's money, really, so she had the final word.

"She has that much?"

"Maybe. I don't know."

She released him.

"You don't get to leave this area for now," she told him. "I'll drive you to Hazeldean. "You can pick up your SUV. We need you to get it out of there."

Derek McVicar took his leave, pleased the interview was over and hadn't taken up too much of his afternoon.

"Come and see me, you and your brother," he told Jay as they shook hands. "We'll get things sorted out regarding your mother's care and her accounts." He stood in the front doorway and pointed to a crimson sun hanging in a sky heavy as pewter. "Will you look at that? You'd think this was the apocalypse."

Jay sat in the back of the car and said nothing as Izzy drove through dense smoke to Cullen Village. Either he was mulling over what they had said or was just plain exhausted. He sat up and took notice, however, when he saw that the canoe was gone, vans were parked outside, and forensic technicians were at work around his family cottage.

"Just get in your car and go," Izzy advised him. She waited until he had driven away before she went inside.

Finn was at home but he was not speaking to his mother. The look he gave Roxanne when she walked in the door was baleful, then he'd stormed off to his room and closed the door.

"He got a message from Carter saying that Jennifer thinks they shouldn't see one another for now. So, no more play dates. It's not surprising, since you arrested Carter's new stepdad," said Matt. "They watched it all happen, didn't they? He says you were real mean, that you picked on Jay. He likes that guy, you know. They were having a good time until they found the body. You made Carter's dad cry."

Roxanne went upstairs and knocked on Finn's door. He opened it on the third attempt. "I don't want to talk to you," he said, and slammed it shut again.

She went back downstairs. She'd give him some time to cool off then she'd try again.

Matt was at his favourite table in the nook off the kitchen, his dogs at his feet, trawling the internet, looking at ads for riding mowers. He'd been told they might need to replace theirs. Outside the windows all she could see was a dull grey miasma.

"Where did you get to?" he asked without lifting his eyes from the screen.

"Bulrush Island. I talked to a woman that Leslie Borthwick had been staying with."

"Couldn't someone else have done that?"

"Not right at that moment." That wasn't entirely true but she wasn't going to say so.

"And it had to happen right then?"

She pulled out the chair opposite him and sat down. "What is this all about, Matt?" she asked. He closed the lid on his computer.

"You didn't think that maybe you should be here? That your son just saw something that scared him half to death and then had to watch you take down his best friend's dad?"

"Jay had no right to take him there."

"But he did. Not because he wanted to expose Finn and Carter to a bad experience but because he wanted to take your son canoeing for the afternoon. He probably got as big a fright as they did."

"You didn't see the body, Matt. Her head was smashed in. There was blood all over the place. It was horrific. The boys should never have witnessed that. That was Jay's fault."

"He made a mistake, Roxanne, and you treated him like he was a criminal. And you knew what Finn had seen but you didn't come home and find out how he was doing. Oh, it's okay. I've talked to him. But didn't you care? That should have been your priority, not messing around in a murder case that isn't yours to investigate. Your kid needed you, and you put the job first. I'm surprised at you. I'm going to go watch the news."

He stalked off into the living room, the dogs following him, picked up the remote and turned on the TV.

Matt had never spoken to Roxanne like that before. They'd had minor disagreements, but this was worse. She knew she was in the wrong. She'd been angry when she'd talked to Jay, furious because what Jay had done had hurt her son. Couldn't Matt see that? She'd gone to Bulrush Island, assuming Matt would cope with any immediate fallout with Finn and she would have time to catch up later. She had got that wrong.

Now Finn hated her and Matt was disappointed in her. Plus, she was off the case, completely. She felt like she would cry.

Roxanne fought back the tears. She wasn't going to let them happen. She went to the fridge, opened the freezer section and lifted out a tub of ice cream. Black cherry, that would do. She grabbed a spoon and ate while she tried to figure out how she was going to sort out the mess she had created.

23

GETTING INTO LESLIE Borthwick's devices had been a breeze. Trent Weiss had been and gone. He was still working on them at HQ when Izzy called him later that day.

Leslie had phoned her husband just before eleven and talked to him for twenty-three minutes, so she had still been alive at 11:19 last night. There were texts on her phone from friends, including one called Jenn Wilson, about staying at Bulrush Island. Some messages were from clients in Saskatchewan. It looked like she had been working on business accounts while she was staying in the Interlake.

She had phoned her brother Fraser a couple of days ago and had also texted Jay about getting together. Prior to Donna's death, the two sisters had spoken to one another almost daily. A week or so ago she had been messaging back and forth with her niece Amelia. They had made a couple of lengthy phone calls not long before Amelia died.

"Too bad we don't know exactly what they were saying, Sarge," Trent told Izzy. But he did think that Leslie's extensive spreadsheets and the notes she had attached to them might provide some clues. It was going to take some time to work through them. Would it be okay with Izzy and Ident if he took the computer home? He had a far better tech setup there than in the cubicle he'd been assigned at HQ.

Dave Kovak had been more than happy to agree if it took that workload off his hands.

Izzy called her brother about finding a place to stay and struck gold. Pete was successful, the eldest McBain son, who now would inherit the family farm, and he was in line to be town mayor. He also had an industrious wife. They owned a couple of places that she let out as Airbnbs. One was a condo by the beach at Fiskar Bay. This week's tenants had cancelled at the last minute because one of their kids had asthma and couldn't go outside in the smoke. Izzy could have it, half price.

"You are so cheap." She laughed. "I'll take it."

Along the lakeshore from Hazeldean, Margo Wishart looked out her window. She wouldn't be able to walk her dog very far through that poisonous haze. She loved the smell of woodsmoke, but only in sweet drifts on a summer afternoon, not this thick, stinking mass of pollution.

She had ventured as far as the berm with Bob earlier and had been able to see the glow of floodlights at Hazeldean, white shapes moving around them, like spectres. The police had been there for hours. She had heard that a third member of the Borthwick family had been found dead. It was the other sister, Leslie. The police didn't seem to have any idea who the killer was, and this was happening too close to home.

A strong wind was supposed to blow in from the south later tonight. By tomorrow morning the layer of ash would be gone and the sun would shine brightly again. That was good, but there was no rain at all coming their way and they needed water badly. Nothing was growing in the dry ground. Even the trees were drooping. All fires had been banned. Roberta Axelsson was worrying that her well might run dry. This was dismal. She and her friends needed cheering up.

She could invite the Applebys for drinks. She'd heard that June had been present when Leslie Borthwick's body had been found and that Herb had discovered Leslie's car, parked over by the railway station. Roberta would love to come and hear all about it.

Sasha Rosenberg sometimes made margaritas in the summertime and Margo herself did a decent gin and tonic. Would it seem in bad taste, given these recent deaths, to have a party? She could invite the Hallidays, too. Do it tomorrow night when the smoke had all blown away. Why not? You needed friends around you in dark times.

Over at Hazeldean, the body had been removed but Dave Kovak's team was still at work. They'd be a while longer, but they would lock up when they were done and let Izzy know if they found anything of interest.

Visibility on the highway was worse because of the dense smoke and traffic had picked up. That was a dangerous mix. It was Sunday afternoon and some cottagers had to get back to their city houses and their jobs. There had already been a collision just north of Fiskar Bay. Izzy had to flash her lights to get through. Constable Ravi Anand waved to her as she drove past.

Wes Melnyk's farmers market was eight kilometres north of Fiskar Bay. It had access roads, a parking lot, an area for goats and a donkey to amuse the kids, and rustic booths to accommodate his vendor, but it was all empty now. He'd closed early and put the animals inside his barn. No one was around except Fraser Borthwick. He was sitting on a bench outside the farmhouse door, smoking weed, adding to the pollution.

Fraser had been stuck there all day because of the weather. He knew he couldn't drive the bike; he couldn't see halfway down the driveway. The filthy air hadn't stopped people coming out in the morning. Wes had told him to direct traffic and given him a lamp to swing like a beacon, but by lunchtime everyone was gone. Just as well. He'd been in need of a nap by then. And now here was another cop come to bug him. Izzy McBain, Mike's sister.

"So, you're the detective?" he said.

"I'm in the Major Crimes Unit." Izzy sat down beside him on the bench. "Has anyone told you what happened at Hazeldean today?"

No one had. He was way north of Cullen Village and he'd been put out to work, out on the road. "What now?" he asked. She told him.

"Leslie? She's dead too? What the fuck! What was she doing there?"

She told him how Leslie had fallen out with her friend at Bulrush Island and gone off to stay at Hazeldean instead.

"She always got on her high horse when she got pissed off," he said, putting out his smoke as if he wasn't affected, but she could tell he was. He looked shaken and puzzled. "Someone smashed her on the head? Just like what happened to Amelia?"

"There's a similarity." Izzy heard horses moving close by, invisible in this blanket of grey. She was glad she was wearing a mask. She should tell Fraser to put one on. Being outside in this dirty air couldn't be good for his lungs.

"This is total shit," he said. "Do we need to be watching out for ourselves? Me and my brother? Is someone going to come for us next?"

"Is there any reason someone should?"

"Nope. Don't think so."

"You and Jay will inherit all your mother's money when she dies, now that both your sisters are gone."

Fraser leaned forward on his elbows and laced his fingers. "Guess we will." Furrows deepened on his forehead. "You saying one of us must have done it, Sarge?"

"Did you?"

"No way."

"You dropped by your brother's barbecue last night. In Cullen Village."

"Yup. Me and Big Sig, but we didn't stay long."

"Where did you go, after?"

He and Sig had eaten some ribs that Jay and Jennifer had given him, then they'd gone to the bar, where they usually went on a Saturday night. "Mike'll tell you. Ask him." Sig had driven him back after eleven. It wasn't late but Wes and the missus had hit the sack already. They worked hard, weekends. Had to get up early so things would be ready for the market.

He'd gone to bed. And no, he hadn't gotten on his bike and driven through this soot, in the dark, with a few beers in him all the way to Cullen Village. What kind of an idiot did she take him for? Plus, he didn't know Leslie was there, did he? Last time he'd talked to her she was living in some fat cat monster house on Bulrush Island.

"What did you talk about, when you saw her?"

Funny she should mention that. Leslie being dead really messed things up for him. But Fraser perked up as he realized he had a very good reason not to have killed his sister.

"We had a deal, me and Les, so I could get some money to keep me going. I was thinking I might stay out here. Not go back to Toronto. I've got good buds here, like Mike."

He kept reminding her that he and her brother were friends.

"What was the deal?" she prompted.

"Well, see, her and Donna used to be kinda partners when it came to lookin' out for Mom. Les said it needed two of them to sign cheques and things when stuff needed to be paid for and now that Donna was gone, I could take her place. Help Les out. Especially if I was planning to stick around here and could check up on Mom now and then. I could sign papers for her, cheques, things like that. I said it was hard to make any money out here to live on and Les said she could maybe spring me some cash."

"She'd pay you?"

"No, she'd give me money that's coming to me. It sounds like there's lots, just sitting in the bank. Hers and mine and Jay's, once Mom's gone. So, some of it's gonna be mine anyway. She was going to figure out how much that was and give me a bit now and then, to live on. An advance, that's what she called it. But see, that's all screwed up now. I won't get it, now she's dead." He groped in his pocket and pulled out a baggie and his rolling papers. His hands were shaking. "This totally sucks. There's no way I'd have wanted to kill her."

"So let me get this," said Izzy. "Leslie wanted you to have power of attorney for your mother as well as her? You would stay here at Fiskar Bay and sign for anything that your mother needed?"

"Yup." He was keeping himself busy rolling another joint, still trying not to give in to his shock at Leslie's death.

"In return, she'd start paying you your share of your inheritance? How much?"

"I dunno. We still needed to figure that out. Enough that I could get by. Maybe rent an apartment. Trade in the bike for a car. It'll be useless here come winter." He clicked a Zippo. The light illuminated his craggy face in the gloom.

"That's not the only cash that's coming your way. Your brother's willing to pay you for your share in Hazeldean, isn't he?"

"Yeah, but it's not anything close to what I'd have got from Leslie. And he's not going to pay me what the cottage is worth. Not according to Leslie or my Aunt Sylvia. She knows how much places are going for around here. Maybe I'll have to take what Jay's offering, though. I hope he still wants it. Maybe he won't now that Leslie's died there, too." He puffed more smoke into the already thick atmosphere.

"Did you tell anyone else about Leslie's offer?"

"The guys know. Of course, they do. Who else do I have to talk to?"

His phone buzzed and interrupted him.

"It's my Aunt Sylvia," he said. "What?" He rose to his feet as he listened and put out what was left of the joint with his other hand. He answered in monosyllables. "When? How bad? No way. I'll be there, soon as. It's my mom," he said, pocketing his phone. "They had to call an ambulance. She's really sick. It looks like she's got sepsis and she might not make it. Can you give me a ride to the hospital?"

The crash on the highway still hadn't cleared. Once more, Ravi Anand waved and Izzy waved back. Fraser slunk down in his seat.

"Folks are gonna think you're taking me in," he whined.

"Hey," Izzy told him. "I'm giving you a ride, remember? Doing you a favour."

The emergency department of the little hospital at Fiskar Bay was packed and the staff was overwhelmed. An ambulance had arrived with casualties from the crash. People coughed, wheezed and limped in the waiting room. No seats were available and nurses were too busy to be interrupted, but Izzy knew her way around. She'd been here many times, first when she was a kid who played hockey and rode horses and had suffered the occasional fall. Second when she'd been a uniformed constable here in Fiskar Bay. When an orderly tried to stop her walking through the door that led to the wards, she flashed her warrant card and found her way to the nursing station. Fraser followed in her wake, leaning on his cane, looking like he might be in need of patient care himself.

"We're doing what we can. Her sister is with her now. Only immediate family are allowed to visit," said a young nurse Izzy had never seen before.

"I'm her son," growled Fraser. The girl's mouth fell open at the sight of this scruffy man. He looked like he lived on the streets but he was related to Lois Borthwick and her sister, Sylvia Olafson? She said she'd go ask and hurried away. Then she came back and said he could follow her.

Izzy noticed a man pushing a trolley toward her dressed in scrubs, a plastic hair cover on his head, a mask on his face. She knew him; he'd been in her year at Fiskar Bay High School. She had to remind him who she was. She pulled her own mask down for a moment.

"Izzy McBain! How're you doing? Are you still a cop?"

She was. "What's going on with Lois Borthwick?" she asked.

He shook his head. Not good. Her organs were shutting down. They didn't have a bed for her. They'd made her comfortable in a corner of the emergency ward; a curtain gave the family some privacy. So sad, but they were doing the best they could do. He couldn't stay and talk, sorry, Izzy. He needed to deliver meds, he said and pushed his cart off down the hallway.

Izzy went back along the blue and pink hallway. Sig Olafson barged through the door at the far end and walked right past her as if he didn't even see her. But Ravi Anand did. He'd just arrived to find out what had happened to the casualties from the accident. He'd spotted Big Sig as well.

"How's it going, Sarge?" Ravi looked exhausted. He'd been on the job for hours.

"Let me buy you a coffee," she said.

The hospital cafeteria catered to patients and their visitors. It was relatively quiet and calm compared to the chaos in emergency. They found a table in a corner. She bought coffee for herself, tea for him and a couple of big cookies. She told him about Fraser, the Borthwick money and Lois Borthwick's illness.

"So, if she goes tonight, he and his brother are both going to be rich?"

"Seems so."

"If Leslie hadn't died last night she'd have inherited a third of the family fortune, and that chunk wouldn't have gone to them?"

"That's right."

"Interesting timing."

"You bet."

They ate the cookies. Ravi Anand devoured his.

"When did you last eat, Constable?" she asked. It had been a while, but he wouldn't have another cookie. Food would be waiting for him when he got home.

"Is there any way that either of the brothers would have known that Lois was on her way out?" he asked her.

"Fraser looked surprised, but that's something I need to find out," said Izzy. "Sylvia Olafson visits her sister every day. She might have noticed that Lois was deteriorating. She could have mentioned it to him."

"Is he capable of killing anyone? He can hardly walk."

"I'm not sure just how disabled Fraser really is," said Izzy. "I think being helpless works for him. But he and Sig Olafson are first cousins. And they're close buddies."

Ravi had met Big Sig on several occasions, some of them memorable. He knew that he was a bruiser. "Would he be stupid enough to kill, just to help out his cousin?"

"If that cousin was going to become very rich as a result? And he might benefit? Maybe," said Izzy.

They went their separate ways, Ravi to his home and family, Izzy to get a key to the beach condo from her brother's wife. She liked what she saw of Ravi Anand. He was smart and not afraid of hard work. Maybe now that she didn't have Roxanne working beside her on this case, she could get him as a replacement. Second him onto her team, if Roxanne was willing to let him go.

24

THE PROMISED WIND blew in after midnight and swept all the sooty ash out of the sky. By the time the sun rose, not a speck remained. The birds raised their voices in welcome and Lois Borthwick's joyful spirit, which had remained intact in spite of memory loss and a failing body, floated away with the sound. Her sister Sylvia had refused to leave her side all night long. Her sons Fraser and Jay had been present when she died. They were all bereft.

It was too early for news of the latest death in the Borthwick family to be out yet. Things were still tense in the Calloway/Stavros household. Matt was behaving like his usual amiable self but Roxanne knew that, in his eyes, she had not lived up to expectations. Finn only spoke to her when it was necessary. She needed to do something to fix this situation. She left them eating breakfast—she still had no early morning appetite and Matt would deliver Finn to summer camp, as usual—and drove to Cullen Village.

The café at the Rec Centre, The Laughing Coyote, was closed on Mondays. She might be able to talk with Jay's family and make amends. Maybe she had gone a bit over the top in arresting Jay. She did realize that she'd acted in anger and she'd scared the boys. She was prepared to apologize and hope that Jennifer Boychuk would relent, that she would allow Finn and Carter to be friends once more. She was glad to see Jay's SUV and a van that must belong to Jennifer sitting in the Rec Centre parking lot. She'd wondered if they might be gone, up early and off to the city on their day off. She went to the door of the motor home, took in a deep breath of fresh, clean air and knocked.

Jennifer opened the door. She was in a short night shift, her abundant brown hair loose around her head and shoulders.

"You," she said, blocking the way inside. "What do you want now?"

"I wondered if I could have a word with all of you." Roxanne tried to smile brightly.

"Today? Are you serious? Don't you know?"

"Know what?"

"That Jay's mother is dead! Two, three hours ago."

"I didn't know." She hadn't even known Lois had been hospitalized. "I'm sorry. How did it happen?"

Jennifer stepped out of the door and onto the steps. Roxanne was forced to back down onto the ground. Jennifer stood above her like an irate angel, her hair like a halo around her head. The door clicked shut behind her.

"She got sepsis. Organ failure. It was natural causes, before you start thinking someone did her in, too. Jay's asleep. He was at the hospital most of the night, so you can't see him. He's just lost his mother. The last person he needs talking to him is you."

"I wanted to speak to him about what happened yesterday," Roxanne said.

"You treated him like a criminal in front of Carter."

"I was just doing my job."

"Do you know how hard Jay's worked trying to get my son to trust him, Sergeant? To be a good dad?" Jennifer folded both arms. "He knows he blew it with his own kids. He didn't spend anything like enough time with them because he was busy with his restaurant. He wasn't going to make that mistake again. So here he was, doing his best, taking Carter and your son out for the afternoon so he could teach them how to paddle a canoe, and what did he find? His own sister, lying dead on the ground. And if that's not bad enough, along you came and yelled at him, then arrested him. Had him driven off in a police car while our son watched it happen. If that's you doing your job, you're welcome to it. You just stay away from us. We don't want to have anything to do with you."

She turned her back on Roxanne, opened the door, stepped inside and banged it shut.

Roxanne was stunned. Was that how she was perceived? Jay bore some responsibility for what had happened yesterday. Could no one see that except herself?

And now Lois Borthwick had died? Less than two days after her daughter, the one who held the purse strings to her large fortune, leaving Jay and Fraser as the only beneficiaries?

She needed to get to her office and find out what was going on.

Izzy wakened in the well-appointed Airbnb at the beach in Fiskar Bay. It was three storeys up with a balcony that overlooked sand and water and seagulls. She could see bright sunshine outside. Town workers in hi-vis vests were picking up garbage. A tractor was dragging a large rake over the sand to make sure it was pristine for the day's batch of tourists.

She'd slept well in a comfortable bed. The shower was efficient. There was a supply of coffee pods but her sister-in-law had drawn the line at providing full service for Pete's little sister at half the normal rate. Usually, she stocked the fridge with juice, milk, muffins and fruit for her renters but all there was this morning was bottled water. Izzy swung the door shut and sighed. She'd have to stop somewhere and get some breakfast. She dressed in her usual jeans, a tank and a tee, sneakers and socks, and went outside.

It might be sunnier again, but yesterday's smog had cooled the air. This was an okay morning to be outside and Izzy wasn't going far. She could walk everywhere she needed to go today and get some exercise. She stopped at her car and found a ball cap and sunglasses. She could almost pass for a tourist.

She jogged her way to a different café from the Timmies near the RCMP detachment. This one was new, made good coffee, people said, not that Izzy cared much about that. She just wanted a regular latte and something to eat. They did an eggy bun. That was fine by her. She found a seat on the patio outside. More town workers were hanging flags from the light standards. Red maple leaves were appearing alongside baskets full of petunias. A banner was being suspended across the street. CANADA DAY!, it proclaimed in bright red letters.

Izzy took out her phone and checked her calendar. Friday would be Canada Day. The town would be packed with visitors for the festivities, so the RCMP would be busy all week, which was probably a good thing. It would keep Roxanne occupied. But it also meant that all of the Fiskar Bay team would be needed. Roxanne wouldn't want to lose Constable Anand to the Major Crimes Unit right now.

Izzy watched a car stop at the nearest intersection. Matt Stavros was driving, a kid in the seat behind him. That must be Roxanne's boy. He'd sure grown since the last time Izzy had seen him. A big rig trundled along behind the car, loaded with wheels and metal tracks and colourful mini-cars. The midway was arriving to get ready for the celebrations.

She drained the last of her latte and checked the time. Almost nine. Chris Olson, the manager at Harbourfront House, should be at work by then. She jogged further west, past the bank and the grocery store and the pharmacy, still closed.

She left the main drag and slowed down to a walk along a leafy street with houses on tidy lots. Roxanne had lived in one of them before she'd moved in with Matt into that big house near Cullen Village. She turned again, in the direction of the lake, toward the path that looped by the sparkling water. Outside the yacht club, a pair of healthy-looking older teens were dragging dinghies to the beach. It looked like a sailing class was about to happen.

Harbourfront House, the care home, was right ahead. Chris Olson ushered Izzy into her office. Chris was her usual large, smooth, assured self. The way that Lois Borthwick had died was not at all unusual, she said, not for someone in an advanced stage of Alzheimer's, as Lois had been. Lois had been prone to urinary tract infections this past year or two. Usually, they were able to clear those up with a course of antibiotics, but this one had persisted. Lois couldn't shake it and it had developed into septicemia. She had very little resistance left, she was so little, so frail. Once the infection had reached a certain point, the end had been inevitable.

"So sad." She folded one hand over the other on her desk, as still as a benevolent Buddha. "Lois was a happy presence around here for many years. She was never argumentative or difficult. Some of our patients can become violent, you know, but you could always count on Lois for a smile. She never said an unkind word."

"When did you know how sick she was?" asked Izzy.

"Yesterday. Her sister Sylvia noticed that she was more confused than usual in the morning when she dropped by to visit. By the afternoon, we knew we needed to call an ambulance. It all happened very quickly."

"Did you suspect that this infection might kill her at any time before that?"

Mrs. Olson pursed her lips.

"She had a fever, but she could have recovered. I never thought she would leave us so quickly. Not that you can predict anything when it comes to old people and their health. You never know when death will strike. In Lois's case, it's saddened all of us. She was one of our best loved residents. She must have been a delight to know when she was younger."

Izzy took her leave. Over at the water's edge she could see a bunch of kids being shown how to get in and out of a boat in the water. One of the boys might be Finn Calloway.

She had a message from Trent. *Call me ASAP.* She'd do that as soon as she got to the office upstairs at the RCMP detachment, but her walk up Main Street took her past the McVicar Law office. Izzy opened the door and walked in.

She got a warm welcome from Matt. He enveloped her in a big hug. When she took off her cap he told her he liked the haircut. His hand rose, like he wanted to rumple her hair, as he would have done when they lived together, but then he seemed to think better of it. His office receptionist sat at her desk and watched.

"Great to see you, Izzy. What finally brings you my way? You've heard the news about Lois Borthwick? That she died this morning?"

"I have," said Izzy. "That's why I'm here to talk to you. I need to know what happens to all her money now."

He led her into the panelled meeting room with yachting photos on the wall. The receptionist brought coffee and little square cookies. He'd help if he could, but Derek McVicar was the lawyer in charge of the Borthwick account, Matt said. He would probably meet with the family within the next few days.

"And then Jay and Fraser will both be rich men?"

"Not that soon. There'll be probate. And as far as I know there's no executor, since Leslie is dead. That's going to hold things up in terms of them getting the actual cash."

"How long?'

"Hard to say."

"Can the Palmers challenge the will?"

"Graeme might since it's old, signed over twenty years ago, before he was born. He could argue that Donna's share should have been passed down to him. Do you think that's why the sisters both died? Because of the inheritance?"

"Seems as good a bet as any." Izzy had forgotten how easy it was to talk to Matt, how relaxed she was in his company. "Leslie, who was the only one of the family who knew what Lois's fortune as worth, died sometime Saturday night and now it turns out the old lady was getting sick by then with an infection that would eventually kill her. Interesting timing, isn't it?"

"Well," he said. "Off the record, I think Sylvia Olafson believed Leslie was playing around with the money and Donna might have been involved in that. This business all began with Leslie and Donna wanting to rebuild that old cottage, didn't it? And Amelia was going to do the same. Now all three of them are dead."

"You know what?" Izzy dusted crumbs off her fingers and got up. "I've got a guy checking out Leslie's accounts right now. I'd best go see what he's found."

Matt didn't hug her as they said goodbye but he did say it had been great seeing her again and he grinned. Matt had a smile that went ear-to-ear and Izzy had never been able to resist smiling back. The receptionist saw and heard everything. She already knew that Izzy used to live with Matt before he got together with Sergeant Calloway, who ran the RCMP here in Fiskar Bay. She and two of her friends were going to be at a baby shower tomorrow night. They would be interested to know what went on in Mr. Stavros's life.

Trent had learned a lot from the notes Leslie had left in her computer. She'd written about her plan to finance rebuilding Hazeldean and to share in the profit. Her calculations were all there.

Her most recent entries had been made that weekend, on Saturday, right before she had died. She had estimated that her brother, Fraser, would inherit about $1.2 million from their mother's estate. She proposed putting the sum in a separate account and pay Fraser a monthly allowance, beginning in July. She thought that the most she could afford to pay him was $2,000 per month. Her last entry read:

Talk with F. re: Plan A. Get agreement signed, PoA application also. He has a bank account? Check.

She had drafted an agreement with Fraser but hadn't filled in specific figures yet.

Trent also knew that Leslie had been skimming money from her mother's accounts for years.

"She tried to write most of it off as expenses, but some of it is just listed as an administration fee. Maybe she became complacent. She'd been doing it for over twenty years and getting away with it," he said to Izzy.

He wasn't close to a final tally but the total must be in tens of thousands per year. And she had given her sister Donna a monthly payment for being their mother's prime caregiver, plus a loan of $500,000 when Donna set up a new office for Bricks and Sugar seven years ago. He'd found no record of any repayment, or any request for a payment, so it looked like Donna had received money that belonged to her mother, too. He'd have full figures for Izzy in a couple of days, unless she needed him for something else?

"No," she said. "Go right ahead."

Izzy rocked back in her chair. Was this what Sylvia Olafson had suspected? Could she have said something to Fraser? Did Jay have any idea? Did the brothers know that their sisters had been stealing money that should have become theirs? Had the two of them discussed this at all? Could they be working in tandem to make sure that they got what was left for themselves?

It was going to be difficult to talk to them right now, when their mother had just died. Maybe she should go track down her brother Mike first. He hung out with Fraser and Big Sig. He might be able to tell her something.

25

LOIS BORTHWICK'S SUDDEN death superseded that of her older daughter as the main topic of conversation at Margo Wishart's cocktail party that evening. Herb Appleby could talk of nothing else. The Hallidays, Roberta, Sasha, and Herb's wife, June, sat around on Margo's deck and sipped their drinks as he held forth.

Lois had been nineteen years old when Herb had first met her. She'd been newly engaged to Will Borthwick. Prettiest girl at the beach, he enthused. Margo watched June stare out over the lake, no expression registering on her face. Lois had been too good for Will, Herb continued. He had known that right from the beginning. She had spent all of her summers at the cottage, as soon as she and Will were married. Came out May long weekend and stayed until September. She'd raised her kids out here. Will came and went all summer long, drove out from the city, didn't take the Daddy Train. He always had the latest make of car. Liked to show it off. He sometimes brought visitors with him. The house was always spotless. Lois could whip up a lunch at a moment's notice.

"She was capable," he said. "Will took everything she did for granted."

Herb himself had been teaching high school back then, phys-ed, and had school holidays off. He and June had boys that were about the same age as Fraser and the older Borthwick children. Herb had taught most of the kids in the area to swim and to ride their bikes. Lois's were no exception. He'd shown them how to handle a boat.

"Didn't someone say that Will had a power boat of his own?" Freya Halliday asked.

Sure he had, but Will just used it for taking friends out on trips. Business acquaintances, mostly. The boat was for show, like his cars.

So usually it was just Lois and the kids at Hazeldean.

"She had her hands full. Those girls looked a lot like her but they behaved just like their dad. Both of them liked to have their own way. There was no stopping them, especially Leslie. They knew they could get whatever they wanted from Will. He just laughed at what they got up to. Real daddy's girls, both of them. Fraser, though, was another story. He was a soft little boy. Will thought he needed toughening up. He wanted Fraser to grow up just like him, and it wasn't going to happen.

"I can still remember Will forcing Fraser to jump off the pier into the lake. He wasn't five yet. Wasn't ready. He was terrified. Crying. But Will made him jump anyway."

"Couldn't Lois have stopped him?" asked Roberta.

"No way. There was no stopping Will when he got an idea in his head," said Herb. "And, of course, it turned out badly. Fraser got into drugs when he was in junior high. His father eventually gave up on him."

"He did get arrested, Herb," June reminded him. "For dealing. Twice." She turned to the rest. "Fraser had quite the little business going on out here by the time he was in high school. I had to ban him from the house. I told my boys they were to have nothing more to do with him."

"Yeah, well, he went off to university and disappeared not long after that. Just about broke Lois's heart," said Herb. "But she got pregnant with Jay around then. There's nineteen years between those two boys, you know. Will was too busy making money to pay much attention while Jay was growing up. He didn't mess around with him the same way as he did with Fraser. I know you shouldn't speak ill of the dead, but Will dying when he was only fifty-seven freed Lois up. It was like she got a new lease on life." Herb was the only one of Margo's guests who had opted to drink beer. He finished his second and waved the empty can at Margo. She went to fetch another.

"That didn't last long," said June. "Lois started losing her memory real early."

Herb shook his white-haired head and reached out a hand for the fresh can. He poured the beer into a tall glass. "Terrible," he said. "And she knew it was happening. She worried about what would happen to Jay. She was forty when she had him, you know, and the disease took hold before she was sixty. Jay was just starting university. She's been shut up in that care home for years. I used to go visit her every summer until she didn't know who I was any more. It was the saddest thing." He went silent. They all drank, wondering what to say next.

June stood up. "Time to go home, Herb," she said. "Thank you, Margo, we must be off." She walked over the grass and up onto the berm. Herb didn't argue. He put down the almost-full glass and followed her like a large, obedient sheepdog. They watched them disappear along the path to their own house.

"Well then," said Freya Halliday. "What do we make of that? He sure liked Lois Borthwick a lot."

"Let me refill your glasses," Margo offered.

They agreed to switch to wine. She had a bottle of pinot grigio chilling in the fridge. It was a beautiful evening, the sky an azure blue turning to yellow then pink over the pale water, and not too hot. The birds were quiet, gone to roost. All they could hear was the croaking of frogs. They moved closer to one another and lowered their voices. Sound travelled easily when it was as quiet as this.

"Herb couldn't have been having an affair with Lois!" Sasha said. "June would never put up with it. She calls the shots in that marriage. You saw how he did as he was told right now. And she'd have eaten Lois Borthwick for dinner if she'd found out. June's tough. I know. I used to play tennis against her."

"June wouldn't have been out here all the time, though," said Freya. "He had teacher's holidays but didn't June work in the bank? Wasn't she a loans officer?"

"Jay doesn't look at all like a Borthwick," Roberta commented. It was true. He didn't look much like Lois either. He was on the small side and the only one with red hair and fair, freckled skin. Lois had been blonde, like her sister, Sylvia.

"What did Will look like?" asked Margo. Doug Halliday had seen a photograph. Big, broad-shouldered, dark-haired until it turned grey.

"Herb's definitely shaken up about this death," said Doug. "He doesn't usually drink as much beer as that."

"I'd be shaken, too, if I lived next to a house where the family was being killed off one by one," Roberta mused. "I was saying just yesterday that place has got a curse on it and they should rip it down."

"That would really rile Herb up," Doug told her. "He's got a thing about old cottages like that. Believes they should all be preserved for posterity."

"And there's a meeting about that tomorrow that I must attend. Lovely evening, Margo, but we must go," Freya announced.

Soon, the party was over. Roberta was driving. She needed to leave, too. Sasha's dog was in the Margo's house, with Bob.

"Come on." Margo picked up a leash. "I'll walk with you." It was the perfect evening for a stroll back along the shore, just a sliver of a moon but stars in abundance. And it would give her some quiet time to sift through all that had been said this evening.

Izzy had not been able to talk with her brother Mike. He'd been working on a contracting job all day and now he was out helping his friend Fraser Borthwick drown his sorrow because Fraser's mother had just died. Wes and Big Sig were with them, as usual.

Fraser puffed smoke towards a clear sky thick with stars. The bar had closed long since. The wind had carried away the woodsmoke that had been hanging in the air and they could breathe again. It was calm and still. They sat on a beach in a small bay just south of Fiskar Bay, a place where they had partied many years ago. They had a bit of a fire going. That was against the rules because of the drought, but they ignored the fire ban. There was no one to see them out here.

They'd talked most of the night about his mom's money and how rich Fraser was going to be. He could stay here, in the Interlake, where he had these good buddies to keep him company. He wouldn't have to go back to Toronto and try to make money the only way he knew how. He'd told his Aunt Sylvia earlier in the evening that Leslie had been going to look after all that cash for him, had said she'd give him a bit of it each month, so he wouldn't be tempted to blow it all in one go.

"Good idea," Sylvia had said. "Talk to your Uncle Art. He can help you to make that happen."

It was awful that Mom was gone but she'd been on her way out by the time he'd arrived. He was glad he'd made it back to the Interlake before she died. That he'd managed to visit with her again. Have a laugh together, even if she didn't remember him or his name.

The problem was that he might not get his hands on the money right away. There was lawyer stuff that needed doing. And he could use some of it right now. The loot he'd got from his trucker friends wouldn't last forever. He couldn't live off Wes much longer. Fraser needed to find his own place to stay.

"That's my cottage, too," he said, remembering nights like these when he used to spend the summer at Hazeldean. Why should Jay have it for himself? "I need it more than Jay does. I'm the one that's homeless. And he's got enough cash to tide him over until we get the big cheque. He was going to buy me out, right?"

Wes was the only one who was half sober.

"Remind me. What was he gonna give you for it?" he asked.

"I asked seventy grand. He said something like fifty. Maybe it was fifty-five." Fraser screwed up his face trying to remember.

"That's crap. See here." Wes grabbed a stick and started writing figures in the sand. "He told you that while Leslie was still around. Back then there were three shares, right?"

"No," said Fraser. "Four. Donna's kids got hers."

Wes did the math. Four times $55,000 in giant figures: $220,000. "That's nowhere like enough for that place," he said.

"It's because it's in such a mess. And Jay says it'll need to be winterized." Fraser lay down in the sand. This was all too much for him to take in.

Wes kicked him. "Don't fall asleep, Fraser. Sit up. This is important," he said. He reworked the figures. "There's three shares now, right? And that place has got to be worth $275,000 at least. Lakeshore, wide lot, a beach, a pier? C'mon. One third of $275,000 is more than $90,000. You could rent somewhere for the winter out here and live on that, easy, until you get all your mom's cash." He waved his stick around in the starlight as if it were a wizard's wand.

"Told you. Jay says it's not worth that much."

"How come Jay thinks he knows?" Mike had been listening. He knew a thing or two about houses and the cost of fixing them up. He worked on and off for the contractors. He'd been in on some renos. Had been doing that today. He could check it out and give Fraser some idea of what the place was really worth and how much it would cost to fix it up.

"We should go have another look," said Fraser.

"Right now?" asked Wes. But Mike was full of beery bravado and he thought it was a great idea. It didn't matter that the police had the place all taped up. If they got caught he could talk his way out of trouble. His sister was in charge of those murder cases, wasn't she? She was Sergeant Izzy McBain of the Major Crimes Unit. No one would see them anyway. It was the middle of the night. He got to his feet and hauled Fraser onto his feet.

They kicked sand onto the fire to put it out and stomped on the odd stray ember.

"I'm going to pass," said Wes, sense prevailing. He had work to do in the morning. Beasts that needed feeding. Big Sig decided to head for home, too. So it was only Fraser and Mike McBain who drove into Cullen Village in the quiet starry hours of the morning.

They put on a light and puttered around the house, talking about what needed to be done. But mainly they drank some more. They found two wine bottles in a kitchen cupboard. There were logs in a box by the big stone fireplace. Mike got a fire going. It wasn't cold at all but they liked the look of it. The room became thickly warm. They talked about possibilities. Replace the windows. Insulate. Put in a furnace. Mike would need to go down into the crawlspace under the house and see what needed doing. He'd work up an estimate. Within an hour, Fraser had dozed off, sprawled out on the sofa by the fire.

Mike finished the last of the bottle and decided to clear off. He'd text Wes and get him to pick Fraser up some time tomorrow. He left the light on in case his buddy woke up while it was still dark, then he found his way to his car, walking the careful walk of someone who has had too much to drink. He backed out of the driveway just as cautiously. Mike knew he shouldn't be driving, but he'd done this many times before. He'd take the back roads home and his sister's buddies in the RCMP would never see him.

26

MARGO FOUND IT impossible to sleep. What Herb Appleby had said last night played around in her head. He had obviously been fond of Lois Borthwick and had revealed more than he should, his tongue loosened by grief and alcohol.

June had sat and listened, as if it was no surprise. She must have known everything. Or perhaps nothing had actually happened. But it did seem that Lois and Herb had spent weeks out here every summer, next door to one another, their children sound asleep in their beds, while their partners were at work in the city.

And there was the business of Jay, the child born years after his siblings, the one who did not look like any of them, the one that Will Borthwick had left to Lois to rear by herself. Jay had a different disposition, too, from the rest of that family. He was sweeter-natured than all of them.

If he was Herb and Lois's lovechild, she speculated in the wee, small hours, having Jay live next door to his cottage would likely have pleased Herb. He could have wanted that very much, enough to make sure that nothing happened to prevent it, like Donna and Leslie and Amelia conspiring to tear Hazeldean down and build a different house in its place.

Was Herb Appleby capable of killing? Could he have lifted Donna Borthwick's body and pushed it off the end of that pier, all by himself? Perhaps. He'd been athletic. Had taught phys-ed Herb still looked like he had been a big, strong man and he was in good shape for his age. He golfed all summer and curled in the winter.

"This is ridiculous," Margo told herself. Her imagination was working overtime. Herb and June Appleby had been good summer neighbours all the years she had lived here. There was not a shred of proof for any of this. She pounded her pillow and eventually drifted off to sleep.

It was almost daylight when her eyes snapped open.

What would happen, she thought, if the police did DNA testing on Herb and Jay? Finding out if they really were related was something that they should know. That meant she'd need to report what she had heard Herb say and what she suspected to the police, but she wanted this to be handled with discretion. She didn't want the Major Crimes Unit and their forensic experts swarming all over the Appleby house without good reason. Margo would have a quiet word with Roxanne and drop the suggestion in her ear, because that was all it was, wasn't it? A suggestion?

She was wide awake now. She got up and Bob jumped off the end of her bed, looking hopeful. She let him out and saw light spreading from the horizon over the lake. It was so quiet outside she could almost hear this old world turning on her axis. It was going to be a beautiful day, like yesterday. Doubt struck again. Why should she spoil it with suspicions about Herb Appleby? She should just leave things be.

"Come on, Bob. Let's go watch the sun come up." She pulled on a long skirt and a cardigan. It was cool out, a welcome change after weeks of heat, and today it might become hotter again. She put on sandals and grabbed a leash.

Margo had only gone halfway along the berm when she saw the light in the window of Hazeldean. That should not be there, she thought. There was still police tape up. She padded closer, keeping Bob leashed, at her side. Was someone in the cottage? Was there any sign of a car? She could not see one, in this half-light. Not that that meant anything. Hadn't Leslie Borthwick hidden her car beside the railway station and walked over?

Then she noticed another light, this one in the Appleby house next door, at a side window. She thought that must be the bedroom. Was Herb Appleby out and about as well? Was he over at Hazeldean? Why would he be there?

She led her dog back home as unobtrusively as she could. It was too early to call Roxanne Calloway. Or was it? Whenever anyone was in that cottage these days, it led to trouble. Someone should go and check it out.

The sound of the phone woke both Matt and Roxanne.

"It's for me," she said. "You go back to sleep."

Roxanne listened as Margo told her a brief version of the story, how Herb Appleby had said things he maybe should not have over drinks last night. That Margo suspected that he might have been in a relationship with Lois Borthwick, many years before. That Jay might have been the result. Now someone was inside Hazeldean and there was also a light in the Appleby house, next door. Her imagination might be running amok, Margo admitted, but what could you expect when so many people had died there recently? Perhaps Roxanne could get someone to come by and make sure that everything was okay?

"I'll do that," Roxanne replied. Matt sat up and watched her put on her uniform.

"Just something that needs taking care of," she told him. "It's still early, just gone five. I'll probably be back soon. Get some more sleep." She kissed him and crept past Finn's door on her way out the house. Matt's dogs raised their snouts, watched her go and snuggled down again.

The sun would be up shortly. She could have asked a patrol to drop by Hazeldean but she was curious and Cullen Village was only minutes away. She would have a look in the window of the cottage and see what was inside. Call for backup if she needed it.

Margo's story interested her. They had been working all along on the theory that this case was about the Borthwick money, but what if it was not? What if it was about an old, thwarted passion? Testing would prove whether or not there was a relationship between Jay Borthwick and Herb Appleby—that was easy—but surely other people must have suspected? If it was true, Herb's wife, June, mustn't have been too happy to have Jay talking about moving in permanently, right next door.

Inside Hazeldean, Fraser woke. He wasn't at all sure where he was or who the woman was looking down at him. He could only see her outline against the single light behind her and he wasn't focusing very well. The wine on top of the beer hadn't been a good idea. He was thirsty, very thirsty.

"Aren't you Fraser?" the woman was saying. "Jay's brother? Are you drunk?"

Maybe he still was. He didn't know how long he had been asleep. Hadn't Mike been here? Where had he got to? Fraser swung his legs around so he could sit properly. Where was his cane? He couldn't get up without it, certainly not when he was feeling as woozy as he was right now.

The woman walked off in the direction of the kitchen. He got a better look at her. Tall. Long, brown hair, tied back in a loose braid. Big boned. Jay's woman. He groped through the alcoholic fog that thickened his brain and searched for a name. Jackie? Janine? Jenny? Jennifer, that was it. She was coming back with a glass of water. He gulped it down, thankful.

"How come you're here?" he asked, the glass empty.

"I was going to ask you the same question," she replied. She was kind of plain looking. Ordinary. Youngish. Couldn't be thirty yet. "It's past five in the morning. The sun's just coming up." She sat down, opposite him. "How did you get here? There's no car outside."

"Dropped by," said Fraser. "I had a buddy with me. Mike. He must have gone home."

"Guess so." Jennifer stretched out an arm and picked up an empty wine bottle from a side table. "You had a bit of a party first? Lit a fire?" A faint red glow remained in the grey ash in the fireplace. "Drank some of this?"

"Yup. Good bottle too. Donna must've bought it." He was beginning to feel better. He should go pee. Where was that cane? He scanned the room. Couldn't see it. The woman was still sitting opposite him. "You haven't said why you're here," he reminded her.

"Just walked by." Jennifer relaxed back into her chair and crossed her legs. "I wake up early because I used to work in a bakery. We started at this time of day and I've got into the habit, so I get up and go for a walk. That way I don't wake Jay or my son. It's sometimes still dark when I set out. Not a soul around, then the sun rises and the birds start singing. It's the best time of day. You should try it." Fraser didn't think so. "I came this way and saw a light on, so I thought I'd better look in. And there you were, sound asleep on the sofa."

She sounded okay. Nice, maybe. Maybe she would make him some coffee?

"I don't know if that's a good idea," she replied, getting up out of the chair again. "We don't want to stay here too long. If the police find out that we've been hanging around we might get into trouble. Maybe we should walk over to the Rec Centre. It's only ten minutes away. I could make you a decent coffee over there. Cook you up some bacon and eggs."

His stomach heaved at the suggestion. And he couldn't walk that far. He needed his cane.

"This one?" She bent down and picked it up off the floor. "It's a nice one. I like it." She rubbed her hand over the yellow handle. Then she laid it down on top of the big table, further out of reach.

"What made you decide to come here?" She perched on the arm of the chair. "Did you come to see where Leslie died?"

It was a good enough reason, but Fraser didn't see any need to lie to her. She was a good listener. Considerate. It might be easier to tell her about his idea than to have to explain it to Jay.

"Well, see," he began. "It's like this. I was thinking I might like to stay hereabouts. But I'm going to need somewhere to live. You and Jay are okay; you've still got your place in town, haven't you? I know you want to move out here but you could wait a bit, couldn't you? I can't. I've got nowhere. I know someone who could help me get the place ready for winter."

She looked right at him, listening as if she was really interested. Fraser rambled right on.

"Y'know, once we get Mom's money, I could maybe buy you and Graeme Palmer out of your shares. You and Jay could buy another place. We could be like neighbours." He grinned encouragement. Outside it was getting lighter.

"I don't think so, Fraser." Jennifer smiled briefly. "You see, Jay and I are going to make this our home. We've got a plan all figured out for this house. We know what needs to be done and what it will cost. We're setting up our own business here, in Cullen Village. We're off to a good start, and I want to raise my son out here."

She sounded sure of that. Certain. But who was she to tell him, Fraser Borthwick, what should happen to this cottage? To Hazeldean? Jennifer wasn't family. Not really. In his indignation, Fraser quite forgot that he had broached the subject first. That he'd thought she might be receptive to his idea. But she wasn't. Now she was an obstruction.

"That's not for you to decide," he informed her. "You're not a Borthwick. You have no say in what happens to this place." He remembered an idea that he had had before. "Y'know what? We were all supposed to be able to stay here for a month, every year, ever since Mom got moved into Harbourfront. That's what, ten years ago? I never got mine, because I was away. That means there's ten whole months, due to me!" he crowed. "I should get to stay here right through to next spring! And by then we'll have Mom's money all figured out."

"That so?"

He didn't like the way she was looking at him now. Whenever people got that look on their faces it meant they were going to tell him something that he didn't want to hear. He'd said his piece: it was time to get out of here. He slid along the sofa to the far end, closer to his cane. He'd leave her here, go outside and text Wes. He might be up already. Find out when he could come and pick him up. But Jennifer was standing again. She reached his cane before he could even try. She held it in her hand. Leaned on it. Her mouth tightened. This didn't look good at all.

"You are all the same," she said. "Except Jay. You and your sisters. You think you own this part of the world, just because you are Borthwicks. That because you've been here a long time, you get to decide everything. But look at you. You're a mess, Fraser. Useless. You don't deserve a single thing. Not all that money you're going to get. Or this house."

He didn't like the way this was going. He wanted out of here. But he did need his cane and Jennifer had it.

"I came out here once," she was saying, "in the summer, when I was eight years old. My mom rented a trailer, at the other side of the highway. We had to walk ten minutes to get to the beach; it wasn't right outside, like here. Mom couldn't really afford it, she'd just left my dad. We had no money but she wanted me to have a holiday. She cleaned houses so she could pay for us to stay for a whole month. This cottage was one of them. My mom used to bring me along while she worked. I wasn't allowed to go out on the pier or go down onto your beach. I had to stay in the kitchen and not touch anything. Donna brought her kids out once. They were still little, Graeme was a baby. She acted like I didn't exist. The only person who spoke nicely to me was Jay. He said 'Hi!' in passing, and he'd smile. He doesn't know that I was that little kid. I'm not going to tell him and neither are you."

The truth suddenly dawned on Fraser. "It was you!" He clutched the arm of the sofa and tried to pull himself upright. "You killed them!"

He watched her swing the cane round to grasp it by the bottom end. The brass handle rose then fell. It smacked into the side of his head and he passed out.

Herb Appleby was a habitual insomniac. One solution was to read, so he turned on the light and picked up a book. This was such a normal occurrence that June wore eyeshades to bed. She didn't even stir. An hour or two with a good murder mystery would clear his brain of whatever bothered him and he might get another couple of hours of shut-eye. On this particular morning, it was almost five when he got up out of bed to go to the bathroom.

The day was breaking, the sky translucent, the birds singing. He opened the back door to look and listen. Was that a light shining in the window at Hazeldean? He looked again to make sure. It definitely was. What was going on? Who might be there? Herb could call the police but the interloper might be gone by the time they got here. He should go see who was there first. Herb went to fetch his dressing gown then picked up a golf club, just in case he ran into some kind of trouble.

The sun was just up over the horizon, bright enough that he could see. There wasn't a car parked in the driveway, but he could hear a woman's voice inside, talking, as he got closer to Hazeldean. He couldn't make out what she was saying. It sounded harmless. Maybe he should go in and have a word with whoever it was. Just as he reached the back of the cottage, he heard a loud crack.

Herb thought he heard a car approaching, but he didn't wait. He prided himself on being decisive. He marched to the veranda steps and walked straight up the steps, golf club firmly in hand, then pushed open the door.

"Anyone there?" he called. Jennifer Boychuk was inside. She was walking backwards out of the living room into the hallway and she was dragging a body. Her head turned toward him and she frowned. Then she dropped the body onto the floor and disappeared into the living room. Herb recognized Fraser

Borthwick, blood dripping down the side of his head. Should he go and help him or turn and run?

Herb hesitated. Jennifer reappeared, jumped over the body and came running up the hallway at him, a walking stick in her hand. Herb staggered back and dropped his golf club. Jennifer was coming after him, fast. She was almost at the door, the cane held like a club. The steps were dark, in shadow.

"Stop! Police!" yelled a woman's voice. Herb had stumbled halfway down the steps. Jennifer was right above him, the shiny handle of the cane raised, about to crack down on his head, when Roxanne Calloway fired her gun and shot her.

27

"WRITE YOUR REPORT, then go home," Inspector Schultz told Roxanne, as soon as she told him what had happened. It was standard procedure when a member of the RCMP fired a weapon in the line of duty and seriously injured a suspect. Roxanne would be off the job while her bosses figured out what to do. Part of the decision depended on whether Jennifer Boychuk survived. If she did not, Roxanne would be suspended with pay, pending an inquiry.

The ambulances had arrived. Jennifer was being transported to Winnipeg and Fraser Borthwick to the hospital in Fiskar Bay. Herb Appleby had given a statement to Sam Mendes and been handed over into the care of his wife, shaken but unscathed. Sam had photographed everything. He'd wait for Ident to arrive from the city to take charge of the scene.

Roxanne called Matt as she drove to the detachment in Fiskar Bay and told him what had happened.

"You okay?" he asked. He could work from home today. Keep Finn here, too, so they'd be here for her when she got back. "Don't worry," he told her. "You did the right thing."

It was still early, not yet seven, when she sat down in her office to type, running though the earlier events, trying to keep the facts straight in her head.

She had arrived at the village shortly after Margo's phone call. She could have called a patrol car to check out Hazeldean but she knew she could reach Cullen Village more quickly. She had decided to go, assess the situation and call for support if needed. She had arrived just after 5:00 am, not long after daybreak.

She had parked on the street and approached the back of the building walking along the driveway at the side. A light was on inside the cottage and she had heard some movement. When she reached the corner of the house she could see along the length of the veranda at the back. Herb Appleby was standing at the open doorway to the house, looking in. Though the sun was barely rising and the veranda was in shadow, she could see the expression of horror on his face quickly turning to fear. He was holding a golf club. He dropped it as he turned and hurried to the top of the steps. He was wearing house slippers and he looked like he couldn't see the steps.

Someone was pursuing him. Aware this house had already witnessed two murders and another suspicious death, Roxanne pulled her gun.

Jennifer ran out the doorway wielding a cane with a heavy yellow handle. Roxanne called a warning to stop. Jennifer did not. Herb had made it halfway down the steps but Jennifer was directly above him. She raised the cane. Roxanne saw the golden handle catch the morning light. Believing Herb in imminent danger, she pulled the trigger.

The woman was more than twenty feet away, moving quickly across the shadowy veranda. Roxanne aimed for the largest body mass she could see—the torso—thinking that Jennifer's arm was most likely to receive the impact. But Jennifer suddenly swung to the right and raised the cane with both hands. The bullet pierced her rib cage.

By the time Roxanne was done writing, she had heard Jennifer Boychuk was waiting for surgery. The bullet had missed her heart and she had not died. Instead, it penetrated her left lung.

Fraser Borthwick was in hospital, too, with a suspected fractured skull.

"Don't worry about it," Ravi Anand assured Roxanne. He'd arrived at work as soon as he'd heard. She was glad to see him.

He would deputize for her until she returned or someone came to be her temporary replacement. Canada Day was coming up. Ravi knew the game plan for the week. He could handle everything for her and she'd be back at work in no time, he assured her. "You did what you had to do. The bosses are just worried about bad press. You know what happens when any of us fires a gun. But everyone's on your side. And Herb Appleby is doing you proud." Ravi had heard Herb on the radio before he left the house.

Herb had been interviewed by the CBC and local print media. He'd made the national news. "RCMP sergeant saves grandfather's life!" "Serial killer shot in the nick of time!" proclaimed the headlines. Someone had found a photo of him, a smiling, white-haired man, anybody's granddad.

"When I saw that woman, she was dragging a bloody body," he said. "She came at me like a banshee. I thought I was a dead man, that she was going to smash my brains in. Sergeant Calloway fired just in time. She saved my life." He was a natural. "The woman who attacked me's got to be the one who killed the Borthwick women, all three of them. Donna and her daughter, Amelia and then her sister, Leslie. If you'd seen the expression on her face when she attacked me, you wouldn't doubt it for a minute."

The thing was, they couldn't prove Jennifer Boychuk was responsible for any of the deaths. All the evidence they had against her was circumstantial. What Fraser had told them gave her a motive. She'd had reason to envy the Borthwicks since childhood. She wanted to own that cottage badly, the one that her mother had once cleaned and where, as a girl, she had been treated as though she was nothing. She had wanted her child to have the privilege of living there, one that she herself had missed. Jennifer hadn't wanted Donna to tear down Hazeldean, build a big new house in its place and sell it. She'd wanted to set up home there with Jay and her boy.

Fraser Borthwick, safely tucked up in a hospital bed, had been able to tell them that Jennifer had told him she was in the habit of roaming the village, alone, in the early hours of the morning. Jay Borthwick had reluctantly confirmed that she often rose at dawn and went out walking then returned in time for breakfast. She had done it in Winnipeg and she continued to do it in Cullen Village. She would have been around Hazeldean just when all three murders were known to have occurred. The timing and the opportunity fit.

She had strong hands and arms. Years of baking bread had built up her muscles. She'd dragged Fraser Borthwick like a flour sack when Herb Appleby saw her, so they knew she was responsible for that attack. Fraser was skin and bone but he was a tall man. He had to weigh more than Leslie Borthwick, the largest of his sisters. Jennifer could have throttled a small woman like Donna Palmer and hauled her off the pier. She could have smashed Amelia or Leslie's head in with ease. But where was the proof?

For now, the RCMP could charge Jennifer with the assault on Herb Appleby and on Fraser Borthwick, upgrading it to attempted murder if the Crown Attorney agreed. That was it.

Why had she not used her taser, Roxanne's superintendent called her to complain.

"Because, sir, murders had already happened at that cottage. Two, maybe three, all within the past month. I believed I was dealing with a killer."

"You didn't know that," he barked.

"It was a fair assumption," she responded.

"We don't work on assumptions, Sergeant," he reminded her. "And why did you go there alone? Why didn't you call for backup?"

"If I had waited, Herb Appleby would have been seriously injured, maybe killed. And we don't know what Jennifer Boychuk intended to do with Fraser Borthwick. He was unconscious and she was trying to drag him somewhere when she was interrupted."

"There wasn't a patrol car in the area?"

"I was closer, sir. I could get there faster and the situation was urgent."

"Yes, Calloway, but you didn't know that when you got the call, did you? You just knew there might be an intruder."

"Yes, sir," she replied.

There was a moment's silence. He had made his point.

"We will hope, Sergeant, that the bullet you fired doesn't kill her. That the damage to her lung isn't too serious and she pulls through. You're off the job for now. We'll get someone out there to run things until we find out how this is all going to pan out. Let's hope it's a temporary replacement. Meantime, you talk to no one. The press has got hold of your name. You will say nothing."

"Yes, sir." Roxanne hung up. It was exactly what she had expected, but a thank-you for saving Herb Appleby's life would have been nice. This was how things were done these days. Public perception of the force was a priority. She needed to tell her team that she would be leaving them for now and she wasn't sure when she would be back.

Fraser's X-rays showed his skull was intact. He had a concussion. He was happy to tell his version of the story to the police and to his aunt and uncle.

"She acted so nice and helpful," he said of Jennifer. "Then she went for me. She put my cane out of reach, where she could grab it first. Just played me along, cat-and-mouse-like. Then she clobbered me with my own stick. Used the big knob on the end. I saw stars! Passed right out! Where do you think she was she taking me, dragging me out of the living room? Was she going to haul me to the pier and tie something tight around my neck and shove me off it, just like she did with Donna? Or push me off the veranda and drop something on my head to finish me off, like happened to Les? Bash me harder, like Amelia, to make sure I was a goner? Maybe if she managed to get off with killing me and moved into Hazeldean with Jay, she'd have done him in, too.

"What is happening with Jay?" he asked.

His Aunt Sylvia shook her head. "Not in good shape, from what we've been told. He's in Winnipeg, waiting at the hospital to find out how she is. They don't know if she will make it."

"Too bad the cop didn't kill her outright," said Fraser, drugs dripping into his system through an IV, comfortable in his hospital bed. Once Sylvia and Art had gone he'd try to sneak a nap, even although the nurses didn't want him doing that. Big Sig, Wes and Mike had texted to say they were going to stop by later. He could tell his story all over again. Maybe they'd bring him a drop of brandy. Medicinal, for his mental health. He'd suggested that in a message to Wes.

Adrenaline was still fuelling Herb Appleby. He held court later that morning in his cottage, enthroned in a big recliner. The Hallidays brought early tomatoes from their garden. They were precious in this drought year: Doug had been watering them daily. Sandy Ferguson showed up with a carrot cake. He'd had to drive to the grocery at Fiskar Bay to get it. It wasn't half as good as the cake Jennifer Boychuk had made for them but it was okay. Jennifer would not be baking cakes for them at the Rec Centre any longer.

They treated Herb like he was a hero. He'd gone to see what was wrong at Hazeldean, all alone. How brave.

"It was the right thing to do," he assured them, not the least bit bashful. "I just didn't expect to find what I did." He didn't mention that he'd dropped his golf club and fled the moment Jennifer had come after him but he did admit that the sight of her was terrifying. Sergeant Calloway had shown up just at the right time. He'd be dead, otherwise.

"We've sent flowers to her house as a thank-you," said June, who had slept through the whole thing. "I wonder how she knew to come?"

"Because I told her." Margo Wishart had found an upright chair in a corner. "I woke up early, too. I saw the light in the window at Hazeldean and I called Roxanne. She's an old friend."

She wasn't going to admit to any of them that she had told Roxanne that she suspected Herb capable of murder.

"If Jennifer dies, won't Sergeant Calloway be suspended?" asked Freya.

"She had no choice," said Herb. "She had to stop that woman."

"She could have used her taser instead," Sandy interjected. He'd worked in administration for the government and thought like Roxanne's superintendent. "She should have tried to stop that woman. Talked the situation down."

"No, she could not." Margo disagreed. "I saw it all happen. After I called Roxanne I went back onto the berm to see what was happening. I watched Herb going to the house and I was going to call to him but then I heard Roxanne's car pulling up. There was enough daylight by then and some light coming from the door of the cottage, so I could see and hear everything. Herb went to the top of the steps in a hurry and called in the door, then he turned away. Next thing, Jennifer came running out the door. Roxanne called to her to stop but she didn't. She lifted that stick. I could see the end of it shining in the light. She was just about to smash it down on Herb's head when Roxanne shot her. It all happened very quickly. Herb was in real trouble. Roxanne did exactly the right thing."

Margo rose to her feet and excused herself. As soon as she arrived home, she got her car keys and drove to the RCMP detachment in Fiskar Bay.

"I need to make a witness statement," she told the young woman constable behind the desk, the one with her arm in a sling. "I saw everything that happened at Hazeldean this morning."

Margo's testimony was one small piece of evidence. It wasn't enough to clear Roxanne of wrongdoing, but she had witnessed Jennifer Boychuk attack Herb Appleby. It helped prove that Jennifer was capable of violent behaviour that could lead to death. Izzy called with fresh news, just as Roxanne was preparing to leave for home.

"Ident found something!" she said. "A fingerprint on that flowerpot she used to smash in Leslie's skull. Jennifer Boychuk left a perfect thumbprint on a broken bit of clay. So even if she does die on that operating table, we know that it's likely she was the murderer. And you know what else my guy Trent found out? The man Jennifer was married to before she met Jay hanged himself at home in their basement! It was investigated, but the coroner decided it was suicide. What happened to him was just the same as Donna Palmer!

"It's total shit that they're suspending you, but it won't be for long. It's just them covering their asses. Take a break. Take the kid to the beach. And don't worry. We're going to get this whole case wrapped up, no time at all."

Roxanne finally went home. Finn came running out to greet her.

"It's true, Mom? You shot a killer? They're saying that you saved his life!"

"He doesn't know that it was Carter's mother yet," Matt told her quietly, as they walked up to the house. "We can tell him later, when the time's right. One bit at a time."

"It looks like I'm suspended," she said.

"Thought you might be. Come on in and you can tell me the whole story."

28

JENNIFER BOYCHUK SURVIVED the operation. She was taken into intensive care, too weak to be interviewed by anyone from the RCMP.

She was, however, charged, with the murder of Leslie Borthwick and her niece, Amelia Palmer. The manner and the timing of their deaths were too similar for it to be coincidence. A jury could be convinced that the killings had been carried out by the same hand. Not only did Jennifer have means and opportunity, she had a strong motive. Too, she had seriously injured Fraser Borthwick, then acted in a way suggesting she intended him further harm. For that, she was charged with attempted murder. She'd also threatened Herb Appleby, pursued him, intending to inflict a lethal blow to the head. That brought another charge of attempted murder.

The first death, Donna Borthwick's, was different. It had likely occurred at the end of the pier, with no weapon but Jennifer's strong hands—if she was the person responsible. They could prove nothing, but Jennifer's husband dying a similar way five years earlier was significant. The evidence from that old file would need to be examined

"She said that her husband had been depressed and talked about ending his life. The investigators at the time believed her," Trent Weiss reported. "He didn't leave a note but the city police, who were investigating, were busy with other cases. They didn't look hard enough." He had forwarded all the documents that substantiated his findings to Inspector Schultz.

Jay Borthwick hovered in the hallway outside the ICU, refusing to leave. He wouldn't be allowed to see his partner, the constable on guard told him, but still he stuck around. Somebody needed to have Jennifer's back, he told Izzy, when she tried talking to him. He needed to be near so he could look out for her.

He'd wanted to keep Carter with him but he wasn't the boy's dad. The police had called Child and Family Services and they had contacted the Boychuk family. Carter's paternal grandparents had been appalled to hear the news but an aunt and uncle with kids the same age had offered to take Carter in. They had already picked him up.

"He hardly knows who they are," Jay complained to Izzy and Trent.

"Let's go find a place where we can talk."

A nurse's aide steered them to the ward's quiet room. Plastic flowers were arranged in a vase in a corner, a box of tissues sat on a low table between a sofa and two comfortable chairs.

Izzy and Trent sat on one side of the table, Jay on the other. He told them how he and Jennifer had met, how they had hired her on contract to provide his restaurant with cakes, but she'd proved to be so good that they'd hired her as a pastry chef and she'd come to work full-time in the kitchen.

"She can bake anything," he said. "She's got such talent." Jay's wife had left him months before and gone off to B.C. with his kids. He and Jennifer had hit it off, right from the start. "It was like she walked into my life just when I needed her." Carter had been six years old at the time, a little guy in need of a dad. And Jay had missed his own boy and girl. He realized that he should have spent more time with them, then they might not have disappeared from his life.

"Did you know that you'd met her before?" asked Izzy. She recounted what Jennifer had told Fraser, that she had been the child of a woman who cleaned Hazeldean one summer, over twenty years ago. That Jennifer had sat in the kitchen while her mother scrubbed the house clean. That he had said hello to her, when she was about eight years old.

"I did?" he said. He'd completely forgotten. He couldn't remember them at all, neither Jennifer nor her mother. "Are you sure about that?"

"That's what she told us."

"I'll need to ask her. She had a hard time growing up," he told them, still eager to find a reason to explain Jennifer's actions. "Her father drank too much and got abusive. She told me she and her mother had to leave the house and go live in a home for battered women for a few weeks. They moved into a basement suite after that. It was all they could afford until her mom met her stepdad, then things improved. He was okay but he put Jennifer to work in the bakehouse while she was still a kid. That's where she learned to bake.

"She's always had it tough. She got married and the guy died, left her alone with Carter. She was only twenty-two, but she did come into some money, not long after I met her. Enough to buy a house. That's what saved us when my old restaurant in Winnipeg, The Sleepy Fox, went under. We had a plan, to move out to the beach. To start fresh. Make a new life together.

"I thought it was great that she liked Hazeldean as much as she did. I brought her out to see it in April and her eyes just lit up. If what you're telling me is true, she's done all of this because she wanted us to live there so badly. It must have been a dream come true for her, that she could own the cottage that her mother once had to clean. She did all this out of love, for me and Carter, for the cottage, for our future together." He looked across the table at Izzy, tears drizzling from his pale, orange-fringed eyes. "Now that's all ruined," he said.

Izzy moved the tissue box closer to him.

"You knew she got up and went walking early in the morning?" she asked.

"She always did." Jay gulped in air.

"And you never wondered, when your sisters and your niece died during the night, if she had anything to do with it?"

"Never." He shook his head in vigorous denial.

"She didn't try to stop you when you said you'd bring Carter and his friend over to Hazeldean to get the canoe, the morning that you found Leslie's body?"

"I didn't tell her that I was going to go there," he said. "I just told her that I needed to go pick up the canoe. It could have been at the marina. Anywhere."

Izzy doubted if that was true. She thought it more likely Jennifer knew the canoe was beside the garage, that she'd trusted he'd have no reason to go to the back of the cottage.

Meantime, Jay was in no state to take care of himself.

"Is there anyone we can call to come get you and take you home?" asked Izzy.

"I'm not leaving," he insisted. "I'm staying right here. I don't care what you say Jennifer's done, there's gotta be a reason. She'll tell me when she's ready."

"You can't talk to her," Izzy said.

"That's okay. I'm not going anywhere." They left him sitting in a chair in the bleak hospital hallway still believing that Jennifer could not be as bad as they said she was, ready to excuse her anything, sure that there had to be a better explanation.

Roxanne Calloway wasn't quite sure what to do with herself without a job to go to. She hadn't been off work since Finn's dad had been shot by a driver high on drugs that he'd pulled over on the highway.

Flowers had arrived from Herb and June Appleby. She'd called to thank them and Herb had been effusive in his thanks. There had been calls from media outlets but Matt was heading those off. She was glad to have him there, taking care of such things.

She should be happy. Matt was thrilled about the baby. He'd suspected when she stopped eating breakfast and he'd been almost certain when she'd started stuffing her face with potato chips at night. But now he knew for sure. A New Year baby!

Finn wasn't so enthusiastic.

"What if it's a girl?" he asked, making his preference clear.

"We have to wait and see." She hugged him. He'd always be her first. And he was talking to her again. Having a mom that everyone said was a hero, who had brought down someone bad, all by herself, had wiped clean his anger. They still hadn't told him that the person she had shot was the mother of his best friend Carter.

"You might not have to," Matt advised. "Carter's gone. It'll just be one of those summer friendships, the ones that come and go."

But no one called from HQ as the afternoon wore on to let her know if Jennifer Boychuk had survived her surgery. Roxanne had never killed on the job before and she wasn't sure how she felt about that. She was sure she'd done the right thing, that if she hadn't acted as she did, Herb Appleby would probably be dead too. The nearest patrol car would have taken more than five minutes to reach the scene and that would have been too late. But being responsible for taking a life was something that did not sit well with her. She hoped that was not what had happened.

She could phone Ravi Anand and ask if he knew anything. Or Izzy. But she stopped herself, aware that as far as the RCMP was concerned, she no longer had the right to know, not when she was off the case. She was suspended. This was a new experience for her, too, and she didn't like it one bit.

She needn't have worried. The phone finally did ring. Izzy, at last.

Jennifer Boychuk was going to live. There were two charges of murder against her and two of attempted murder.

"And the fifth?" asked Roxanne. "That's Donna Palmer, right? They still can't make up their minds?"

"Listen to this," said Izzy. "Trent's spent hours checking out what happened when Jennifer Boychuk's husband died. He's supposed to have hanged himself, which is so like what happened to Donna. Trent's sure it wasn't properly investigated at the time. We've just been to see Schultz. He's glad it was the city police who screwed up but it makes all police, including the RCMP, look incompetent when something like this happens.

"We all think you'll be back at work in no time. They're sure now that Jennifer's a killer, so Herb Appleby would probably have died if you hadn't made it there in time and caught her in the act. The bosses are going to be more worried about the media finding out that she might have murdered her husband years ago and the city cops missed it. If she'd been caught back then, the Borthwick women would still be alive. If the press gets hold of that, and they probably will, no one's going to question why you needed to use your gun on her.

"So relax. Everything's going to be fine. Enjoy the rest of the week off, because that's probably all you're going to get."

Roxanne hung up and instantly felt hungry.

"Let's go to the Red Shack and get burgers and fries," she said. Finn was gleeful. Roxanne seldom agreed to buy that kind of food. The shack was right by the highway at the edge of Cullen Village. There were picnic tables in the parking lot, like the ones that had been laid out for the barbecue last Saturday at the Rec Centre. Jay and Jennifer's café would no longer happen. Those tables would have to be put away and the festive lights taken down.

The Red Shack, however, was a summer institution, beloved of residents and tourists alike, and it was busy. More than one person stopped by their table to thank her and shake her hand.

"Good on you, Sarge," she was told. Finn was impressed.

The mayor of Cullen Village sat nearby with his wife, enjoying a hot dog and a milkshake.

"We've got a petition going insisting that you be reinstated," he came over to tell her. "You saved Cullen Village from a serial killer, and it's not the first time you've done that. They should be awarding you a medal instead of suspending you. I'll be sending it off to the assistant commissioner in the morning, and I'm copying it to our local MLA as well. Meantime, you'll be free on Canada Day? How about you come and join us in the parade? Be my guest, up front in the lead convertible?"

Roxanne had always had to work at Fiskar Bay on Canada Day. The crowds were larger there and more likely to need attention. But she had been told that Cullen Village held its own little local parade, with antique cars and tractors and kids on decorated bikes. After it, the village got together to sing "O Canada" in a park near the Rec Centre and they cut a celebratory cake. She'd be glad to join them, she told the mayor. Once they were done here they'd have to go see what they could find to decorate Finn's bike. He could be a part of the parade, too.

"Just hope the rain holds off," said the mayor. The weather forecast said clouds were going to roll in by Thursday. "Bring an umbrella, in case you need it. Isn't this just like it? We've been waiting for weeks for this drought to break and here it comes on the one day we don't want it." But he smiled as he said it. This hot weather would finally end. The grass would turn green again and the trees would stretch their leaves to drink in the welcome moisture.

Margo Wishart and her friends, Sasha and Roberta lounged in Sasha's backyard in the shade of a large old Manitoba maple tree. The dogs, Bob and Lenny, had both been for a cooling dip in the creek that ran by. Cold beers beaded with moisture lay on a table.

"I'm glad they made an arrest, but it's too bad it's her. She and Jay sure could cook," said Sasha. "What do you think will happen to Hazeldean now?"

"Bet it will be sold." Roberta had taken possession of the only lounger and lay with her legs stretched out. "I hope whoever buys it doesn't tear it down, but they probably will." They all nodded in agreement. That was happening to many old cottages along the lakeshore these days. Hazeldean would be demolished and a big, rectangular slab would go up in its place. "I guess we'll never find out if Herb Appleby is Jay Borthwick's father, either."

"I suppose not." Margo was rather glad. If Jay had come to live permanently next door to his supposed birth father, that could have caused tensions in the Appleby household. It had been a secret for more than forty years and it would remain that way. Herb could keep quiet about it and if June knew, which Margo suspected she did, she could continue to ignore it. She liked having the Applebys as her neighbours during the summer months. Things would return to normal in her quiet corner of the village as long as the bulldozers didn't roll in.

"You took your time telling me about the baby," Matt said, late that night as they lay in bed, his hand on Roxanne's pregnant belly. "What was that about?"

"I knew you would have kept quiet if I asked you to, but you would have wanted to tell everybody," she said. "And once Finn found out, and he would have, the secret would have been out. And then I'd have had to tell them at work, too. You know how it works. I'd have been stuck on office duty for the duration."

"That's what you do, though, most of the time, don't you? You manage the detachment from your office. The only thing different was the Hazeldean murders. Did getting involved in those cases matter that much to you?"

"I guess so." She yawned, sleepy, full of food and sunshine. "It was interesting and I like solving difficult cases."

"Does the job that you have bore you as much as that?"

Roxanne lay on her back and thought about it. Maybe it did. She'd been in charge of the detachment at Fiskar Bay for four years now and she knew exactly how everything worked. It no longer held much in the way of surprises. But that was what she had opted for. Expecting excitement on the job was unrealistic. Her work was all about day-to-day policing.

"I chose to leave the Major Crimes Unit, Matt. And that was before you and I got together. Before we decided that we were going to live here. I wanted to be safer than I was in Major Crimes, after that time when I got my throat cut on the job and almost died. I wanted to know that I'd live to see Finn grow up."

"Yet you walked right into danger this morning."

"Not really. Jennifer never saw me coming. I had the advantage."

"You went and tackled a murderer singlehanded, Roxanne. She was dangerous. It could have gone the other way."

"I suppose so. But I didn't think that I had a choice."

"Do you want to go back?"

"To the MCU ? I can't do that," she said. "They cover the whole province. I could be sent anywhere, for weeks on end. We've got Finn and a new baby coming."

"I'm right here," said Matt. "Derek McVicar is talking about retiring by this time next year. He's been dropping hints that I can buy the business if I want, then I'd be my own boss. So I'm not going anywhere and you wouldn't be away on the job all the time. We could manage, with daycare. Or a nanny."

She thought about that. Then she said, "No. You know how it works in the force. You don't step backwards in your career. The only way to go is up through the ranks and I'm not sure I want to do that. I don't want to be an inspector—that's way more administration, not less. I knew when I took the Fiskar Bay job that this was as far as I was probably going to go. So here I am."

"You don't need to be stuck in a job that doesn't interest you anymore, Roxanne." Matt wrapped his arm around her.

Was he right? Did she have options? It had been a long and eventful day. Roxanne was too tired to think about it right now. When she had this baby, she would have a whole year off. There would be plenty of time then to decide if she wanted to make any other changes to her life.

"Let's go to sleep," she said and snuggled up close.

"'Night, Roxanne." Matt lifted his arm and turned off the light.

Acknowledgements

THANKS, AS ALWAYS, to the good folks at Signature Editions, especially Karen Haughian and Ashley Nielsen, and to Douglas Whiteway, my editor. I count myself very lucky to have you at my back.

Kirsty Macdonald and Ann Atkey read the first draft of this book and gave invaluable advice. Thanks for all the good questions and phone conversations as the book progressed.

Andrew Minor answered my questions regarding policing and Nikki Phelps provided answers about some legal matters.

Finally, thanks to Sylvia Robinson, in Scotland, whose ancestors lived at Hassendean House near Hawick, in the Scottish Borders – the original Hazeldean.

About the Author

RAYE ANDERSON IS a Scots Canadian who taught Drama and ran theatre and community arts programs for many years, notably at Prairie Theatre Exchange in Winnipeg, in Ottawa and Calgary. Her work has taken her across Canada, coast to coast, and up north as far as Churchill and Yellowknife. She's also worked as far afield as the West Indies and her native Scotland. Raye has been a resident of the Interlake since 2007, and recently moved to Gimli, Manitoba. Her first crime fiction novel, *And We Shall Have Snow* (Signature Editions, 2020) was a finalist for the Crime Writers of Canada Best First Novel Award and was also shortlisted for the WILLA Literary Award. *And Then Is Heard No More* (2021), the second book in the series featuring Sergeant Roxanne Calloway of the RCMP, revolved around a fictional Winnipeg theatre company and was a *Winnipeg Free Press*/McNally Robinson Book Club pick in 2022. Raye returned to the Interlake as the setting for her third and fourth books, *Down Came The Rain* (2022), which takes place during a wet spring and this, *Sing a Song of Summer*, which unfolds over one hot, dry summer.

Eco-Audit
Printing this book using Rolland Enviro100 Book
instead of virgin fibres paper saved the following resources:

Trees	Water	Air Emissions
3	1,000 L	219 kg